DEATH GOT NO MERCY

Dude, did that fuckin' dog just answer the question?

Cade doubted it. But that dog was definitely trained to perform a couple of tricks, and if the skinny kid had taught it to get up and do a little dance when it got asked a question, it was probably trained to disarm or disable an opponent. If they were regularly checking on the cannibals, the dog would need to be able to defend them. That was just common sense.

The dog sniffed the air again, then started padding in his direction.

"Well, it looks like Doobie's got the scent of something!" said the short girl. The dog was sniffing and walking in Cade's direction. He gripped the knife tight.

"Yeah, like, he's got the munchies, right Doob? Maybe somebody, like, made a sandwich nearby!" The boy licked his lips, leading with his face, throat exposed. Cade let them get a little closer.

The girl wagged a finger at them. "Well, don't get too far off, you two! There have been some spooky goings-on around here and –"

Cade moved. The dog had to go first – that was obvious. He rolled out of cover and grabbed the mutt in a headlock, bringing the blade of the knife down near the base of the skull, between the second and third vertebrae, neatly severing the spine as it buried in the dog's neck. The dog gave a strangled bark and went limp as the skinny kid jerked

"*It's* [...]

W[...]OM

An Abaddon Books™ Publication
www.abaddonbooks.com
abaddon@rebellion.co.uk

First published in 2009 by Abaddon Books™, Rebellion Intellectual Property
Limited, Riverside House, Osney Mead, Oxford, OX2 0ES, UK.

10 9 8 7 6 5 4 3 2 1

Editor: Jonathan Oliver
Cover: Mark Harrison
Design: Simon Parr & Luke Preece
Marketing and PR: Keith Richardson
Creative Director and CEO: Jason Kingsley
Chief Technical Officer: Chris Kingsley
The Afterblight Chronicles™ created by Andy Boot and Simon Spurrier

ISBN: 978-1-906735-15-9

Printed in Denmark by Norhaven A/S

THE AFTERBLIGHT CHRONICLES

AL EWING

DEATH GOT NO MERCY

Abaddon
Books

WWW.ABADDONBOOKS.COM

For Jon, Matt and, most of all, Tom

CHAPTER ONE

THE DUCHESS

Skrr-rr-retch.

The knife was a combat knife, and it was sharper than a knife had any right to be. Put to use the right way, it'd cut bone, and, even in the hands of an amateur, it could gut a man from stem to stern and spill his steaming guts out on the dusty ground.

The trick was, when you sharpened it, to drag the blade over the whetstone, gentle-like. Cade was a man who could be gentle when he had to be.

Wasn't what you'd call his main skill, however.

Right now, the knife was only cutting wood, but Cade gripped it like he was cutting through a man's skull. And a man who was alive, at that.

Skrr-rr-retch.

Cade sat on the steps of his trailer, bringing the knife slowly up against the wood, letting it bite in and then flicking his wrist up so as to carve one small shaving at a time off of the piece in his hand. The work was slow and Cade's body was still – an intense kind of stillness, like that second of quiet before the artillery tears into brick and slate and flesh and leaves nothing but mist behind. When Cade was still and silent like that, there was a danger about him. That ain't to say clichés like 'coiled spring' could quite apply to the man – even the suggestion of potential motion was missing from him. But put your ear to his chest, the old-timers in Muldoon's used to say, before the bad times came, and you wouldn't hear a heartbeat. You'd hear ticking.

Across the way, the Duchess was laying out solitaire. She'd found a poker set in Bill Aughtrey's trailer after Cade had taken his body out to the back lot for burning and burying – once upon a time she might have felt a little out of kilter about playing with a dead man's cards, but too much time had passed. They were just nice things going to waste, and the Duchess made it a point of pride to never let anything go to waste, especially not now Duke was in the ground more than two years.

Even in her middle sixties, even playing solitaire, looking at the Duchess was like looking into a burning fire. Every move she made, she shifted against her T-shirt – low cut and ugly pink, off the shoulder, what she called her 'show-off' top. She leaned – playing the ace of spades down into the space she'd marked for it – and the bounty of her breasts leaned along with her, heavy and gorgeous against the tight ugly pink cotton, moving just on the edge of Cade's vision.

She knew what she was doing. They did the same damn thing every day.

Skrr-rr-retch.

The knife cut deep.

Pretty soon, Cade figured, he was going to have to stand up and turn that damn card table over. The Duchess would say something appropriate and Cade would say something appropriate back. Then he'd carry her into her trailer and put her down on the old mattress and they'd get to it. The Duchess knew it. Cade knew it. Hell, the rusty bedsprings in her trailer knew it. It was coming, it was inevitable, and Cade knew it because it happened every damn day.

Not that Cade was complaining, exactly. There wasn't a hell of a lot else for either of them to do.

It was a routine they'd fallen into, on account of how routine was about all that was left for anybody after the bad times, unless you wanted to go stone crazy. But it was a pretty damn good routine for all that.

Cade just hoped she wasn't playing a winning game when he sent the cards flying. Be a shame to wreck that.

The knife handle twitched. The blade cut.

Skrr-rr-retch.

Woody Dupree was due any time. Another ritual. Woody would come and bring the insulin, and they'd maybe play cards a little. Or maybe they wouldn't. Maybe Cade would knock over that card table first, and they'd be in the trailer getting to it when Woody arrived, and he'd just have to sit awhile. Cade wasn't a rude man by nature, but sometimes it happened that way anyway.

But eventually they'd all be sat around the card table with a beer each and they'd talk about the weather, or about something Woody'd read in a book, or maybe about how the vegetable patch was doing.

The last three living people for miles. They'd sit. And they'd talk.

Mostly Cade and the Duchess and Woody Dupree didn't talk about the bad times – mostly they skirted around it, like old rats around poison. But occasionally someone would say something. A subject that big, that black, someone had to say something. Woody might mention his mother, or the Duchess would make an off-hand comment about Duke, and all of a sudden all of those old ghosts would be back in the room and things would get colder. The night would end in silence and pain and a few tears, with Cade left to watch the other two feeling things he couldn't.

Best to leave the past in the past, Cade figured.

Skrr-rr-retch.

More wood shavings fell on the ground, the fresh ones joining with old and rotting ones from the day before and the day before that.

The Duchess laid down another card, her body shifting on the edge of Cade's eyesight.

Cade cut.

Skrr-rr-retch.

He didn't even really know what the hell he was carving.

He just cut.

Skrr-rr-retch.

Cade was considering standing up and turning the damned card table over when he heard a rumbling noise from down the track, and turned his head to see Woody's pickup rolling up next to one of the empty trailers, saving him from his thoughts. The Duchess looked over and waved as Woody opened the driver's door and stepped out, then walked around to the back of the truck. Cade figured something was wrong right then.

Generally, Woody brought the insulin a box at a time, on the passenger seat. But now there was a big crate of the stuff in the back of the truck.

The Duchess' smile left her face, and she looked puzzled instead – puzzled and a little fearful.

Woody was breaking the routine.

Woody still lived in the same house over in Muir Beach, about a couple miles away from the trailer park, and he spent most of his time there. He was a solitary man, even before, and since his mother died along with the rest of the folks in Muir Beach he didn't seem to need or want any company, beyond the time he spent with Cade and the Duchess. Sometimes he wouldn't come to the park for days, and when they'd head into Muir Beach to find him and drag him out for a beer in what was left of Muldoon's – another ritual they tried to keep to every week at least – he wouldn't answer his door. Him bringing the insulin to the trailer park every week was a way for the Duchess to keep an eye on him.

Woody was a fella who needed taking care of, she figured.

His hands shook as he tried to get a hold of the big crate. They shook most of the time, these days.

"Gimme a hand with this, Cade? I don't want to drop it."

Cade stuck his knife in the ground, got up and walked over. The crate wasn't that heavy, but Woody wasn't much of a physical specimen and besides, he had the shakes pretty bad. Cade figured it was best he took hold of it.

By now the Duchess was looking worried. She was scratching lightly at the needle marks on her arm, saying nothing as Cade laid the crate down inside her trailer. Cade figured he'd best ask the question.

"Woody?"

Cade was a man of few words.

Woody sighed, looking down at the ground.

"That's the last crate, Cade."

Cade narrowed his eyes. The Duchess spoke up, a tremor in her voice.

"Now, that can't be right, Woody. I – I thought there was plenty left in Brenner's..."

Woody shook his head, not looking her in the eye. "I thought so too, I did. But, uh, the crates in the back room of the store, the ones that have insulin written on the side, they're... well, they're all full of eye drops. I guess they ran out of eye drop crates at the factory, or there was some sort of mix-up or something... anyway, that's the last. There's sixteen boxes in there."

The Duchess shook her head, getting to her feet. She was blinking slowly as it dawned on her.

The Duchess had known the insulin would run out eventually, but she figured they had enough for a year, maybe two. Long enough to work something out.

"Woody, that'll only last about four months. What happens after four months?" There was an edge of panic in her voice.

Cade shrugged. No sense he could see in panicking. "We get more."

The words hung in the air for a moment. Woody swallowed. "Um, yeah, that's why I brought the whole crate up in one go. See, uh... I figure there's going to be more in the city, so I'm taking the truck down that way, and loading some boxes up..."

He tailed off.

The Duchess looked at him, blinking. "Jesus Christ, Woody,

you wanna go down to Sausalito?"

Woody shook his head. "Sausalito's gone. I was thinking Frisco."

Cade looked at Woody. Woody who was out of shape, who still lived with his mother's ghost. Woody and his shaking hands and his twitch that wouldn't go away, talking about how he was going to take the pickup truck down all the way into San Francisco.

Ed Hannigan had taken a car down that way to see how things were there, about a couple of weeks after the last broadcasts finished and even the emergency band on the radio wasn't giving anything but static. He never came back.

After a couple more weeks, Woody had driven after him a ways. He'd stopped when he came to a skeleton hanging from a sign by the side of the road. He told Cade later there was an orange glow lighting up the horizon.

Sausalito on fire.

Since then, the three of them had pretty much given the cities up for lost, and now Woody Dupree wanted to go down and load up a few crates of insulin, because he felt guilty. He was terrified. You could tell just by looking at him.

Cade shrugged his great shoulders once, reaching to scratch the hairs at the back of his neck. It was pretty damned obvious Woody was about to get his fool self killed.

Hell with it.

"I'll go."

Woody looked at him like a drowning man looking at a rope. He shook his head, licking dry lips. "No, it's okay. I should have checked the crates earlier. It's my fault, I'll..."

"I'll go, I said."

Cade wasn't a man you felt comfortable arguing with, at least not when his voice carried that tone to it. Woody looked down at the ground. "Are you sure?"

The Duchess spoke, her voice dry as Martini. The scare had gone out of her, and Cade was glad of that. "If it's my life on the line, I want Cade to go. No offence, Woody."

Woody nodded. "I'll..." He swallowed hard, unable to keep the relief off his face. "I'll leave the truck here. If... if you drive down to the town tomorrow morning, I'll help you load up with stuff." He licked his lips again. Nervous. "You know. From the gun store."

"Sure." Cade said. He didn't smile, but he probably would have made an attempt if he'd thought of it, for Woody's peace of mind as much as anything else.

Cade was never what you'd call the smiling type.

Woody looked at his shoes for a bit, and then waved, feeling foolish. His face was red as wine, and his eyes were wet, and Cade couldn't help but feel a little sorry for the man. The bad times had left their mark on him and he wasn't ever going to be the same, but he was a decent fella who wanted to do the right thing, and Cade knew that he hated himself right then for passing the buck along. Cade almost wished there was a way he could take that off the man's shoulders.

There wasn't, though. Not a way Cade could figure, at least.

Woody finished waving and turned. "I'd... I'd best get moving, if I want to get home before the sun..." The sentence trailed off, and then Woody turned and trudged back down the hill, leaving the truck where it stood, looking foolish.

They watched him leave, and when he was out of sight the Duchess eased the fullness of her body back into the picnic chair she'd been playing solitaire in and made a show of picking up her cards. Her hands trembled, just a little.

Cade went to pick up his knife.

"Hey."

Cade turned. The Duchess was smiling, or trying to. She was still scared, he could tell. It wasn't just the possibility of losing her insulin supply – or her life. It wasn't even losing him – he knew a lot better than that. She didn't much like Cade, except in bed.

What scared her was that tomorrow would be the end of the routine.

The Duchess shot a glance at the card table, and then a glance at him. Then she half-lowered her lashes, leaning back and raising her hands up into her dyed-blonde hair. "You want to come turn this over?"

Cade nodded, and went.

CHAPTER TWO

THE BAD TIMES

Cade met up with Woody the next morning, outside his mother's house.

Cade didn't know much about her, but then he hadn't known much about Woody before the bad times – carrot-topped, slightly overweight, working under Jim Robinson at the Post Office. Soft voice, hunched back, liked men better than he liked girls, and if Cade ever needed to kill him the best way was probably to sever the pulmonary artery. That's all Cade had known about Woody back then. He remembered Woody's mother as a kindly-faced woman in her middle seventies with the same soft round chubby look to her as her son. Mothered him a lot. Made brownies for the boys at the bar come Superbowl time. Nice woman, if you thought about such things, which Cade didn't.

She'd been one of the first, as he recalled.

Cade's constant silence made him a repository of confidences for the town of Muir Beach, and he was happy enough to listen to people's troubles, just so long as he wasn't imposed upon to care.

That night in Muldoon's he'd been drinking alone, watching Duke lose at pool to some hitchhiker come down from Seattle and breezing through town on the way to a stag weekend in Mexico, when Doc Hackett had sat down at his table, a double whisky in each fist, and it had all come pouring out of him.

Woody's mother had come in to see the Doc about a cough she'd had the whole afternoon that had turned bloody. Right there in his office, in the middle of telling him about it, her lungs had rotted down to liquid in her chest – she just keeled over like a sack of potatoes and let what was in her chest flood out over his white tile floor. He'd seen seven other people do the same thing - that or flow out through their ass – and there were more coming in, and the nurses were coughing their guts up too, and half the people in the street, and... and he needed a drink, god dammit.

Cade passed his own whisky across. The Doc downed it to keep the previous two company and went into a coughing fit, finally spitting a mix of blood and meat back into Cade's glass. Then he went into the toilet and never came back.

Cade had sat and drank, listening to the people in the bar starting to cough. He could've said something, but he figured there wasn't much anybody could do, and there was no mileage in starting up a panic. If this was his last whisky, he wanted to drink it in peace.

Jerry Muldoon closed the bar early – he was coming down with the flu or some such, he said, and besides most of the patrons had staggered out long before – and he died twenty minutes later, while Duke and the hitchhiker were singing in the streets, drunk as lords, not seeing the bodies in the doorways or hunched in parked cars. They were singing Meat Loaf, as far as Cade could remember – I Would Do Anything For Love, with Duke singing the female part in a high, shrill voice. He punctuated every line with a hacking cough until he had to stop, and when the hitchhiker, whose name Cade never learned, leant over and puked his guts in the street, there'd been blood in the vomit. The boy stared at it a second and then slumped face first onto the pavement, the seat of his jeans turning red as he bled out.

Duke made it home, at least, although he didn't know who the hell the Duchess was when she let him in. He called her by the name of a whore he'd known in Abilene while his guts turned to liquid and pooled on the kitchen floor.

Cade buried him the next day. Duke had touched a lot of people in his life, but only the Duchess was there to mourn him.

Everyone else in Muir Beach was dead.

They'd got a hard dose of what was going round – Cade had heard tell of folks hanging on for maybe a week or so with it, but Cade was kind of glad that wasn't the kind anybody in Muir Beach got.

Bad times should be over with quick.

Cade shook his head. He figured there wasn't any point in dwelling on it. He pulled up the truck next to Woody and leaned to open the door.

Woody nodded slightly and walked around to get in. His eyes shifted uncomfortably to meet Cade's for a moment, and Cade could see the skin beneath them was baggy and black. It was a sign of what kind of nights the man had had recently. Last night he probably hadn't slept at all. Apparently people didn't sleep too well when they were guilty, or at least Cade had been told that once. He had no way of knowing.

Cade hadn't felt guilty about much of anything in a while.

Woody muttered a hello as he clambered into the passenger seat. Cade didn't say a word in reply.

It wasn't a calculated gesture, or one made out of dislike of Woody. Cade found Woody pretty much as bearable as he found anybody else. But Cade wasn't a man who said hellos and goodbyes – it was one of those social conventions he never did see much point in, like giving up your seat or opening a door for someone. Cade didn't see the point in that. Or shaking hands. Shaking hands was the worst.

If you reached out your hand to someone, you exposed the wrist. It was the easiest damn thing in the world to grab that hand and carve down the wrist with the blade of your knife. Then the other guy's busy trying to stop eight pints of blood hitting the dirt and he's no damn good in a fight, which means you can drive your knife right in the man's eye and kill him stone dead in less than a second. Shaking hands just seemed like a risk that wasn't worth taking.

That's the way Cade saw it, anyway.

Woody sat – nervous, fumbling with his hands. Then he reached across to grab hold of the seatbelt and draw it across what remained of his pot belly. He spoke softly, without looking at Cade, fingers fumbling with the seatbelt catch as it rattled in the slot. "I couldn't sleep last night, Cade. I felt terrible. It's my fault, all this."

Cade shrugged and shook his head.

"It is, though. I mean it, Cade." He sighed. "She was relying on me. She was relying on me and I let her down. I should have looked in the boxes, or at least... I don't know. It's – it's our most valuable resource. More than canned food. We've got more of that than we know what to do with. I... I should have..." He paused and swallowed, his eyes wet, still fixed on the road ahead, unable to go on. He seemed not to be able to look at Cade.

Cade didn't say anything.

"She could die." It was almost choked.

Cade didn't say anything. Not much to say. Woody wasn't to blame. Some damn fool had marked or packed the crates wrong and there'd been no way of telling. If Woody couldn't see that, there wasn't much point in discussing the subject. He'd have to work through it on his own time.

They drive through Muir Beach in silence.

Muir Beach was a small town – small and secluded, with about a hundred and fifty houses in all, and the trailer park just up the mountain. Everybody knew each other for the most part, even if only by sight, and while there was plenty to gossip about, the folks had respected Cade enough not to pry into his business too close, which was the way he liked it. Muir Beach had become his home after the business with Fuel-Air and the Captain and Sergeant A, which was a business Cade didn't like to dwell on too much. He didn't exactly regret anything he'd done, or even anybody he'd killed, but it'd been a hard day to live through and it was better kept in the past.

Muir Beach had seen better days.

Woody and Cade had managed to clean the bodies out of the places they went regularly and a couple other places besides, but for all that, the town had a rotting, decomposing stench to it, that got on the clothes and the skin. It was one reason the Duchess had moved out to the trailer park after Duke died. The air up the mountain was a hell of a lot cleaner, at least once they'd burned the few bodies that'd been in the trailers.

Woody'd stuck around. Cade didn't dwell much on why that might be. Punishing himself, probably. Cade looked over at him as he sat up suddenly, looking confused and pointing out of the passenger side window.

"The, uh, the gun store's down that way."

"We don't need them."

Cade used the 'we' out of courtesy.

"Um. Are you sure?" Woody finally looked at him, wet eyes wide and uncomprehending. "I mean, you don't know what kind of trouble you're going to run into there. You – you need something to defend yourself."

Cade shrugged. He never did like guns. They just weren't that much use unless you were on a battlefield, at least in his opinion, and Woody's idea that a gun'd help defend a man was full of holes. If someone saw you had a gun, they'd be more likely to shoot you, not less, and a gun wouldn't stop you getting shot either – not unless you were faster than they were, and that was a gamble, not a guarantee. But Cade's real problem with guns was that guns jammed. Guns broke. Guns misfired. They needed cleaning all the damn time. They could get taken away from you and used on you if you didn't know what the hell you were doing, and most people didn't. Guns were just plain unreliable.

When it came to killing, Cade liked things to be reliable.

That's why he carried a bowie knife.

"Hardware store's got everything we need." he said.

Woody paused, looking at Cade out of the corner of his eye,

but didn't say anything more.

Instead, he looked out at the empty streets, as if he was wondering what it was going to be like to have to walk them all alone.

Cade didn't spend too long at the hardware store. He was mostly there for chain.

He settled on two lengths of it. The first length was of the kind strung between posts to make fences with; every third link was decorated with a diamond-shaped decorating weight. This was chain designed primarily to look pretty and line driveways and lawns, and there wasn't all that much in the way of call for it here, but the hardware store kept it in anyway, for reasons that died with Bart Oakley, who was in charge of ordering and died with his face in his cat's litter tray. The chain was useful, in that it was heavy and strong and the decorative weights on it would crack skulls and gouge out eyes should the need present itself. Cade looped it around his waist like a belt and fixed it in place with a combination padlock, which he closed and locked with one number off 0-0-0-0, in case he needed it quickly.

The other chain was lighter gauge, a little thicker than you'd find in a door chain. The sign next to the roll said it was the strongest on the market, and Cade took about five feet of it. It was a good length for strangling, and if looped on itself it'd hurt without killing. A good swipe of this would blind a man, which could come in useful. He looped it around his right bicep, putting it in place with another padlock. Then he though, hell with it, and took another length of the same chain for his left. Might as well.

A man couldn't ever have too much chain, in Cade's opinion.

Woody looked dubious, and that was good. Cade knew most people would look at it the way Woody did – as a decoration or an affectation. That was very good. That meant that when they took away his knives, they wouldn't take the chains. And they probably would take away his knives, Cade figured, even if he didn't know who 'they' were quite yet.

He had two knives. The combat knife, the bowie, his favourite and the one he knew best, was strapped to a holster on his belt. He also had a switchblade decorated with a skull, picked out in white ivory, that fit neatly in his pocket, waiting to come out. Both of these were good blades, although the switchblade was kept more for sentimental value, or as close as Cade got to sentimental, anyway. He made sure to keep them both in good working order. Cade figured between them and the chains, he'd have enough to work with.

The knuckledusters were insurance.

Woody watched in silence as he loaded up, then moved to get in the passenger seat again. Cade shook his head.

"I'm going to head out to Frisco from here, Woody."

Woody swallowed and looked at his feet. Cade figured he could walk from here without any problems, and he waited patiently while Woody searched for the right words.

"Thanks, Cade. For... for taking this on, I mean. Uh, when do you think you'll be back?"

Cade shrugged. "No idea. Depends."

Woody's head lifted. "On what?"

"Don't know. Might need to kill some people. Depends on how many and if they kill me." He scratched the back of his neck, frowning. He wasn't used to talking as much as this, and it sat wrong.

Woody nodded and looked at the ground again. Cade didn't feel like prolonging this any longer, and he figured he should cut it off where it lay.

"See you, Woody. Visit the Duchess regular. She worries."

With that, Cade figured he'd done about enough big speeches. He stomped on the accelerator and the roar of the engine drowned out Woody's reply.

Driving out past the far edge of town, towards the woods that lay between home and the big city, Cade felt something. Saying he felt his load lighten wouldn't be true – Cade was a man who didn't really lighten or otherwise – but there was something that lifted, all the same. The routine of two years of sunrises and sunsets.

Cade had a job to do in San Francisco. He was going to have to do what he did, and it'd been a long time since he'd done it. It might even be fair to say that he missed it, as much as he let himself miss anything or otherwise.

Cade was going to have to kill people again.

He might have smiled at that.

But he wasn't the smiling type.

CHAPTER THREE

THE VOICE IN GERMAN

Duke had a story he used to tell. Kind of a story about a story.

There was a fella once up Russian River way – and Duke always said how dumb they were up Russian River way – but anyway, this fella made his money driving a big rig, an eighteen-wheeler, from a supply depot in Jenner down through the woods to Sausalito. Electrical goods for the most part, there and sometimes back – repairs, Duke figured – and occasionally he'd run a little coke down there from his cousin, or bring a load of reds back to Jenner with him if the Sausalito boys gave him a good deal. Usually his route took him through the Muir Woods area which, by a coincidence, were the same woods Cade was headed through now.

One time, this fella, the dude from Russian River, saw a body laying in the road in a pool of blood. Just laying right in the road and looking deader than hell. So this fella stopped, got out of his cab and went to check, whereupon the dude laying in the road got himself right up and pulled a Mac-10 out from under his belly, stuck it in the dumb fella's face, jacked his truck and drove off into the sunset with a hundred thousand dollars worth of Japanese cameras and half a kilo of coke under the front seat. They found the truck abandoned in Tiburon with the coke still sitting there, and the fella ended up doing about fifteen in San Quentin. War on drugs and all.

Turned out the blood on the road was ketchup.

Now this wasn't the end of Duke's story – it was just the point at which he got in another round of whiskies and maybe took a trip to the head if he had a mind to. The rest of the story went like so: one time Duke was taking the Mustang on a road trip down to Daly and the best way to get there was on the road through the Muir Woods, less you wanted to carry on down the highway and get backed up for your trouble. It's worth mentioning at this point that it'd been ten or eleven years since dumb-fella-whose-name-Duke-forgot got jacked up and busted, and in all that time Duke hadn't ever heard of anyone else having any kind of a similar experience – not in the Muir Woods, anyhow.

Lo and behold, as Duke would say, he'd driven roughly about a mile into the woods when he saw a body laying in the road. Not looking deader than hell so much this time, but laying on his front with one hand under his belly, like he'd hidden something there. Duke stopped the Mustang and got his shotgun out from under the blanket on the back seat. Then he walked towards the fella in the road, real slow, checking the situation out. There wasn't even any blood on the road this time and Duke figured he'd best shoot first before the guy got his Mac-10 or Uzi out or whatever else he had and sprayed Duke with a few hundred rounds.

That was when the man vomited up his breakfast all over the road, which was evidently two bottles of bathtub liquor. Damn fool had just passed out in the road.

"I damn near shot up a drunk 'cause of that dumb Russian River bastard," Duke would say, ordering another round of whiskies.

"What the hell was that fella's name anyway?"

The lesson according to Duke was that if it's a choice between taking the Muir Woods shortcut and going around the highway, you should go around the highway.

Cade didn't feel like going around the highway.

So he ran the truck on the road through the woodland, letting the giant redwoods rising up either side pass him by. Cade figured they hadn't much noticed the human folks dying, but they'd take advantage just the same. Gradually, those redwoods were going to spread out, first of all obliterating this little road, then the big highway, then any of the empty towns in their way, until they'd reached a size big enough for them to feel comfortable in. Muir Woods had been hemmed in by the people for too long.

Cade wasn't what you'd call an environmentalist, on account of how he didn't get too involved in politics on a general principle. He didn't figure he needed any more excuses to kill folks. Life provided enough as it was. Still, he figured it was only right that the great redwoods would take their land back over the generations, for practical reasons if nothing else. People wouldn't be gone forever. Those trees needed to get their numbers back up a little, if only so that men could come and chop them down again when the time came.

That was about all the thought Cade gave the subject.

He drove the woodland road in silence.

There wasn't much point in having the truck's radio on, since there was no stations to pick up anymore. On the few occasions he and Woody had clustered around Bobby Terrill's radio set – Bobby Terril had boasted back before the bad times that he could get any station in the world with his setup, and Woody believed it – they'd heard nothing but crackle and static, apart from one voice in German, talking about who knew what.

Woody had been excited at that, and Cade had let him be. It'd lasted about half an hour, and then Woody realised that neither of them knew German and while it was nice to know that some German guy had gotten hold of a radio, they didn't have any way of talking back. Still, Woody took Bobby Terrill's radio set into his home and listened to the German voice sometimes on dark nights, long after Cade had lost interest in who else might be wandering around out there, and after the Duchess had decided it was better not to hope too hard.

Once, Woody'd turned up at Muldoon's during one of Cade and the Duchess's drinking sessions, all excited. "He was speakin' English today! Kinda, anyhow. See, I couldn't figure what he was talking about at first, but it was all thees and thous and it had a kind of rhythm to it and I figured it out pretty quick – it was Shakespeare! The man was reading Shakespeare, can you believe it? Out loud, I mean."

Cade had shrugged, and the Duchess had smiled maternally. "That's real nice, Woody."

"Ain't it? I figure he's been reading stuff over the radio to maybe keep himself sane. It's a good idea, y'know? I mean, maybe I could do that. Read books to whoever's listening. If we could broadcast, I mean."

"That sounds like a real good idea, Woody," slurred the Duchess, lifting up her eighth whisky. "So, you worked out how to do that? I'd like to hear it. You got a good voice. Ain't he got a good voice, Cade?"

Cade shrugged. Woody shook his head, not losing his smile.

"Nope. I figure, uh, we need a transmitter or an antennae or something. I dunno, I'd need to look it up, and I don't think we've got the books here. Still, it would be nice, wouldn't it? Sending all that literature out into the world. I got some Ed McBains I could read – you know, like those old detective plays that used to come on the radio. Wouldn't that be nice?"

The Duchess had laughed, and poured him a tall whisky, and they'd talked into the small hours about the books they liked to read. Turned out the Duchess had a thing for Harlequin Romances and J.P. Donleavy, of all people. Woody liked crime novels, most especially Donald Westlake in his Richard Stark days, the Parker novels.

Cade didn't read, at least not fiction. Nobody was surprised.

A few shots of whisky after that, with the Duchess passed out on a couch in back, Cade had asked Woody if he'd ever tried tuning in and finding something from the States. Maybe there was someone reading books in American. Maybe, said Cade, coming to the real point of the matter, the Government had managed to get themselves together again. Maybe they were organising, or broadcasting. Maybe there were some good times coming.

Woody had been laughing and playing with the dead shot glasses, making cracks about old brat pack stars he'd have liked to take to bed, but with that question he suddenly sat up straight, all the good humour draining out of him like someone had pulled a plug at the bottom of his soul. Woody'd looked at Cade, pale and drawn, and downed his next whisky in one gulp. "Good times ain't coming, Cade."

Cade blinked. Woody swallowed, trying to clarify. "I mean they ain't organising, Cade. Folks are broadcasting, but... they, they ain't organising." His eyes were suddenly wet. "And they ain't reading no great literature out either, or any Harlequin Romance books or Parker novels or anything else. Trust me on that, Cade. They ain't."

Cade had shrugged and let it go. He'd had a pretty good idea of what Woody had been hearing when he'd tuned away from that calm voice of Germany, and he figured it wasn't anything he needed to trouble himself too much about, and especially not something he needed to burden Woody any further with.

Anyway, he'd know for sure now, or soon enough at any rate.

Cade left the radio off, and the only sound was the dull growl of the truck's engine and the occasional rustle from the trees as a bird took off and flew. Cade kept alert – in these woods, it wasn't uncommon for a deer to head onto the road, and if he wrecked the truck it was going to be a long walk. Not to mention the possibility of dying from being crushed to death by a dead deer.

Cade wasn't a man afraid of dying, but that'd be a pretty damn foolish way for a man to go.

In the event, he didn't see any deer. What he did see in the road was a man. Or a boy. Young adult probably fit him best, Cade figured.

The young adult in question was all of eighteen years old, certainly not much older than that. He was dressed in old, grubby jeans, boots, a t-shirt with a confederate flag on it and a lumberjack shirt. He had sandy hair, close-cropped, and a pronounced overbite. And he was laying in the road, looking like he was injured. But there wasn't any blood.

Cade thought about Duke's story – that time Duke nearly shot the drunk because of what had happened to the fella from Russian River.

Guess things did come in threes at that. Funny how it works out.

The young fella had his hands on his belly and his face suggested real pain. His posture as he lay suggested maybe a couple of cracked ribs, like he'd been beaten and left there to die, although there weren't any marks on his face beyond dirt.

He was laying right in the path of the truck. He didn't look to the layman's eye like he could move himself. If Cade didn't want to roll right over that boy and splatter him on the trail, he was going to have to slam on the brakes. Then he was probably going to have to get out of the car, keeping one of his knives ready at hand, and check to see if the boy was all right or if he was faking. And he wasn't exactly trained as a doctor.

Hell with it, thought Cade.

Then he slammed his foot down on the accelerator.

The boy's eyes went wide in shock and he had just about enough time to let out a squealing cry, like a pig in an abattoir, before the front left tyre hit his head and burst it open like a melon, spraying blood, brain and skull fragments across the dirt roadway. The truck skidded slightly, the front wheel churning in the boy's face as Cade gripped the wheel, fighting the swerve – then the neck cracked as the head went under the wheel. There was a jolt as the limp body thudded under the back wheels and was left behind.

Cade had figured the truck's shocks could take the collision, and he was happy to see he wasn't wrong. He probably couldn't have hit a deer head-on that way, but then again, a deer was a sizeable animal. A kid wasn't going to do as much damage, especially when he'd been laying down.

It wouldn't have troubled Cade much if the young fella had

been what he appeared to be. Things like guilt or remorse weren't especially in Cade's nature, although there were nights he had bad dreams, especially on the subject of Fuel-Air and Sergeant A.

But all the same, there was a certain satisfaction when it came to being proven right about something.

So when the two men charged out from behind the tree with the shotgun, Cade felt a little better. He could keep his foot on the accelerator, keep going, but there was a good chance they were going to blast away with that shotgun, maybe take out one of the back tyres. Then he'd have to abandon the truck. That'd be a real shame. Not to mention the fact that if he drove off now, they'd be waiting for him on the return leg.

And he'd gotten a little rusty. It'd do him some good to get back in practice on these folks.

Hell with it. If he was going to go to the trouble of justifying it to himself, he might as well just do it. At least driving over the kid had thinned them out some.

Cade put his foot on the brake and the truck came to a screeching halt. And then he stepped out of the truck and raised his hands.

The man with the shotgun had sandy hair in the same shade as the young feller's, grown down into a mullet, along with the same pronounced overbite and the addition of a ratty moustache. The other man had the same. There were some physical differences – mullet a little longer in front on one, belly a little pronounced on the other – but the only real difference was in their t-shirts. The one without the gun had a stained *BURN THIS FLAG* tee, the other was wearing one advertising the Scorpions on their last tour. Scorpions' face was red and there were tears running down his cheeks, so Cade figured he was related to the boy somehow, but it was pretty obvious both these men were kin of some kind. Brothers maybe.

The man with the shotgun opened his mouth and screamed.

"Y'all killed my boy! Y'all drove over him like he was nothing!"

It was like an animal howling. The barrel of the shotgun was pointed right at Cade's chest. This was the moment. If Cade ran, or flinched, or looked like he was going to do something, Scorpions was going to pull the trigger. Cade just stared.

He figured Scorpions had a bit more to say on the subject.

"We was just going to rob you, you know that? We was just gonna take your fancy truck and your stuff, and then you killed my boy! My youngest! I dunno how I'm gonna tell Maw her youngest boy's dead..."

Cade wondered if Maw was a term of endearment or if Scorpions had gotten his mother pregnant. It wasn't outside the realm of possibility. Scorpions had the barrel pointed at Cade's face now, and he was moving closer.

Not quite close enough, though. Cade waited.

He could be patient when he had a mind to be.

"...but I reckon the tellin's gonna be a mite easier if'n I blow your head off and take her your goddamn brains in my hand, you son of a bitch! Look at me! Look at me when I'm talking to you! *Look at me!*"

Cade wasn't looking at Scorpions. He was looking over at Burn This Flag, sizing him up. Burn This Flag was looking back, a little wary. His mouth was half-open, like he was trying to work out what was going on.

Cade figured Burn This Flag wasn't the smartest in the family.

"Look at me! I wanna see your eyes! Look at me!"

The barrel of the shotgun was nudging Cade's chin.

"*Look at me! Look at me, goddamn you...*"

Cade made his move.

His right arm moved suddenly, almost a blur, grabbing the end of the barrel and twisting it to the left, while his left hand grabbed it further down, twisting it right. The gun went off, discharging close to his left ear, leaving nothing in it but a ringing noise. Cade hoped that wasn't permanent. He hadn't figured on the gun going off.

Rusty.

The shotgun landed on the ground between them as Scorpions clutched at his hand. His trigger finger was bent upwards, at a right angle. He stumbled back, looking at Cade with wide eyes, his mouth open in shock.

His face stayed that way while Cade took the combat knife out of his belt and cut his throat with it.

Cade sidestepped most of the blood, but still felt a wet gush of it hit his side. He'd probably need a change of shirt later. Burn This Flag was still looking at him, blinking, his mouth opening and closing like a fish. His legs were shaking a little. He wanted to run, Cade could tell. But he just couldn't make his legs do it.

Cade had seen that happen to people he'd killed before.

As he walked up to Burn This Flag, the redneck let his bladder and bowels go, soaking the front of his jeans with a growing dark stain as the back sagged under the weight of his mess. His eyes were still staring ahead and his mouth was still opening and closing, trying to form even one word, when Cade drove the point of the combat knife through his forehead and into his brain.

Burn This Flag took one step backwards and crashed down, convulsing on the floor. Cade figured he'd let the man thrash a little and then get his knife back. Then he'd carry on the way he'd been going, past what was left of Sausalito and into San Francisco. Not much point hanging around.

He didn't hear the growl.

His left ear was still ringing, and they came on his left. It was the big shape in his peripheral vision that warned him, but he wasn't expecting what he saw.

An old woman of about eighty or ninety, with wispy grey hair and that same damn overbite, standing in a worn polka-dot dress. That wasn't so surprising to Cade. He figured there'd be more from the family around these woods. What was surprising was what she had with her.

On the end of a chain leash, there was a brown bear – a grizzly. Up on its hind legs, teeth bared, eyes red. A grizzly bear in a killing mood, and this old girl had domesticated the damn thing somehow.

Cade was rarely surprised by anything. But this was one of those times.

After all, bears weren't common to the Muir Woods.

Cade scratched the back of his neck. The combat knife was stuck in Burn This Flag's skull, and he'd need a second to pull it out. He figured he most likely didn't have a second.

He looked at the bear.

The bear looked back at Cade.

The old lady looked around at the three bodies. Then she let go of the leash. Her voice was high, reedy and a little raspy. Cade figured this was Maw.

"Sic 'im, Yogi."

And Yogi did just that.

CHAPTER FOUR

THE BEAR

Now, your standard grizzly bear stands about eight feet tall and weighs about eight hundred, maybe eight hundred and fifty pounds.

Which is a hell of a lot of bear.

Yogi was a little taller. Cade figured that one good swipe from Yogi's claws was probably going to take his face off – just unzip the flesh from off his head and tear it loose like peel off an orange.

Hell of a thought. One swipe, knocking your head to the side, maybe cracking your neck, so's the one eye you got left gets to see something wet and red flying off to the side like a pink deflated balloon. Something with a nose and a mouth, wrapping around a tree, while your grinning skull waits there for the jaws to crack down on it and burst it just like an egg in a grown man's fist. Thought like that'll keep a man up nights.

It didn't trouble Cade overmuch, mind, but Cade had a habit of not troubling himself with the details. The important thing at this particular moment was to pick a weapon and stick with it.

He had maybe less than a second. Not much time at all – not near enough to go for the switchblade, or pop one of the lengths of chain on his arms. He'd have to take the bear on with just his hands, which was going to be a problem. That said, Cade didn't worry too much.

He had the knuckledusters on, and Cade was a man used to making do.

He snapped his right arm forward, slamming his fist into the bear's stomach, then did the same with his left, then his right again. The three punches took less than a second to throw, and he felt one of the bear's ribs go with the last one – on account of the lead weight sitting on the end of each fist, turning every punch into something like being hit by a sledgehammer.

Cade wasn't under any illusions. The bear wasn't about to get any easier to fight. Fact was, now he'd wounded it, it was going to be pretty damn mad – killing mad – and eight hundred and fifty pounds of killing mad bear could probably tear a man right open without even letting the thought cross its mind.

He'd just have to kill it before it did that.

The knuckledusters were simple but effective – studded lead weights that fitted his fingers neatly. They were a good pair of tools, and Cade had gotten a fair amount of use out of them in his time. Cade wasn't generally known as a man who got into bar fights – not as a rule – but once upon a time, he'd been ambushed in an alley on the way back from a long session at Muldoon's. Sore loser who didn't like having his money taken away from him by a straight flush and figured he could take it right back. Cade wasn't of the same opinion.

Cade had never learned the man's name. They'd found him in the alley the next morning and identified him using dental records, from the bits of jawbone laying a few feet away from what was left of his face. Cade never heard anything more about it, so he assumed the detective in charge of the case hadn't had much luck. Too bad.

The knuckledusters were useful, all right. But that was then and this was now, and there was a hell of a difference between a drunk with a blackjack and eight feet of pissed-off woodland killer.

Cade had his work cut out for him, in other words.

One of the razor-sharp claws came for his face, ruffling his hair as he ducked under it. The damn bear was howling up a storm now – Cade could see that in just about a half second the animal was going to spring forward and slam all that weight down on him. And while Cade was pretty capable of lifting a thing when he had a mind to lift it, he wasn't about to lift eight hundred and fifty pounds of bear, most especially angry bear. Not if that bear decided to grab his head in its jaws and crush it like a damn eggshell and then pull what was left off of his neck like a chicken drumstick.

Yogi roared at the top of his lungs, showering Cade in bear spit. Another swipe from those claws... Cade veered back, getting far enough out of the way not to lose any more than a button off of his shirt, then stepped back inside the bear's reach and swung his left. Cade had a pretty fearsome left hook and with the knuckleduster on, it could kill a man without trouble. But a bear's not a man.

The lead weight slammed against the side of Yogi's head, caving in half of the beast's teeth and most likely fracturing the jaw into the bargain – at least if that hard, flat *crack*, like a rock breaking underneath a chain gang hammer, was anything to go by.

It was a hell of a punch, no doubt about that. But it was a lucky punch, and Cade wasn't going to stay that lucky for long.

Next thing he knew, he was flying across the dirt road with a warm gash opening up in his side. In the half-second he'd taken to register his own hit, the damn bear had backhanded him. On account of not having hearing on his left side, maybe. He slammed into the dirt, the impact knocking most of the wind out of him and sending a wave of fire through the fresh wound on his side.

Yogi was already lumbering towards him as he rolled back

onto his feet. At least he could get on his feet and still keep his guts inside him. Cade figured that meant he hadn't been tagged that bad – maybe a deep cut, but nothing a few stitches wouldn't cure, if the bear didn't decide to stick that smashed muzzle in it and root around for whatever it could get.

He braced himself as the bear charged.

Cade lashed out again, aiming for the head – a solid right, impacting above the eye with an unholy crunch, leaving a dent. The bear's momentum kept it moving, those eight hundred and fifty pounds slamming into him like a freight train, knocking him off his feet and damn near crushing the breath out of him. Cade aimed another punch up, into the jaw, a left hook that landed with the power of a drop hammer. Then a right, into the throat, crushing the windpipe. He felt it go – felt his hand sink into the flesh, rupture the organs the animal needed to breathe – and then he was buried in fur with eight hundred and fifty pounds crushing down on him, breathing bear. This was it. If the damn thing wasn't dead by now, it was going to rear up and those jaws were going to rip him into bloody pieces before it even thought about breathing. The pain from the broken jaw would just make it bite harder while it could.

The bear didn't bite. The jaws lolled, drooling spit and blood. The body shook, convulsing, as Cade managed to work himself out from underneath the dead weight of it, careful of the still-twitching claws.

The damned thing was dead, all right. So much cooling meat. Cade had killed it when he'd cracked the skull, probably put a few pieces of bone right into the animal's brain.

Lucky punch.

Cade stood, the corner of his mouth twitching slightly as his fingers moved over the gash in his side. Not even deep, just plenty bloody. Ten or twelve stitches would see to it.

Just as soon as he'd done something about the old woman.

She was standing, looking at him, a cold stare that didn't blink once. There was a lot of hurt in those eyes. Hurt and hate and frustration, because the fight was over and she'd thrown her best at him and she didn't have much of anything else to throw.

And he was still standing.

"You killed Yogi."

Cade nodded. It was a fact.

"You killed Yogi and you killed my boys." She swallowed, shaking her head slowly. "They was just going to rob you some. You didn't have no reason to kill 'em for it."

Cade nodded again. He didn't feel the need to say anything. She was right. He hadn't needed to kill 'em. But Cade only fought one way, and people didn't get up again after it. That was just the way the man was.

Nobody said anything else for a good minute. Cade looked at the dead bear, and the old woman looked at Cade until he turned those grey eyes of his in her direction again.

She shook her head. "It ain't right, that's all I'm saying. Ain't meant to happen this way, not to the family. We had the good blood – we could all of us live through the sickness. Good blood, kept in the family, that's what pappy said. Allus had it. We all kept our bloodline pure."

Cade looked into her eyes, old and confused. Crazy as it was, there was a hell of a lot of logic to it. There was that one blood type that the plague didn't hit, Cade knew that from the news reports and presumably these people did too, before the news reports quit on them. Inbreeding might keep that special strain of blood flowing.

Once upon a time, these people were probably the scum of some community down south or in a trailer park somewhere even people as damaged as Cade and the Duchess wouldn't end up. A bunch of inbred hicks, a sick town joke. And then the bad times had come and turned the whole damned world into the punch line. And suddenly the hillbilly scum family everybody laughed at turned out to be the last survivors. Any of them who could read or switch on a wireless would put two and two together and the first thing such a clan'd do sure wouldn't be to stop screwing the hell out of each other. Keeping it in the family would go from general policy to an article of faith.

Keep it in the family and you kept the blood pure.

The old woman's eyes glittered, hard little stones in the grey flesh of her face. "Who's gonna keep it pure now? Got Maybelle and the baby waitin' back in the woods. Their brothers are dead now – so who's gonna get 'em with child? Who's gonna keep that blood pure? You tell me that!"

She was crying.

"We was gonna start again! Gonna – gonna –" She groped for the word, clawing the air with her fingers. "Gonna repop... repopulate the world! You killed the world today, yes you did, killed the whole damn world! Killed the future of the world..." She shook her head. "You best kill me too. You better had – better put me in the dirt right now! Because *I'm going to come after you!*"

Cade looked at her. She was thin as a rake – malnourished, probably full of cancer.

She grinned, and there was one tooth in it. "I'm going to come after you! And I'm gonna kill you and anyone you love like you killed *mine,* boy –"

Hell with it, thought Cade.

He figured you should take your elders at their word.

He swung his right into her face, the lead weight smashing just above her eyes, crushing the skull inward and turning the frontal lobes to jelly. She tottered back for a step or two, her head dented in like a car bonnet after a death-crash, whatever was in her bladder and bowels hitting the ground with a wet slap, then tumbled over like a rag doll. Twitching on the ground, she looked like nothing quite so much as a puppet with the strings cut.

Cade figured she was probably just crazy, but there was a chance she had some clout – maybe she could have caused him trouble on the way back. He was better off dealing with her now. Anyone coming across the scene would probably put the picture together, but Cade'd be long gone by then.

He reached down and gripped the handle of the combat knife, tugging it free of Burn This Flag's skull. Cade wasn't a man who worried himself a great deal, but there was a troubling aspect to the encounter. These were probably the most screwed up people he'd ever encountered outside the confines of his shaving mirror, but they made some sense. Their blood was an antidote to the thing that'd murdered a planet, so inbreeding made sense. Screwing your own family, bearing children by them, that made sense. Pretty good sense, in fact.

That worried Cade.

He wondered if there were crazier people waiting for him in Frisco. More dangerous people. And if there were, he wondered if they were going to start making sense to him too.

When Cade got out of the woods, he put the truck in gear and pointed it south, down Highway 101. Behind him, to the north, was what was left of Sausalito and Marin City. Part of him had been hoping Woody was wrong about that, but one look at the column of smoke still rising up towards the horizon was enough to set him straight. Woody wasn't wrong. Sausalito had most likely been razed to the ground, and the chance he was going to find what he needed there was slim to none.

San Francisco lay ahead, across the Golden Gate Bridge. Cade gunned the engine, narrowing his eyes.

There was something strung across the bridge. Something white and flapping, half-burned, stained with blood in places. A banner. Cade strained his eyes, and read:

HIPPY DONT LET THE SUN SET ON YU HERE!!!

Cade didn't figure that was a good sign.

CHAPTER FIVE

THE ALPHA MALE

Cade kept the truck on Highway 101, past the cemetery and along Marina Boulevard. The parks and suburbs around the Presidio looked as gutted as Sausalito had been – wrecked houses, smoking timber where trees and fields had been, dead bodies nobody had bothered to clear up. A lot of them looked dead from the bad times – bled out on the street or on the porches of their houses. Some of the corpses looked like they'd died some other way, though – there was one in particular, a pair of legs dangling by almost-rotted trouser cuffs from a telephone pole, the top half laying propped against a fire hydrant, mostly lost to rats and scavengers.

Across the street, there was another sign, of sorts. A fat fella – had to weigh a good three hundred pounds, and all of it blubber – was sitting naked on the road ahead, placed so that Cade had to swerve around him. He slowed the truck, taking a good look.

The man was naked, and had been posed and propped up with a stick, sharpened and pushed into the meat of his back. His head had been severed, and the neck was ragged, as though it'd been pulled off. What was left of the head was sitting in the man's lap, and flapping out of the open mouth was something Cade thought at first was a thumb, until he got a little closer and saw it had a foreskin on it.

Carved into the chest were some words. It took Cade a few seconds to read them.

Helter Skelter.

Not good at all.

Something bad had happened out here. Probably the same bad thing that happened to Sausalito, to Marin City. The destruction seemed to get worse as he went further down the boulevard, the last of the suburbs a still-flaming vision of something out of hell – then suddenly he took the truck past the line of Baker Street and he was on the city grid. And things were different.

He slowed the truck down to a crawl. The streets were empty, and they were mostly clean. There weren't any bodies laying anywhere – he figured they'd been dumped into the Marina, or piled up elsewhere, out of sight. Maybe even buried. He glanced right, down the length of Broderick Street. The same story. Clean, deserted, no dead, no garbage.

Cade figured he'd just crossed a boundary line. Either whatever had torched the Presidio had been turned back here... or it'd started out here. The hairs on the back of Cade's neck were itching a little, the way they had out in the desert when the officers were talking about their damn-fool strategies. Those hairs on the back of Cade's neck were an antennae, of sorts. They flared up when something got to smelling bad.

Cade had to admit, this smelled pretty bad.

He figured he had a couple of options, as things stood. He could find the first pharmacy, load up with as much insulin as he could handle and get the hell out. Thing was, that wasn't much of an option for two reasons.

One, if he loaded up the truck with one drugstore's worth, he'd buy the Duchess maybe another year at most and then he'd need to do it all again, and he'd be a year older and a year slower and have a year less gas for the truck. And then the year after that – well, it just wasn't sustainable, was Cade's thinking on the matter.

No, Cade needed to find a big supply of the stuff, which meant he'd probably need to ask some questions, which meant, judging by the state of the Presidio, that he'd need to kill a few people. That was fine by Cade.

The other reason was a matter of security, and it'd been half in his head since he'd seen Sousalito, and now he'd crossed the bridge, he was sure of it. Muir Beach was a ways away from San Francisco, but if they'd trashed the Presidio and the suburbs, then gone for Sausalito, then Marin, then who knew where else up to the north – well, it was a matter of time before they headed west and got to be a serious problem. Whoever did what he'd seen, there was a hell of a lot of them. Either they were out to the north and he'd need to run them down, or they were here and he'd need to burn them out.

Either way, he needed to ask some questions. He needed to ask a few just to get the lay of the land, because it was pretty damn clear to Cade that San Francisco was as foreign a country as he'd ever been in and he didn't have a damn clue what the customs were or who the local boss was. All he knew for sure was that there wasn't a single soul on the streets.

Not one soul, alive or dead.

Which was a little weird in itself.

There's a hell of a lot of weight on a dead body. Woody and Cade had done the best they could with the hundreds of bodies in Muir Beach, although in the event Cade had done most of the actual work, cutting the bodies down and lugging them a piece at a time. Woody wasn't made to haul bodies, though he did as many as he could before he started crying and throwing up, and Cade didn't want to trouble the Duchess with it. Cade didn't exactly care about people, but there were a small number of people he nearly cared about, and he came the nearest with her. He wasn't about to put her through a nightmare he could take on his own self.

It had taken months to even make a few places in Muir Beach liveable again. That was a small town of a hundred and fifty homes and no cable TV, and they couldn't clear it entirely – had to give about two thirds up for lost.

San Francisco was a whole damned city. There were more people on five or six blocks than in the whole of Muir Beach. And by the looks of things, it was clean as a hospital wing.

Frankly, that just wasn't right.

The air blowing in through the truck window was clean, with no trace of that rot that blew through Muir Beach when the wind went the wrong way. But it still stunk to high heaven for all that. The hairs on the back of Cade's neck were buzzing like death row.

"Hell with it," he muttered, and jerked the wheel right, turning the truck down Cervantes Boulevard. He wasn't going to be getting anywhere pissing about the edge of town.

His eyes narrowed as he crawled down the street, checking the buildings one by one. Something about halfway down the Boulevard caught his eye, and it took him about a half second to work out what the hell it was.

Neon.

BLARNEY'S, flickering on and off in green with a little shamrock. An irish bar.

With a neon sign.

Those neck hairs were dancing tango.

They had electricity – probably something rigged up in back, a cheap gas-powered generator, maybe, but someone had to rig that up and run it. And nobody was going to the trouble of making a neon sign flicker without a good reason. Neon signs were what Cade would call a hell of a luxury.

What that was, was a beacon. Maybe an invitation.

"Hell with it," muttered Cade, and parked the truck.

As he got out and closed the door – Cade knew better than to slam it – he was listening. There was a sound on the wind – low voices, men's voices, singing softly. Cade stopped for a moment, breathing in the clean air. There was something about that song that halted even him, something that gave him a little pause.

Not the soft tone of the melody, or the reverence, but that such a thing should be at all.

Amazing Grace... how sweet the sound...

Cade scratched the back of his neck, and his mouth twitched towards a frown for a second. Cade wasn't generally a man who allowed himself to be spooked by much of anything but he had to admit to himself that this was a touch spooky no matter how you cut it.

Back in the desert, Cade had been in a humvee with a guy named Fuel-Air. That wasn't his name – his name was Billy Dominguez – but the Sergeant figured nicknames were good for morale, so if someone looked like he was bucking for one, Sergeant A made sure it stuck. Fuel-Air got more Ripped Fuel than air, according to Sergeant A, so he ended up on a permanent caffeine and ephedrine rush. That made him a hell of a driver on no sleep, but made him a hell of a talker besides, which wasn't the best company for a man like Cade, who gave the impression in a conversation that he lost a year of life for every word he said.

Fuel-Air pissed Cade off no end. He never shut up, and he had a way with a phrase, short little explosions of profanity and bitter sarcasm mixed in with all the shitty DVDs he used to rent before he joined up. Fuel-Air Bombs, according to Sergeant A, who was a lot funnier in his head than he was in real life. Still, he cared about his men, and he did his damnedest to keep them alive.

He wasn't like the Captain in that respect.

No sense dwelling on that, though.

Fuel-Air was dead now – dead before the bad times hit, which was probably best. Cade didn't think Fuel-Air could've coped with losing his guts out of his anus. That would've been *some five-star fucked-up undignified Stephen King shit* as far as Fuel-Air was concerned. He'd have complained about it every damn second he was dying. Probably would've been one of the ones who lasted a week, just so he could discuss it at length.

Cade blinked and pictured his voice, yelling over the dull engine roar of the humvee droning in the background. Always yelling, always talking.

"This is some five-star shit, dog, some five-star Silent Hill *strange-ass* Children Of The Corn *shit! They're gonna put fuckin' bees on your head or some shit like that, man, like Nic fuckin' Cage!"*

He was dead before that film came out, though. Cade shook his head. He didn't know what the hell he was thinking about that boy for. He'd hated the little bastard.

Time to get to work.

Cade walked to the door of the bar and pushed it open, and the singing stopped.

The first thing Cade noticed was that all the taps had been torn out of the bar, and instead of booze on the shelf behind, there was bottled water. All kinds of brands, sparkling and still, rows and rows of glass and plastic bottles and not a single drop of anything alcoholic between them.

Each of the bottles had a cross drawn on it in magic marker.

That spooky feeling was getting worse.

Cade didn't like where things seemed to be headed. He counted the men – ten sets of eyes staring in his direction. Ten men, a couple bigger than Cade, and none of them looked like a man who wasn't used to fighting.

And he'd done interrupted their choir session.

This would not end well.

The muscles in Cade's back tensed, but he spoke gently, calmly. Truth to tell, Cade didn't really have another way of speaking but calm, and soft, and low. A lot of folks found that menacing, but Cade just wasn't the shouting kind. He hoped he didn't sound like he was trying to be menacing now. He wanted some information.

He didn't want to kill anybody.

If it came to a fight, Cade pretty much only knew one way of fighting, and that was fighting to kill. So if things got a little untoward, there was a good chance none of these people would be left in a position to say a damn word about Sousalito or any other subject you could name. They'd be a little busy being dead. Cade didn't want that. At least not just yet.

"Sorry to disturb you." he said, as a courtesy. "I've got some questions."

One of the men was chewing a stick of gum. A blonde guy, maybe six-five, had an alpha-male look about him. He stopped chewing, and his voice was a slow, lazy drawl, heavy with scorn.

"You a hippie?"

Cade considered the question. No, he couldn't say he was. He shook his head, keeping his eyes on Alpha Male.

"You look like a hippie."

Cade lifted his hand to his face and tried to remember the last time he'd looked at himself in a mirror. Cade pretty much avoided looking at himself in a mirror unless he had to. It wasn't a guilt thing, exactly. Cade wasn't a man who felt guilty as a rule. But it was a pastime he couldn't say he got an awful lot out of.

His fingers brushed through his beard. It was pretty furry there, all right. A good three months of growth.

And now he came to think about it, the Duchess had been saying she needed to cut his hair again. It'd been about eight months since she'd done that. She was saying he was getting to looking like a damn mountain man.

Cade ran his fingers through his hair. It was pretty long at that.

This was something he should've considered when he saw that sign on the bridge.

"I said you look like a hippie, boy."

Alpha Male was pressing his point. Cade was a fair-minded man when he had a mind to be, and he surely had to admit that there was a certain logic to Alpha Male's position. Cade probably did look a bit like a hippie, at least going by his hair, and his beard. Mind you, there was the big splatter of slowly drying blood on the side of his tank-top, and all over his fists and up his arms, but maybe in this light they just looked a little grimy.

Hell with it.

"Guess so." Cade nodded. No harm in being agreeable. "All the same, I've got some questions." He paused, looking at the men. The ones with glass bottles were carrying them by the neck now, like clubs. Cade figured he could see where this was headed.

"Hoping you could answer them."

One of the men smashed his bottle against a table, the water splashing onto the ground along with shards of glass, leaving him with a weapon. Cade looked in his direction for a moment.

"I'd be obliged." said Cade, softly. He figured there wasn't much else apart from that to be said.

Alpha Male spat.

"You got a nerve, hippie. You're a long way from the Hashbury now, you know that? Satan doesn't have the power to help you here. This here is God's city." He grinned, and the grin lit up his face. There was malevolence there, but also a kind of fervour, a sort of ecstasy that shone out of those blue eyes.

It hit Cade, suddenly, that this talk of God and Satan wasn't an excuse.

Cade had met a lot of folks in the past who used talk of Jesus to excuse themselves when they figured they'd give Woody a punch in the mouth for sleeping with who he did, or take a tyre iron to Lou Greer's caddy because Maisy Greer was white, or tell Frank Bellows' eldest she was Lucifer's own murderous whore because she'd gotten herself pregnant and decided not to keep it. Cade had come across a fair few of those folks, and usually it was people like Frank Bellows – who didn't appreciate some damn fool making his only daughter feel even worse about something that wasn't their damn business to begin with – who'd ask him to make their acquaintance.

For the most part he'd gently let them understand that Muir Beach wasn't the best town for them to make those excuses in. Generally that didn't take more than a couple of fingers.

Those folks were just of a certain mind, Cade figured. If they were in some country where folks weren't quite so fired up about God and his particular wants on a subject – Sweden, maybe – they'd find another reason to bully folk. But Alpha Male believed every word, and so did the other nine.

In another moment, they were going to do their damnedest to kill him for the length of his chin hair, because in their minds, that's what Jesus had told them to do.

Cade couldn't help but wonder if they'd come up with that one on their own.

He cracked his neck, and popped the chain from round his waist. There was the sound of another bottle breaking. Then a third.

Alpha Male grinned.

"Praise be."

And then they charged.

CHAPTER SIX

THE FIGHT

As it turned out, Alpha Male was the first to go.

Alpha Male had a real name, of course. It was Marvin Wilton, and he'd been a basketball hero in college before settling down with the prom queen, who also sang regularly in the local church – which had unfortunately been wrecked during the roughest days of the bad times, like a lot of churches had been. He'd had three children, all of whom were now dead, and before the bad times hit he'd been a pillar of his community, albeit a little judgemental when it came to some of the people he shared San Francisco with. His neighbours would have been shocked to see him acting this way, had they lived. They wouldn't have thought Marvin Wilton capable of this kind of wanton violence.

But the bad times changed people.

Not that Cade gave a damn about Marvin Wilton. Cade had turned not giving a damn into a science, and if someone had tried to tell him Marvin's life story Cade would have found something else to do by the second trimester. Alpha Male was Alpha Male, and that was the name he was going to die under as far as Cade was concerned.

It was a legacy of his time in the humvee with Sergeant A – Cade wasn't much on people's actual names. As far as he figured, he was facing down Alpha Male, Combover, Man-tits, Skinny, Budget Ben Affleck, Ears, Never Forget, Tall Fella, Other Tall Fella and Global Hypercolour.

To be honest, he didn't even give them that much thought. But if he'd wasted a second looking at them, that's what he'd have called them, and it makes what happened next a little easier to describe.

What happened next was Cade doing what Cade did.

The heavy gauge chain whipped out, the combination lock on the end whirling through the dusty air like a mace until it slammed hard into Alpha Male's mouth. Marvin's perfect teeth cracked and splintered on impact and he reeled back, spitting out enamel fragments and blood, the remains lacerating cheeks and gums as he screamed – and then Cade swung the lock down on the top of his skull with as much force as he could bring to it. There was another flat *crack* and Alpha Male dropped like a sack of coal, bleeding from one ear. He was one of the lucky ones. He'd lost most of his teeth and he'd never be able to count to a hundred again.

But he'd live. For a while, at least.

In a matter of days, he'd have the jugular torn from his neck by a cannibalistic ex-finance director who hadn't bathed in two years, but that was in the future.

Man-tits lunged with a broken bottle that'd once been full of some Brand X Perrier substitute. Once upon a time, drinking something like that in Blarney's might have been taken as the sign of a man who wasn't in full possession of his manhood. It might even have earned a medium-level ass-kicking, like as not from Man-tits himself, who was the type to take offence at that kind of thing. But things had changed some since the bad times hit. According to the Pastor, alcohol was the work of Satan, and refined sugar likewise. Water was good for the system and good for the spirit, although anything that still managed to struggle out of the taps in San Francisco wasn't likely to be either of those and it was best to stick to the bottled variety, as passed out by the Pastor himself, blessed by his hand. Man-tits had come to believe very strongly in the Pastor and his word.

Man-tits was a man who believed strongly in a lot of things, especially if they were told him in a loud voice and it was implied that he was some kind of communist queer-boy if he didn't buy into them. Man-tits was just that sort of fella.

Cade shifted to the side, then used his free hand to catch Man-tits by the wrist and break his arm at the elbow, making sure to twist it so the broken bone pushed up through the skin. Then he snapped his head forward hard enough to break Man-tits' nose. He could've left it there, but Other Tall Fella had a bottle of his own and was bringing it round to slash at Cade's throat.

Cade grabbed Man-tits by the hair and swung him across, and Other Tall Fella's bottle went right into his neck, carving it wide open. Cade took a step back, doubled the chain in his fist and swung it so it raked across Other Tall Fella's face. It didn't do his complexion a whole lot of good.

The diamond-shaped weights in the chain – that made it look so nice and pretty when it was strung on the edge of a man's lawn – burst both eyes and broke a mess of teeth, which pretty much put Other Tall Fella out of the fight. His fellow men of God pushed him out of the way when he started screaming. He stumbled back, tripped over his own shoelaces and then toppled back like a falling tree, until the back of his head met the corner of the bar with a crunch that finished him off for good.

Probably for the best, considering.

That left seven.

They were a little wary now, though their blood was still up. Cade took a step back, and they took a step forward, shuffling around the bodies. Cade was swinging the chain in his hand, round and round, a slow circle. It made a little *ch-chink* sound every time it went round. A little whisper of metal on metal.

Ch-chink, ch-chink, ch-chink.

Global Hypercolour stepped forward, sweat dripping down his forehead and off his nose, big hot-pink stains spreading out from his armpits and down his chest. The rest of the T-shirt was purple, aside from the Global Hypercolour logo in white. Cade had never understood the appeal of those things.

He whipped the chain out, around Hypercolour's neck, then jerked him in, like reeling in a fish, grabbing the big man in a headlock and twisting his neck quickly until he heard it snap. It was as quick a death as he could make it, but Tall Fella and Combover were already rushing his flanks, and now his good chain was tangled up around Hypercolour's throat. Combover had a broken bottle, Tall Fella just had his fists, and Bargain Ben Affleck was coming up in front to make three.

Cade didn't need to think too hard about it. He took a step back and caught Tall Fella's ear in the fingers of his right hand and Combover's bottle in the left. Then he pulled. Tall Fella had his centre of gravity a little far forward as things stood – the tug on the ear, hard enough to rip the cartilage, send him stumbling forwards until his feet met Hypercolour's thrashing body, and then over he fell. Cade kept his grip on Combover's wrist and moved the broken bottle so Tall Fella tumbled face-first into it. It made a sound like a shuriken hitting a twenty-pound steak.

Bargain Ben crashed into Tell Fella and the two of them went down to the ground while Cade popped Combover's arm out of its socket, and once Ben was down on the floor Cade brought his boot down on the back of the man's head hard enough to smash his face into the barroom floor. Cade figured he probably wouldn't look too much like Ben Affleck after that, but that was his own lookout.

Tall Fella was screaming his lungs out through what was left of his own face, so Cade gave him a kick in the side of the head to shut him up and then swung a right hook around to break Combover's nose and put him out as well.

The whole thing had taken about fifteen seconds so far.

Cade was a pretty quick worker when he had a mind to be.

He cracked his neck again, looking each of the last three square in the eye. Skinny and Ears looked like they might listen to reason at this point – especially with a couple of the bodies still thrashing and voiding their bowels on the floor – but the fella with the crying eagle tattoo and the Never Forget underneath it, he was going to be a problem. It wasn't just the tattoo. It was in his eyes. Never Forget wasn't a man to start talking in a situation like this.

Fella had something to prove.

Cade figured he'd try talking anyway.

"I've got some questions. Hoping you could answer them."

Ears swallowed. Skinny looked down at the dead, his face pale. Never Forget just stared. His lip was curling into a sneer. Cade didn't know whether it was on purpose or if his face was just built that way. He nodded, then spoke one more time.

"I would be obliged."

Never Forget spat on the floor.

Cade shrugged. Hell with it. Least he'd tried to do things the easy way.

"You got a nerve, you –" said Never Forget, and that was as far as he got, on account of the next second Cade's combat knife was lodged in his throat and he couldn't get the next word out through the blood flooding out of his mouth.

Cade was a man who was willing to give a fella a chance when he had a mind to.

But he didn't always have a mind to.

Cade went into a roundhouse kick, aiming the steel toe of his boot into Skinny's chest, snapping a rib and sending the man down to the floor. In the movies, folks tell you a broken rib ain't much of anything. They're liars. A broken rib's a hard thing to work around, especially when it breaks off bad and ends up going into a lung. Cade had made damn sure it'd gone into a lung, and now Skinny wasn't going to get up again in a hurry. He had his hands full just taking a breath without screaming.

That left Ears. He was already raising his hands to surrender, but Cade didn't catch it in time. Cade wheeled around in another roundhouse – what Duke had called his Chuck Norris move – and brought his foot up a little higher this time. The steel toe cap slammed into one of those big elephant ears hard enough to burst the eardrum. Then Cade followed up by smashing an elbow into the man's face.

That's another thing the movies tell you is easy – driving a man's nosebone into his brain hard enough to kill him stone dead. It's a hell of a trick, especially with the elbow.

Maybe Cade just got lucky.

Still, after he'd stepped back and taken a breath, he didn't feel quite as lucky as all that. Skinny'd passed out pretty much right away, which meant there wasn't anybody likely to answer his questions. He had a few more of them than before. Cade was a man who could put two and two together if he had a mind to, and he'd figured on there being some kind of old-time religion operating in Frisco – when the bad times hit, a lot of people had made some snap decisions about religion – but damned if he knew how far it spread or what the hell else might be going on. He wasn't any closer to finding any insulin, and he damn sure wasn't any closer to finding out what'd done for Sausalito.

He'd killed a bunch of folks, sure, but there came a time even that wasn't much consolation.

"Hell with it," muttered Cade, and reached down to tug his knife free of Never Forget's windpipe.

That was when he heard the voice.

The voice had a thin, reedy quality, a kind of soft hissing rasp that made it seem like a snake talking. It had a way of taking its time over the vowels, drawing them out before biting the consonants into harsh little snaps. The kind of voice that would make a man feel uneasy in the depths of his stomach, make him draw in his breath a minute and take a step back.

The Pastor had a way of making folks hear his word.

"Oh Lord..." It came out *Oooh, Loor-r-rduh.* "Oh Lord, oh, Lord, what hast thou sent to tempt your faithful servant now? Why, a demon of vengeance, Lord, sowing wrath and murder among the faithful. Lord, thy tests are strange and terrible, yes indeed, but your servant shall not flee, oh no, oh no..." He clicked his tongue. "Turn yourself, Demon. Turn yourself to face the Lord's best-trusted servant."

Cade turned himself.

The man was about six-five, thin as a rake, and dressed in black with a white band at his throat – a man of God. Cade figured this was probably the fella calling the shots around here. The right person to ask, anyhow.

He nodded. "I've got some questions. Hoping you could answer them." He nodded down at the dead and the dying at his feet, and the growing pool of blood on the floor. Then he locked eyes with the man in black. "I'd be obliged."

The Pastor smiled, a smile that seemed to crack his thin face into a thousand wrinkles, but never touched his eyes, which were grey as Cade's own but with a touch of ice in them. Cade always figured you could tell a lot about a man from his eyes. From the look of it, this was a stone cold son of a bitch, and violent with it. Cade wasn't too happy about that.

Town probably wasn't big enough for two.

The Pastor let his face drop back into its normal expression – a serene half-smirk, eyes heavy-lidded, that gave the impression of a rattlesnake shaking its tail. "Well then, my son. I shall oblige you. Please, follow along with me." He nodded, stepping back through the door. Cade could see at least six men behind him – big fellas, armed with aluminium baseball bats.

That told Cade something. Muir Beach now had a population of three, and that was counting the trailer park. Now, admittedly, it'd been hit hard, and it was a small community. But all the same, it said a lot about a fella that he could get so many men together, train them and arm them – and the big fellas did look like they'd had training for some kind. Plus, this Reverend or Padre or whatever had no way of knowing Cade wouldn't just go to work on these six like he had on the fools in the bar. Which meant they were expendable into the bargain.

Cade was surely considering going to work. Something about the fella's smile, and those grey eyes of his, made Cade figure he'd be a hell of a fool not to. Put the son of a bitch down and find his answers another place.

The Pastor smiled, all teeth. "The Lord must be obeyed, my son."

Cade gripped the handle of the knife. Then he relaxed, put it back in his belt, and nodded.

"Hell with it."

Cade figured he could handle whatever the thin fella had to show him. And if he couldn't – hell, he'd have time to regret it later.

And he did.

CHAPTER SEVEN

THE PASTOR

"This-a-way, my son. This-a-way, to walk in the very footsteps of the Lord..." And a chuckle like animal bones cracking underfoot. Then the Pastor turned back to his shuffling walk, one foot dragging after the other, the shoulders jerking back and forward in time with the steps. It was eerie, like watching a cobra trying to walk on its tail like a man.

The more Cade saw of the Pastor, the less he liked it. Those damn neck hairs were standing up to be counted.

The streets were still clean, and apart from the Pastor and his guards, there still wasn't a soul to be seen in them. Cade followed along - the way he saw it, if he wanted answers, he could either walk in the very footsteps of the Pastor's God or just kill the guards and beat the answers out of the Pastor.

There were a couple of problems with that second option, attractive as it was. For one, Cade had done things to people occasionally that folk would call torture, and there wasn't anything about it that was reliable for getting information out of anybody. The only thing torture was good for was torture, and unless you were ready to own the fact that there wasn't any kind of purpose or reason to it besides that, you were fooling yourself. So Cade had to shake his head a little when he heard some damn fool talk about using it for an interrogation on the Iraqis or whoever the hell it was this week. That was just fool's talk from a bunch of clowns who figured the only way they could get another bunch of clowns to vote for them was by showing how very badass they thought they were. 'Course all it did was show they were clowns, but a clown's gonna vote for a clown anyhow.

Cade was a mite cynical when it came to politics.

Anyhow, aside from the practicality of beating a confession out of the Pastor, it was pretty obvious the man was crazy as a broken-backed snake and he was likely to say any damn thing that came into his head. Best Cade could do was follow along as the man's guest and hope he picked something up.

Hell, if Cade acted godly enough, maybe the Pastor'd help him out with his insulin problem, or at least tell him what happened to Sausalito. Acting godly wasn't something Cade had much practice in, but he figured if he kept his mouth shut, that'd about do it.

Keeping his mouth shut was something Cade specialised in, after all.

The Pastor smiled, bobbing his head and moving with that gentle, sinister, shuffling gait as he led them down Cervantes Boulevard to where it intersected Fillmore Street. Ahead of them was the Moscone Recreation Centre – a big grey and white building. Cade shot the Pastor a look. It wasn't exactly a threat, but there was a hint in his eyes that he could just as soon go straight to the killing if he was forced to, and he'd take a certain amount of pleasure in doing just that.

The Pastor smiled his cracked-face smile, his eyes as cold as January morning. "They had basketball here once. Did you know that? One of the best places in the city, I was told." He chuckled softly, like a glass file rubbing against a shard of bone. "We have other entertainments here now. Oh yes, we do…"

Cade was starting to wonder if beating the Pastor's head against the concrete until it cracked open wasn't the best plan after all. Cade wasn't a man to be unsettled easy, but there was something in the Pastor that just didn't strike him as right. Part of him was already clocking the positions of the guards with their baseball bats, working out who to kill first, who'd make a good shield, who he should take his blade to and who he could just disarm and put down with a simple neck-breaker or a dislocated leg. Cade had a pretty good strategy worked out by the time they pushed the doors open and walked down to the basketball court. That was when the smell hit him.

He'd spent a day at the San Diego Zoo, once upon a time. Hell of a place to spend time, and even a man like Cade could find a point of interest in it. He'd spent a while in the monkey house, on account of he liked watching them – Cade was of the opinion that monkeys were people with most of the bullshit taken out of them. Not that the smell of shit there wasn't overpowering, but you got used to it quick. Cade had spent a good couple hours there, watching the monkeys do what the monkeys did. After a while the smell stopped bothering him, and he didn't even notice it. When he'd gone to get himself a Coke from a vending machine, the fresh air had smelt sweet as rosewater. A few minutes later, he went back to the monkey house and there it was again, strong as ever. Monkey shit. Didn't matter if you'd gotten used to it – one breath of fresh air and you were primed for it all over again.

The nature of shit was to stink. There was a lesson in there somewhere.

This was a similar situation. Cade had lived around Muir Beach, with its corpses and old bones, for a good couple of years. He'd smelt some sweet air in the Pastor's territory, but now it was like heading back into that damn monkey house. Only this time the smell that was hitting him wasn't monkey shit.

It was dead folks.

Rotting dead folks.

Cade had a feeling he should start the killing there and then. But when the doors swung open and he saw what the Pastor kept on those courts, he figured he'd hang on a little longer. He figured anything that fucked up had a hell of a story in it.

The Pastor smiled, breathing out his words in a soft hiss, like air escaping from a balloon. This time the smile touched his eyes, and they shone.

"Oh hear, sinner man, oh hear... oh *hear* the word of the Lord! Oh, *behold,* sinner, let thine eyes *feast* on His word and His work! Sinner man, can you not see it? Can you not see the *glory* of the Lord your God?" He laughed, and the laugh was a rustle of pages in an undertaker's book.

Cade could see a hell of a lot. He could smell a hell of a lot, too.

He maybe wouldn't call it glory, mind.

Set up in the basketball court were about a hundred wooden crosses, and nailed to each cross was a rotting skeleton. Once, there'd been people on those crosses – living people – with nails pounded through their wrists and ankles for who the hell knew what. And they'd been left there until they'd died, one by one. After that, the putrefaction had set in – the writhing maggots that still coiled and squirmed over the last scraps of a long-vanished face, the seeping, blackened mire that clung to thighbones and scraps of mouldering cloth. A couple of the ribcages were homes to rats, that skittered and gnawed on the bones, giving the cadavers a kind of twitching motion, a parody of life that stilled the heart and sickened the gut.

Cade knew for a certainty that the Pastor came in here every chance he could, to watch it happen, day by slow day. And he knew for a certainty that – while his men might have helped hold them still and keep them in place – it was the Pastor his own self who'd nailed every one of those souls up onto their crosses with his own withered hands.

He heard the sound of a breeze rushing through a graveyard. The Pastor was breathing it in. Savouring it. His brittle body shook like a leaf in a storm. Cade had seen folks taking their first hit from a needle who didn't look half so transported as the

Pastor did in the presence of his works.

Cade wasn't a blushing virgin in the ways of death, and he figured he knew a thing or two about horror. He'd seen a hell of a lot and done a hell of a lot too. He'd figured he had a pretty good idea of how bad the world could be when it had a mind to be.

Now he knew he'd been a damn fool all the while.

He turned to the Pastor and nodded, once.

"It's something at that." His voice was steady, and level, and his eyes were boulders. Cade wasn't a man who got mad exactly, but those few who knew him as well as any could would have said he was as close as he could get to it.

An eyebrow twitched. Questioning. The voice dropped, just a shade quieter than before and cold as stone. The question was almost under Cade's breath, but there wasn't a body in that room who didn't hear it.

"How come?"

The Pastor was still smiling that weird cracked-skin smile of his, eyes still sparking for joy. When it came, his voice was just as quiet and just as focussed. "Perversion. Men laying with men and women with women. Godlessness and atheism. The worship of drugs that steal the soul from the body, a terrible affront to the Lord... but that wasn't the question, was it? No, no, it wasn't the question at all..." Another chuckle, like a trickle of cut glass along a knife blade. "You're not concerned about their crimes. You want to know why I chose this path. Why the *Lord* chose it... well, sinner man, you will hear it. Hear now the word of the Lord..." He closed his eyes, reverentially.

Cade marked the positions of the Pastor's men again. Then he listened. He figured he'd more than bought his ticket. He ought to get the whole show.

The Pastor walked between the crosses, occasionally putting his hand on the bones, breathing in deep. "When I was a young man, I decided to serve as a chaplain in Vietnam, to bring the word of the good Lord to the men fighting there for freedom from the seeping coils of communism..." He turned, and gave Cade another of those cracked-face smiles. "I was young, you understand. Naïve. I did not heed the Lord, nor did I understand his word, nor his glory. I knew very little."

His smile was wide as a cat's. His eyes were like two rivets nailed in his face.

Cade had a feeling he knew where this was going.

"The firebase I was stationed at had been long abandoned by command, and the men there were now fully under the power of demons, oh yes... I saw it with my own eyes, oh Lord, the debasement of the spirit in that dank and lonely place! You say hell is not real, sinner? I saw it! The degradation, the fall –" His voice rose, calling out like he was giving a firebrand sermon from a pulpit. "I say to you, *the very fall of man!* And there were times, oh yes, sinner, there were *times* when I could no longer *feel* the hand of the Lord upon me! When I could not *hear* his foot treading in the shadow of my own, when instead – instead I heard a hoof! *A cloven hoof!*"

His nostrils were flaring, and his shock of white hair was plastered up on his head. The eyes were bloodshot, where before they'd been clear. Cade wondered if the man was working himself up to a stroke.

Might save him the trouble.

"I felt the most alone I've ever felt in that place, with those men who were destroying themselves faster than the Viet Cong could do it, those men who had been abandoned and who had abandoned themselves and their souls in turn. Oh Lord! Didn't I *tell* them, Lord? Didn't I *warn* them what was coming? But I could not teach them! For I could not teach what I did not know, and sinner, I did not truly *know* my God! I did not *hear* his word! Not then!"

The Pastor hissed the words, eyes narrowing.

"Not until those devils came for *me!*"

He whirled, stabbing his fingers at the guards, who dropped to their knees, faces transported in joy.

"Charlie rose against us, rose *up,* I say, and murdered every man in that camp, whether he fought against them or lay in stupor! The ground ran red with *blood,* I tell you, *red* with the blood of sinners! And in that fire and fury I felt you *rise,* oh Lord! I felt your *hand* upon me! I felt you *working* in the fire and in the blood! In the screaming and in the dying! I felt you, Lord, and your name was *death!* And *Hell* came with you to that place! And I prayed, Lord, oh I *prayed!* I prayed for you to *enlighten* me! To show me the *way!* To bestow upon me the *reason!* I prayed for a *sign,* oh Lord, and a sign *came,* oh yes, oh, my *Lord,* my *God... a sign did come!*"

Cade blinked. He got the impression the Pastor had kind of forgotten he was there, and to tell the truth he could see how that might be. Cade had lost himself for a second in the fire and fury of the man. He could figure how other folk might end up losing themselves for good.

"I was the only one to survive. They saw me praying, saw me kneeling, and the spirit of the Lord moved in them. And they *took* me, oh Lord! They dragged me under the earth! To their *tunnels!* They beat me with sticks and with stones! They cut me with *knives!* They broke my legs again and again until I *begged* to be killed! I spent three years in a bamboo cage, three feet by three, oh Lord! I faced *torments! Torments of Hell itself!*"

The Pastor gulped air, steadying himself on one of the crosses. Cade wondered how a man could breathe in gulps of that rotting air without passing out – the stench of the corpses was still in his nostrils with every breath he took, and his stomach did a slow, lazy roll every couple of minutes. The smell of a body that's been dead a long time was a hell of a thing to put up with, even for Cade.

Eventually, the thin man spoke again. He seemed to acknowledge that he was speaking to Cade now – the fever in him had passed. "The good Lord spoke to me. For three years... the Lord, the *good* Lord, was my helper through those terrible days and nights. He spoke of his plan for the world to me, you see. That one day, one day, there would come a terrible *scourge* upon the Earth... and those of purest heart would be saved for the final task, oh Lord, the most *sacred* task... the culling of the last sinners from the Earth." He chuckled, sweat beading on his brow. "You've a great power in you, boy, a great power. The Lord hath placed a terrible *judgement* in your hands..."

Cade narrowed his eyes. This was starting to get a mite personal.

He turned towards the door. "Got things need doing." Cade never had believed in wasting words.

The Pastor smiled.

"You've a great power in you, and I have great power in *me*, son. I have scores of pure souls in my flock, all waiting to do the word of the Lord and work for his glory, Now correct me if I'm wrong, but the kind of things a man like you might want to get done... well, they could need that great abundance. Many hands make light work, they say. And you have set yourself a great task..."

Cade stopped, and turned his head.

"Oh, I can tell just by looking. You have the look of a man on whom the Lord has placed his hand. A man with a mission." He chuckled. This time is was like the shattering of a test tube containing some deadly bacillus. "I will help you, if you will help me, my brother. Place your hand in mine and I will place the hand of the Lord in yours, and He will guide you in your works and bring you aid from every corner of this great city. Only aid *me* when the time comes. Help me in my time of need, my brother." The Pastor smiled his crack-faced smile, and ran a hand over a thighbone, caressing it. His eyes glittered. "Help the Lord in his righteous work."

Cade took a look around the room – at the skeletons hanging from the crosses. There were men there, and women too. A couple of kids. He could see one skeleton at the back, rotted down to bones, and it was no bigger than a chicken's might be, held to the cross with a single nail.

A baby.

Cade took a deep breath of the air in that room. The heavy, sick-sweet, rotted air.

Then he gave his answer.

"Deal."

CHAPTER EIGHT

THE FLOCK

It was a lie, of course, but it seemed to be good enough for the Pastor.

Cade was glad to get out of that room. The same air in the corridors that'd seemed tainted when he walked in now seemed sweet on his tongue, and he took a long breath of it. Then he turned to the Pastor, shuffling along next to him with his cobra walk.

"You did the sign?"

The Pastor narrowed his eyes, confused. Cade almost sighed. If there was one thing he hated, it was using a bunch of words when a couple would do.

"Sign on the bridge. Figured someone had a problem with hippies. Figured it was you." Cade didn't elaborate any further than that. Either the Pastor'd know what he was talking about or he wouldn't, and that'd be an answer in itself.

The Pastor chuckled his little dry-bone laugh. "Yes it was, my friend, indeed it was. Or rather, it was the work of my people, performing a public service for the glory of the Lord. The goodly in this city, the *saved,* feel it best to warn off them that'd spread their sin and wickedness, their *pestilence,* to our beautiful city..."

"Huh." Cade grunted, cutting the Pastor off before he got started. Cade wasn't in the mood for a big speech. He had things to find out. "You burn Sausalito?"

The Pastor chuckled softly. "No, my son, no. When the Lord visits the terrible necessity of taking life upon us, it is with purpose, yes it is, a *great* purpose, the cleansing of *sin* from the community... so that the chosen people of the Lord might go about their works without its taint amongst them. Now what you speak of there is a thing of *chaos,* my friend, of chaos and *damnation,* a *serpent,* I say, let loose upon the earth, a terrible beast of rage and flame, yes indeed..." He stopped, suddenly, his whole body shaking like a leaf in a breeze. Then he tilted his neck and turned those cold grey eyes on Cade, seeming for a moment to look deep into him. He hissed out the words, spitting them like venom. "The *Devil's* work!"

Cade stared for a moment, then nodded slowly.

"So who did?"

The Pastor frowned sternly, drawing himself up, the snake-walk quickening in pace. "You should learn to heed my words, sinner man, heed them well, for they come from the *Lord,* yes indeed, from the very mouth of the Lord on high! Didn't I *say* it was the Devil? Didn't I *say* we were fighting those that spread their sin? Did you not *believe,* oh sinner?"

Cade figured he'd caused some offence with the question. Hell with it. He knew who the Pastor was getting at. "The hippies."

The Pastor grinned, and the grin didn't touch his eyes. "The *hippies.* The *godless.* Satan's own. They burn and they destroy, yes they do, enact the Devil's commandments and bring the Devil's punishment down onto all that stand in their way. It's the truth I bring you, brother, the truth of the Lord. Do not doubt." He chuckled, a high, snickering sound, like a rat skittering in a ribcage. A ribcage of glass. "I speak the word of the Lord!"

Cade nodded, but what the Pastor had to say didn't seem right. He'd been down the Haight-Ashbury a couple of times back before the bad times, and while it wasn't the Summer of Love anymore by any stretch, most of the folks he'd seen there were peaceable enough folk, and the man walking next to him definitely wasn't that.

Still, Cade knew how the bad times could change a body. Wasn't nothing quite like losing everyone you ever knew to make you crazy. He figured he'd reserve judgement until he knew the score a little better, but he was going to need to head east pretty soon and check on Haight-Ashbury for himself.

Right now he had other problems.

He heard the sound of the crowd through the front doors before he saw it. Somewhere between a hundred and a hundred and fifty people were choking the street outside – men at the front, the biggest first. At the back, Cade could see the womenfolk, huddled, not looking up. That made some sense, at least. Maybe Cade could be charitable and say that the Pastor didn't want the womenfolk hurt, but he was building a new society for himself that nailed people to crosses for reasons provided for him by a voice in his head claiming to be an Old Testament God of death and pain and damnation. Traditionally there wasn't a big role for womenfolk in a system like that.

A couple of the women were pregnant, and Cade figured probably more of them were than showed. Breeding the new generation of the saved.

Cade looked around the crowd, and frowned. There were a hell of a lot of them, and though he wouldn't put it past the Pastor to baptise him into the faith in front of an audience, it was a lot more likely that he'd brought these people around because he figured even Cade couldn't kill a hundred people.

And Cade couldn't. Not these hundred, anyhow.

It wasn't just the women. Cade had never killed a woman – though he'd been accused of it – but he wouldn't have a problem if the circumstances came up. It wasn't the numbers, either. Cade didn't have a problem with dying, and he'd take as many of these sons of bitches with him before he went. The ten or so that finally did for him would know they'd been in a fight, that was for sure. Neither of those reasons would have been enough to stop Cade going to work right there.

It was the children.

Little faces with big eyes, peeking between the women's skirts. Maybe eight or nine. Ready to hide if things got bloody, but brought out to see something. A show. A lesson, maybe. Their mommas had brought them to see the sinner.

Cade drew the line at killing kids. As weak spots went, that was one he could about live with.

Cade looked at the Pastor. He didn't bother saying anything. He was a little curious how the Pastor'd got the word out – maybe one of his guards had passed a signal while Cade had been watching the Pastor froth at the mouth in there – but beyond that things were pretty clear.

The Pastor smiled back, and stepped into the crowd. Not a word was said as they swallowed him up. Just an eerie silence, like they were all waiting for Cade to speak. He didn't bother.

"The children of the Lord," came the Pastor's voice from inside the throng. "They who have heard the word, the good word of the Lord in their ears. *You* want to join my flock? A *sinner?* A *killer* of goodly men? Your sins are black, I tell you *black,* inside your soul!" The voice rose, an edge of hysteria creeping in. "You call yourself my brother, with your hands steeped in your black and evil sins! If you touch me, you *defile* me! Your sins are black as *pitch!* You must be *shrieved,* oh sinner, you must be *purged,* your sin must be driven *from* you..."

Cade frowned, taking a step forward. The crowd took a step forward too.

As one.

"Hell with it." he muttered.

The Pastor's voice laughed, his bone-rattle laugh. Cade cast his eyes through the crowd and couldn't see a sign of him. It was as though he'd simply melted into the mass of people. "Oh, sinner. *Oh,* sinner... your sins have found you *out!*"

The crowd surged.

Cade had a couple of choices at this point. He'd left his good chain back at the bar, but his best knife was in his belt and he could get his knuckledusters on quick, maybe pop a chain from his bicep, then wade in. Swing the chain in a wide arc, slash the knife with the other hand, cutting through a swathe of people – the ones he didn't blind with the chain would find their guts hanging on the floor. Then he could advance into the mob, slashing, cutting, keeping a wide circle around him, and then...

What?

Cade had fought big groups of folks before, but it'd take a lot of doing to fight a crowd this size. Most likely he'd tire, or leave an opening sometime – with that number it'd only take one. That was when they were going to drag him under. If most of them were dead on the ground, that'd just make the rest more likely to kill him. And even if he killed a good hundred men – and he figured that he probably could, given time and a hell of a good dose of luck – then what? Start on the women?

The children?

Cade could do that if he had to. But it'd most likely be a death sentence to start, and he wasn't sure there was too much of a need for it. If he was gonna die here, he'd die here.

But he was willing to gamble on the Pastor having something else in mind.

He stepped into the crowd, hands raised, and the crowd folded around him. Dozens of men, jostling and pushing at him, herding him through into the middle of the street, hands roaming and pushing at his back, grabbing at his shoulders and forcing down.

For a second, Cade resisted, and then someone behind him kicked into the back of his knee, sending that knee crashing into the concrete. Cade's expression didn't change, even when they forced him onto his back. He didn't make it easy for them – he fought as much as he could. But the trouble with Cade was that so far as he was concerned, fighting meant killing, and he'd decided he wasn't going to kill any of these people.

Not just yet, anyhow.

Cade wasn't a man who enjoyed being held down, and he

flexed his arms as well as he could, but there were two or three big men for each arm or leg. He wasn't going anywhere.

"Oh sinner man... are you prepared to embrace the Lord your *Master?*" The voice was soft and almost soothing as the Pastor stepped out of the crowd, shuffling. He had a pair of railroad spikes in one hand – big, sharp steel things, giant nails. In the other, he had a hammer.

Cade was starting to wonder if he'd gambled wrong.

He flexed, but they had him pinned. He still wasn't going anywhere. Suddenly he was very conscious of how warm the tarmac was against his back.

He didn't bother saying anything. There wasn't much to say.

Gently, almost lovingly, the Pastor pressed the tip of one of the spikes into Cade's palm. Then he brought down the hammer.

Cade didn't flinch. The spike went through the palm, kicking up a gout of blood as it lodged fast in the tarmac. The Pastor raised the hammer again, and brought it down hard enough to drive the spike another inch in. The pain was like a red hot knife carving all the way down Cade's arm, and he wondered if he'd be able to use his hand again when he got that spike out.

If he got that spike out.

Another blow from the hammer and the spike was deeper into the road. Then a third. Each of those blows of the hammer was like someone sticking battery acid into Cade's palm and shooting eight hundred volts down his nerves. It was a hell of a thing to take and not flinch or cry out, but Cade didn't figure crying out was going to profit him all that much, and flinching was just going to tear his hand up worse.

Another blow. The sound of the hammer on the spike was like a ringing bell. Cade started wondering about infection. The spike was most of the way into the tarmac now. The Pastor stood, panting slightly. "Oh Lord," he breathed, his face flushed, his eyes shining. "Oh Lord."

The Pastor was stronger than he'd looked, to swing the hammer that way. Cade wondered how many times he'd done this before.

Probably a few.

That gamble was starting to look like the worst bet Cade had ever made.

Cade's thoughts were starting to run away from him a little. He tried to focus. He'd been a damn fool to let himself get took. He could've run. Running wasn't his nature, but all the same, he could've hid out, got his answers another way.

He could feel his forearm getting sticky as the blood pooled under it.

The pain was gigantic.

The Pastor moved to the other hand, pushing the point of the railroad spike into the flesh. Cade was ready for it now, when it came, anticipating that first brutal blow of the hammer. But the Pastor was ready too. The hammer didn't move.

Cade looked up and saw that cracked, crazy-paving smile, the eyes glittering above it.

All he could hear was the slow, steady tic, tic, tic of someone's watch.

Cade scowled.

The son of a bitch was making him wait for it.

Cade's lips twitched, nearly baring some teeth. He came pretty damn close to saying something about that. Then he realised that even a cross word was giving the son of a bitch a measure of satisfaction, and the hell with that. Cade took a deep breath, and relaxed, letting the pain in his pinned hand be its own thing, not touching him.

Above the crowd, the sky was a slowly deepening blue. The first stars were starting to come out. Cade looked up at them, letting everything else fade away.

Crang.

The hammer came down, hard, and another white wave of pain smashed down Cade's arm, then crackled and burned like hot coals as the hammer rose and fell, rose and fell, rose and fell. The Pastor wanted to get it done quick now, Cade figured. Good for him.

The men in the crowd let him go and stood back. They still hadn't said a single damn word, which might have shown an impressive command of internal discipline under other circumstances. Right now Cade wasn't concentrating too hard on that. He was pinned, arms spread wide, palms nailed to the tarmac, and that was where he was going to be staying. He figured he could probably pull himself free if he wanted to – except that'd drag those metal spikes through the flesh and bones of his hands, tear them both apart. He'd probably cripple himself for life.

Might have to come to that.

The Pastor knelt down, grinning like a snake in a gerbil's cage.

"*Oh,* sinner, your sins are black as *pitch*... but have faith. Trust in the good word of the Lord. Oh, sinner, *hear* his word!" The Pastor's bony hand crept to Cade's combat knife, pulling it out of Cade's belt. Then he laid the blade against Cade's chest and the black fabric of his tank-top. "You got the *Devil* in you, sinner! You got the hand of *Satan* on you!"

He laughed, and it chattered like skeleton's teeth rattling in a cracked glass jar. "Cast him out, Lord! Cast... him... *out!*"

Then he cut.

Down first, through fabric and flesh, then across, the blade bit, slicing as keenly through Cade's skin and muscle as it did through anything else. Carving a bloody cross.

Cade swallowed. That was just overkill – plus it wrecked a pretty decent vest. He just hoped nobody he'd cut up earlier had any kind of blood diseases. These days there wasn't any telling. A man should be careful.

The Pastor stood, passing the knife to a man in the crowd. That was it. The whole mass of people walked away, not saying a word, most of them heading back down Cervantes and filtering off into the streets and buildings. Within five minutes, Cade was alone.

The agony in his hands and chest had become a steady drumbeat of pain. He could feel the blood matting what was left of his top and the hair on his chest. He was very conscious of the hard blacktop under his head, and how uncomfortable the chains on his biceps were, all of a sudden. He wanted to flex a little, but with the soft tissues in his hands pierced by a pair of railroad spikes, that wasn't a good idea.

Cade breathed in, and breathed out. Far away, a dog howled. It was going to be a hell of a long night.

CHAPTER NINE

THE GHOST

Another man might have screamed.

That's not to say a man couldn't deal with being nailed to tarmac in the middle of the street without screaming. That would certainly be possible, if a mite unlikely. But another man might have found himself gasping out, or grunting, or groaning, or making little noises every time he breathed to help himself deal with the pain. Another man might, after the first nine or ten hours rolled past and the pain in his hands turned into an itching that didn't stop, and the freezing night turned into a baking day, and all in total silence, with just the blowing of the breeze to listen to – well, another man might start to cry. Or start howling in the night like a damned wolf, shrieking at the top of his lungs until those lungs gave out and his vocal chords ruptured, just to break things up, just to hear a sound, any sound at all...

Not Cade.

Cade just lay there and took it.

It wasn't until the sun dipped below the horizon again, and he realised how dry his tongue and throat were, and how he'd been laying there with his mouth open for a couple hours because he'd forgotten to close it and his throat was like sandpaper – it wasn't until then that Cade made a single sound, and even then, it was a slow sigh.

As if to say, *Hell with it.*

He didn't say a word until the second day.

That was when Fuel-Air turned up.

He was sitting on the tarmac next to Cade, his boonie hat pushed back on his head, grinning. He looked wired.

Holy fucking shit, dude, he said, although Cade didn't hear him exactly, more felt him speak. *That's some Jesus Christ on the motherfuckin' cross shit. You messiah-acting motherfucker.*

Cade scowled.

Serious, dog, this crazy fuck's got some sort of king-size fucking hard-on for your ass. I mean, this is some awesome shit, man.

Cade swallowed. "Reckon?"

He could hardly hear his own voice – it was a rasping croak, like a toad baking alive in the middle of the desert. That wasn't any damn good. He could use some fluids pretty soon. Maybe Fuel-Air had some Red Bull or Jolt Cola or something.

Sorry, dog, all I got is coffee granules.

He was eating them raw. Cade shook his head. Goddamn Fuel-Air.

What, I'm supposed to be bringing some magic sponge for your ass? Man up, bitch, you can handle this shit. You did a year in the hole and you didn't blink, man... shit, you were one Steve McQueen-ass motherfucker, know what I'm saying? This should be a walk in the fuckin' park.

"Had a drink back then." Cade didn't know why he was talking to Fuel-Air. It just encouraged him when he was alive, no reason why it should start making the boy see reason now.

Something about that didn't seem right, but Cade couldn't put his finger on it.

Hate to bring this up, dog, but that was urine. You were

drinking piss the whole time you were there.

Cade almost shrugged, then remembered his hands. They were almost numb now. He rolled his eyes instead. Piss was sterile, and he'd needed the liquids. Come to think of it, he wouldn't say no right now.

I ain't gonna piss in your mouth, man. I know how you fuckin' think, dog, and that's some very homo-erotic I Am Curious Yellow shit and I ain't fuckin' doing it. Shit, man, is that even legal in this state? What I look like to you?

Cade took a deep breath, counted to ten, then let it go. Goddamn Fuel-Air always managed to annoy the hell out of him. Maybe the Duchess could talk some sense into him when they got back. Had they met?

Why hadn't they ever met?

Cade closed his eyes for a second, fumbling for the words. "Fuel-Air... aren't you..."

He opened his eyes. There was nobody there.

Hell of a thing.

The sun crawled across the sky, beating down like an oven. Like a kiln. Baking the tarmac until it burned hot all around Cade, baking him just the same. The heat made his hands scream, and the carved-open wound on his chest throb and itch, pulsing raw and red. The sun blazed into his eyes, even when he closed them, and it seemed to pulse to that same hellish drumbeat.

Another man might have passed out.

Cade just took it.

By now it wasn't just his hands, or his chest. His whole body was itching, aching, wanting to move. His leg kept twitching. Shaking. He couldn't seem to stop it. Every time his leg jerked, it sent a little bolt of pain down his arms from his hands.

His mind kept coming back to the heat.

The noon sun up above him was a like a blowtorch searing him, burning him alive, just sitting up there without a care in the world. Roasting him to death and there wasn't a cloud in the sky to stop it. He tried not to think about it, and then he had to swallow with a mouth as dry as bone on sand, or blink away the sweat in his eyes, or shift his weight and feel the burned skin scream at him for it, and there wasn't much option but to let his mind revolve around it, coming back to it again and again, like a planet revolving around the sun, that damned burning sun...

So in the end, Cade just took it. He could take it. Cade had taken things like that his whole life. That was pretty much all he did, was take things. Take and take, soak up punishment like a man on the ropes in the final round. In the desert, they'd said Cade was made of stone. Cade was a rock.

If you hit it hard enough, a rock would crack.

Cade suddenly decided he was going to rip his hands free.

Hell with it. It'd hurt like the devil, but it'd be worth it. He'd like as not never use his hands again, but he'd be able to sit up at least, get out of the damn sun. Get some water. Ruined hands – he could take that. Cade could tough it out. Just a matter of gritting his teeth, flexing and...

Semper Gumby.

Cade blinked, and turned his head. Fuel-Air was sitting a ways away. He had some dip in a can and he was chewing on a wad of it.

Stay flexible, dog. Semper Gumby, you know? This ain't something you can tough out, man. Gotta adjust yourself. Go with the flow.

Cade blinked, and then breathed in, counted to ten, and breathed out, letting his head rest against the cold concrete. He was pissed off with Fuel-Air – he was always pissed off with Fuel-Air – but he was more pissed off with himself. He'd near as dammit persuaded himself to tear his hands to pieces, and for what? Nothing he wouldn't get later. There'd come a time when he'd need to make that choice, but that time wasn't yet. Not by a long shot. Fuel-Air was right.

Goddamn Fuel-Air.

"You said to man up?"

Shit, dog, you gonna hold me to everything I fuckin' say? I told you fuckin' ages ago, ass. Circumstances have fuckin' changed. You gotta adapt your strategy, you know? This is some ungrateful-ass shit right here, bitch. Fuckin' ingrate pussy. I'm spending my fuckin' Sunday keeping your sorry ass company and

you're acting like a whiny bitch. I'm fuckin' ashamed of you, dog.
He spat. *I ain't spittin' in your mouth either, dude. You know you
were gonna ask.*

Cade rolled his eyes. "Didn't know it was Sunday already."

*Every day's fuckin' Sunday here, dog, like in that emo-ass
song. You're in God's country, ain't you been told?* He laughed,
a little snort, then spat another thick wad of tobacco-spit onto
the road. Then he wiped his nose on his sleeve and carried on
talking.

Fuel-Air never could shut the hell up.

*So it's like I was saying, man, this Reverend dude, he loves
your ass. All this shit right here is some kind of* Man Called
Horse *ritual shit, dog. He's testing your ass, 'cause you're so
goddamn perfect. Shit, you saw those dumb assholes in the bar,
and if you hadn't been such a bitch and let them nail you down,
you could've taken those baseball bat wielding motherfuckers
easy. You're one deadly-ass motherfucker, dog.*

Cade shot Fuel-Air a look, then rolled his eyes again. Kid wasn't
worth the spit it'd take to hold up his end of the conversation.

*Fine, be that way. Point I'm trying to raise is that you're a
motherfuckin' stone-ass killer, dog. That's some fuckin' useful-
ass shit right there. Fuckin' Pastor ain't got one motherfucker in
his army who could fuck shit up good as you. Why'd you think he
didn't kill you? Hell, he didn't even nail your damn legs – 'cause
he needs you to walk for him later. Shit, I figure the only reason
he ain't put you to work right away is that maybe he's worried
you're not as stone-cold a motherfucker as he figures. Maybe
you're gonna fold or betray him or some shit. So he puts you in
the jackpot, dog, gives you the fuckin'* Passion Of The Christ *shit,
see if you make it. If you're dead, fuck it – you ain't no problem
no more and he gets his bone on from nailin' you up. Probably let
you rot out here, make a roadsign out of ya. This way to fuckin'
Albuquerque. Helter Skelter. But if you make it, he knows he's
got a fuckin' gold mine.*

"Might kill him." Cade was considering it.

*What, after days with no food and water and big fuckin' holes
in your hands? I ain't sayin' you couldn't, but he could probably*

get his hundred motherfuckers to kick your ass all over again, only this time they'd cut your head off and shit. Or maybe he'd just keep doin' this shit over and over. Up to you, dog.

Cade nodded. Fuel-Air made some sense. That worried him. That, and something else dancing in the back of his mind. He closed his eyes, breathing in through cracked lips, then breathing out.

There was no getting around it. He'd have to say something.

"You're dead, Fuel-Air."

Fuck you. What are you, Bruce Willis now? Fuck you, bitch. You don't get rid of me that easy.

He heard the kid snicker, and spit. Cade felt it landing on his cheek.

No, that wasn't spit.

It was raining.

Cade relaxed as the drops fell faster and faster, hitting his cracked, parched lips. He saw the flash of the lightning through his closed eyelids, then heard the thunder boom overhead. The storm had come out of nowhere.

When he opened his eyes, Fuel-Air was gone.

Time passed.

At first, Cade lay there, his mouth open, drinking in the rainwater, refreshing himself and quenching that terrible thirst that had built up over the past couple of days. But after a spell, the rain wasn't refreshing or soothing. It was just rain. And it kept on. And on.

The sun had sunk below the horizon again. Cade knew better than to miss that burning heat, but all the same, when he tried to bring it to his mind, he couldn't remember the way his skin had seared and his throat had seemed to scrape like a match lighting every time he swallowed. He just remembered he'd been warm and dry, and now he was wet and cold.

Scratch that. He was freezing. His bones were freezing inside him and he could feel every drop of rain chilling him colder yet, like meat in a locker. Cade was probably the toughest, meanest, most ornery son of a bitch you could ever hope to meet, but he was a man for all that, a human being, and he was getting pretty close to his breaking point. He let his mind spin, looking for distractions, looking for something to keep him from that rain, that chilling ice rain, the ice storm beating down upon him harder with every second that passed, pooling in the bloody scar on his chest and the holes in his hands, so the itching and the pain came in icy waves, something to keep him from coming back and back and back to that, over and over...

He couldn't think of a damned thing.

He should have figured he was in trouble when he'd seen Fuel-Air, that stupid, doomed little bastard, always talking even though he was dead. Goddamn Fuel-Air...

Cade narrowed his eyes, then he turned his head and asked the question.

"Why not Duke?"

What the fuck you on about now, dog?

Fuel-Air was standing in his utility dress, the rain dripping off his helmet. He still had that goddamn grin on his face, like a damned skeleton. Cade shook his head, trying to get the rainwater out of his eyes.

"Duke's dead. Why you?"

Fuckin' Duke? What the fuck is this, election day? You wanna pick the guy who you like having a fuckin' beer with or the guy who gets you out of the fuckin' shit when it hits? Duke was fuckin' army, dog, what the hell do those fuckers know when the shit goes down? I'm the dude who drives the fuckin' humvee and gets you through the shitstorm. You know how many times I saved your ass, bitch?

Cade frowned. If he was going to go crazy, he figured he had a right to pick. He wasn't going to start arguing with a dead man, though. Wasn't any profit in it. His head sank back on the tarmac and he relaxed.

Shit, dog, what the fuck do you want? Some fuckin' Patrick Swayze Ghost I-ain't-gonna-quit-you best buddy motherfucker treatin' you to a fuckin' beer and a game of cards while you rot your ass off in the fuckin' street? Fuck, I kept your ass alive in the fuckin' desert, bitch, I'm keeping it alive here... you got tough when you needed to get tough, and now you're nice and fuckin' flexible and Semper Gumby and shit, letting all this bullshit slide off your ass while you wait it out. You been doing everything fuckin' right in this fuckin' ass-ugly situation you made for yourself. You know why, dog? You want to take a guess?

Cade didn't speak.

'Cause you hate me. He laughed. *Shit, dog, ain't you worked that out yet?*

Cade nodded. The little prick had a point. Maybe he'd have given up in front of Duke. But damn if he was going to screw up in front of goddamn Fuel-Air.

Cade spat, and Fuel-Air's ghost grin widened a notch or two.

Attaboy. Figure you last the night, we're almost done. Just stay cool like Ferris Bueller and shit, don't let it get to you. Almost done, dog. I guaren-fuckin'-tee it. Just stay loose.

"Semper Gumby." Cade muttered the words, and closed his eyes, letting the torrents of water trickle off him and onto the road. Things could be a hell of a lot worse. There could be a dip in the tarmac right about where he was nailed to the road – that'd drown him. Hell, they could've cut his balls off. A man could still be a good killer without any balls. They could've stuck his dick in his mouth like they did with the fat guy on the road in.

If that was them. And not some other bunch of crazy bastards Cade hadn't met yet.

Things could always get a hell of a lot worse, Cade figured.

The rain kept on lashing him, pooling in the wounds in his palms, washing the dried blood off his hands and chest and off the road and carrying it into the gutters. Cade turned his face to the side, so it wouldn't drown him.

Then, finally, he slept.

In his dream, the Duchess was sitting in front of him, naked as the day she was born, her breasts falling their full distance without the support of her bra, the blue veins on her thighs visible as her legs spread. She grinned, in that way she had, laying down cards on an old card-table - tarot cards, and every one was Death.

"You got to be ready, Cade. Things are going to get worse and you're going to feel them getting worse right in your soul, but you can't go making mistakes. You just bought something, and you'd better use it, that's all. And watch out for Fuel-Air."

She held up five Death cards, and smiled, starting to sing softly, the way she did sometimes in the mornings.

"Gotta know when to hold 'em, know when to fold 'em..."

"You should've showed up earlier." Cade said. He was wearing his uniform, behind the wheel of a humvee he didn't know how to drive. He needed some coffee. Maybe the Duchess had some of those instant granules – he could eat those raw. "You got coffee?"

The Captain barked back at him, face red as a damn beetroot. *"Wake the hell up! Danger close is coward talk! Wake the fuck up, pissant! Just wake the fuck up!"*

Cade woke up.

The rain had stopped, and the sun had come out and dried him off while he slept. It was high noon. His palms throbbed, a regular, hot drumbeat of pain. It didn't feel so bad, Cade reckoned.

In fact, Cade felt pretty good.

He turned his head, and saw someone standing next to him, wearing black.

"Fuel-Air?"

It wasn't Fuel-Air.

It was the Pastor.

CHAPTER TEN

THE GENERAL

"Easy now, children... easy now. The Lord's touch is *gentle,* yes it is..."

The Pastor crooned softly, keeping his eyes on the spike as it slowly worked free. The man holding the long-handled pliers gave careful little tugs, trying to do as little damage as possible, but the blood had started flowing again despite that. Cade's right hand was already free, and he held it up in front of his face, slowly opening and closing the fist. Every time he did it, his hand seemed to catch fire and burn, the pain igniting his nerves like electricity. He was a little amazed he could move his fingers at all, after what the Pastor had done. The man must have the mind of a surgeon.

Or maybe he'd practiced a hell of a lot.

Anyway, Cade figured he'd feel pain any time he held anything for a long time. Maybe for good.

Cade would probably come to resent that later. Right now, he didn't mind it so much. Not now the spikes were coming out.

The spike in his left hand pulled free with a little rush of blood, and Cade raised that one too, the blood trickling down his forearm as he tested it. This one was a little harder to close – he was going to have to watch himself if he used that hand to work with, and hitting with it was going to be murder. He was going to have to test that out soon.

No time like the present.

Cade stood, his feet unsteady for a second from the long hours on his back. The Pastor watched him, careful as a hawk. Then Cade wheeled and punched the man with the pliers in the forehead, hard enough to send him crashing onto the tarmac, out cold.

The Pastor didn't blink, but Cade did. His mouth twitched. His hand was in agony, glowing like a hot coal. He growled slightly when he spoke. "Wanted to check."

"Oh, I understand, my brother. A soldier in the service of the Lord must test himself." He chuckled, and it still made Cade uneasy, even after all that he'd done already. Shattered glass tumbling from a polished skull. "We should get your wounds seen to, lest the Devil enter and infect the flesh. The sin is driven from your heart, but your body may still succumb to the evils of Satan..." He smiled, and turned, shuffling up Fillmore Street towards North Point. Cade followed, leaving the man with the pliers where he lay.

Cade didn't bother asking the Pastor why he'd had the sudden change of heart. He figured a man who liked the sound of his own voice that much would let him know the reasons soon enough, and in the meantime he'd stick with Fuel-Air's theory – that the Pastor was testing him to see if he'd break, either nailed to the road or after. Testing him to see if he was going to try and kill the Pastor right now. Cade could tell when a gun was on him, and he figured there was a fella at a window somewhere who had orders to make damn sure that if Cade raised a hand to the Pastor it'd be the last thing he ever did.

Cade wasn't in the mood to raise a hand to anything except

maybe a sandwich and fries. After close on three days laying on tarmac with just rainwater for drinking, he'd noticed how hungry he was. Unless he got some food in him pretty soon, he wasn't going to be much use to anybody, never mind the Pastor.

The Pastor turned his head and smiled that weird smile of his. He seemed to know what Cade was thinking.

"We have food and drink, and a place to rest in my sanctuary. My place of peace in the midst of war, where my flock gather to come together in the glory of the Lord. You have seen my purgatory, my brother, now shalt thou know my paradise, oh yes you will. Now shall you understand the *joy* of service to the Lord..." He chuckled his bone-rattle laugh as they turned to move west up North Point Street, heading towards some kind of big supermarket. Cade figured that was where they were headed. It made sense. Lots of room, lots of food – hell, if they'd rigged up a generator to the PA system he could even give sermons. Seemed like a pretty sweet setup.

He flexed his fingers a little, frowning slightly at the firestorm of agony that ricocheted up his arms. There was still a steady throb of pain in both hands and Cade knew it wasn't going away. Maybe not ever. It wasn't going to stop him doing anything he needed to do, but it was an additional distraction he didn't need.

The Pastor glanced at him. "You have a choice ahead of you, brother. Many are tested, yes, but few are chosen to serve in the glory of the Lord. Now your sins have been wiped from your soul and you are again clean, born anew. Tell me, are you still willing to serve the Lord in all of his splendour?" His voice was soft, but there was a keen edge to the question.

Cade shrugged. "Might as well." He shot a glance at Fuel-Air, who was leaning in a doorway with a jar of Ripped Fuel, grinning that smart-ass son-of-a-bitch grin.

Told you so, dog.

Goddamn Fuel-Air. It was a little unsettling to see him again. He remembered the Duchess telling him to watch out.

Well, he hadn't done any harm so far. Might have kept him alive, in fact.

Fuel-Air grinned.

"Got my knife?" Cade looked over at the Pastor, not blinking. He was pretty fond of that knife, and he'd sharpened it and got the balance the way he liked it, and it'd be a hell of a shame to start from scratch. If he had to start from scratch, he'd have to seriously consider snapping the Pastor's neck and using his body as a shield against sniper fire.

He might need to do that anyhow. He hadn't decided yet.

"We have your knife, and we have your chain – the big one with the weights, I mean. We've got all the tools you'll need to be a warrior in the service of the Lord your God, and that's what you'll be, make no mistake." He smiled, turning his eyes up. "The Lord your God has a *mission* for you, my brother, a mission of great import, oh yes, a mission *vital* to the work of God on Earth..." The Pastor was starting to breathe faster, his hands waving and clutching the air as he warmed to his theme, still shuffling with his broken snake-walk. "Will you *follow* his path, oh my brother? Will you bring your sharp sword to *bear* on the unbelievers, the tools of *Satan,* the followers of the Horned *Goat?*" The words were spat, his eyes rolling in his head in a fever.

Cade shrugged.

"Sure."

The Pastor led Cade up Buchanan Street, around to the front of the place. "There are powers in this city, oh faithful servant, yes there are... powers ranged against the glory of the Lord, powers arrayed to *destroy* his works, to commit acts of *murder,* to foment crimes of *perverse lust!*" He walked faster as his hands shook and danced, weaving between the abandoned cars still sitting in the parking lot.

Cade figured that line about murder and perverse lust sounded a little like the pot calling the kettle black, but there wasn't much mileage in saying so – leastways, not until he'd got his knife back. "The hippies?"

"*Lust and murder! Satanism and destruction!* You saw their handiwork yourself – do you think *your* community will be safe if their filth is left *unchecked?*" He hissed it, looking at Cade with that odd ferocity of his as they passed through the doors. Cade frowned. The man had a point. If the hippies – whoever the hippies were, wherever they'd set up – were the ones doing the burning, Cade needed to deal with them.

If they were. Cade wasn't in the habit of trusting people who nailed him to the middle of the street.

The supermarket had been gutted and rebuilt – most of the shelves had been dismantled and taken out, their place taken by a sea of mattresses, most crusted with piss and filth, and the occasional tent-like structure. Dozens of people – men, women, some of the children Cade had seen earlier – were sitting on the mattresses, some singing softly, some reading from Bibles. A couple were eating from tins, taken from the still-standing shelves on the far side of the supermarket. These shelves were stocked entirely with cans and a small quantity of canned drinks, as well as a vast reserve of bottled water – Cade figured any food with an early sell-by date had been eaten long ago. The shelves were guarded by the big men with the aluminium bats from before.

It was a crude setup. Cade could've put something better together in two days, and working alone at that. Most of the men and all of the women looked thin and pale – the kids looked malnourished, with that greyish skin Cade had seen a lot of. The food was probably rationed, maybe one can per meal if they were lucky. Cade looked around, and saw a set of double doors, locked up tight with strong chain and a padlock. That would be where the supermarket storage area was. Cade figured there'd be more food back there.

Unless they were using it to keep something else.

A picture was starting to develop. The hippies, the Satanists, the defilers – if they had control of the Haight-Ashbury, they'd be near Buena Vista Park, Golden Gate Park, the golf course, Corona Heights – all kinds of decent farming land. Cade had slung the word 'hippies' around pretty casually along with everybody else, before the bad times and after, but he knew it could mean a hell of a lot of things; some teenager with long hair, some fella with liberal views, hell, pretty much anybody in San Francisco as was, if you were standing outside it. But now Cade was thinking about communes, collectives, organised groups of people living off the land, growing crops like the Diggers in the sixties. Hell, if they had a working generator or two, they had hydroponics on their side too. As far as food was concerned, they'd be sitting pretty.

Meanwhile, the Pastor's people – who'd maybe been used to having things done for them, used to putting their faith in a higher power and slobbing out in front of a TV set or a pulpit while other people got their snack packs ready for 'em – didn't have a clue where to start when it came to farming and weren't in a position to do much about it except pray and keep on praying, because their crazy Pastor had seen to it that they only had one book to read. And now food was running short – what they needed was someone to grow food for them, someone who already had the knowledge. Maybe a slave class, maybe just some warm bodies to turn cold so all their food stocks could be stolen and taken away.

Cade liked this theory. It fit pretty well, and it meant that the fella who'd killed a hundred-odd people for his Old Testament God and then nailed him to a road for three days on top of that was the bad guy in the equation. Cade'd know exactly where he stood, and that'd be pretty damn good to know. Trouble was, there was a big piece missing that Cade couldn't get to fit.

Somebody'd burnt down Sausalito, and Cade was pretty sure it wasn't the Pastor's people. He didn't trust the Pastor, and the Pastor might have been lying – hell, he probably was lying about a hundred things – but these people liked their territory a little too clean and tidy for them to be burning everything outside of it. Still, even that could be worked in. There was just one thing that couldn't be.

Helter Skelter.

That wasn't a Jesus thing. The Pastor hadn't done that.

That was someone else.

Wasn't any way around it, Cade figured. He was going to need to investigate anyhow. Might as well do it for the Pastor as anyone else.

Still, he figured he should set a couple of things straight first of all.

"You run this?" He gestured around him.

The Pastor looked at him, one eye narrowed. He drew himself up to his full height and launched into a speech: "It is my calling to lead the chosen people of the Lord to their salvation, and to bring *fire* and *fury* upon the –"

Cade cut him off. "Reckon you need a war chief. Like a General. You need them hippies dealt with – kept an eye on at least. That's my job. You run things here." By Cade's standards, it was a hell of a speech. A regular sermon.

The Pastor scowled, which seemed to crack his face up as much as smiling did. "I *have* a mission for you, my friend. A chance, a very *special* chance, to be a warrior in the glory of the Lord. To do his will upon this earth. To be his *sword* in the *war* on the forces of Hell. Now the *fool,* in his vanity and pride, might want *more,* but to him I say –"

Cade sighed. "War needs planning. Scouting. Intelligence. Won't get it done otherwise." Cade was getting pretty damn tired of explaining every little thing. He shrugged. "Not like you've anyone else worth a damn."

The Pastor raised one eyebrow, then looked past Cade, over his left shoulder.

Cade turned.

The man standing behind him was blonde, tan and about a head taller than he was – a muscle beach type. The fella's muscles had muscles on them. Cade figured this guy didn't have to worry himself overmuch about food rationing – he was obviously getting a hell of a lot more than his share. There was a smacking noise as the big man slapped a steel knuckleduster into his palm in a slow, golf-clap rhythm. Cade reached into his pockets for his own.

He didn't bother looking at the Pastor. "Another test?"

The Pastor smiled. "Meet Jurgen, brother. You could call him my General."

Jurgen grinned, speaking slowly, in a thick Austrian accent. "Der Leader already hass an advisor to help him with makink decisions. I am in charge of planning der long war against der Godless – he hass no need of a girlie-man like you."

Cade nodded, looking up. The man had to be a good seven feet tall, and he was a walking advertisement for steroid abuse. Great thick veins like cables stood out on the man's biceps. Cade didn't say a word.

Jurgen smirked through gapped teeth. "I am talkink to you, girlie-man. I haff business vith der Pastor. If you want to be useful, you can try cleanink der toilet. There iss a lot of sshit in it." He smirked a little wider, jabbing a finger into Cade's chest. "I think you would be good at pickink up sshit, girlie –"

Cade moved.

There was a snapping sound as he yanked the finger backwards and broke it. Then he moved with his left, wincing slightly as the fist slammed hard between Jurgen's thighs, smashing against the steroid-shrivelled bits of flesh he kept there. The punch sent a wave of molten lava up the nerves in Cade's arm. Hurt a hell of a lot.

There was some consolation in knowing it hurt Jorgen a hell of a lot more. He doubled over, making a high-pitched whining sound as his eyes bulged, at which point Cade let go of the man's finger and pulled back his right.

Jurgen tried to straighten up, but he couldn't make it before Cade's fist slammed into his jaw. Cade didn't get angry as a rule, but he'd been nailed to the street for three days, putting up with Fuel-Air of all people, and that didn't do much to ease a man's temper. There was a fair amount of anger in that punch, and a hell of a lot of power, and the lead knuckleduster he'd slipped out of his pocket besides.

The impact tore the jawbone off Jurgen's face, sending a gout of blood spattering over Cade and onto the floor, the flesh of the face torn to strips as the jawbone dangled by a thread of muscle. Jurgen's eyes bulged, and he raised his hands to his face.

Cade's hands got there first, closing about the dangling jaw and tearing it free. Then he swung it around, smashing it into Jurgen's temple, sending him crashing down to the ground. The Pastor nodded approvingly.

"With the jawbone of an ass, he will slay his thousands. The Lord was right about you, brother, yes he was."

Cade nodded. "You need a new General."

The Pastor smiled. "Why? The old one's still alive."

Cade tossed the jawbone aside as Jurgen raised his head, scrabbling helplessly with his remaining fingers at what was left of his face, his tongue flapping uselessly as blood and drool mingled on the cold tile floor. Cade brought his fist down once, crashing the lead weight of the knuckleduster into the back of Jurgen's head, smashing the skull into fragments.

Jurgen slumped forward, deader than hell. He hadn't thrown a single punch. A couple of the children started to cry.

The Pastor turned, raising his hands to the crowd. "Be not afraid! For even the angel of *death* himself was but a noble *soldier* in the army of the Lord! Brother – name?"

"Cade." said Cade.

"Brother Cade is here to do the will of the Lord and pro-*mote* his glory! Brother Jurgen was *weak!* The *Devil* was in him! Brother Cade is a strong right arm for the Lord, a man who will do works of *greatness* in his name! Do you not *believe* in the Lord? Do you not *love* your Lord? If you love your God, do not fear! Only the *godless* need fear! The hippies! The *pre*-verts! *Satan's own!*"

The children had stopped crying. They were looking at Cade, mesmerised. If they'd seen a monster standing there before, they were seeing something else now. A biblical hero, ready to slay his weight in unbelievers.

Cade suddenly realised there wasn't a toy in the place.

The kids didn't have toys. He'd figured the adults weren't allowed books, but there wasn't even a magazine or an old newspaper. There wasn't anything that wasn't food or water or a place to sleep. Or a bible. He already knew nobody drank, but that was the tip of the iceberg – the Pastor had taken everything from these people except the chance to kneel and pray to his Lord.

Cade was almost impressed. The man knew how to put a cult together.

One by one, the men and women stood, bowing their heads

and saying their amens. Cade leaned forward and muttered. "We should talk."

"In the morning, Brother Cade." The Pastor smiled, walking into the crowd, laying on hands. Cade followed a pace or two behind. He wasn't in the habit of feeling good about himself, and he felt a mite ambivalent now, but he had to admit he'd played this one pretty well. He had a home base now, while he was in San Francisco – somewhere he could lick his wounds, get food supplies and hopefully medical care, if the Pastor allowed things like band-aids and stitches in his handmade heaven.

He was going to need to kill the Pastor, of course. That went without saying. Probably he'd need to kill a good load of the rest of these fools into the bargain.

But he figured that could wait.

At least until the morning.

CHAPTER ELEVEN

THE WALK

Morning came soon enough.

Cade had managed to get some sleep and a little food – pork and beans out of a can – and now he was in the Duty Manager's Office, looking at a map of the city the Pastor kept there. The thin old man stuck one bony finger out, drawing a line across the map, marking the edge of his territory.

"Pass this line, and you're outside my reach, Brother Cade. All you have is the Lord at your back, and you must trust, you must *trust* and *believe,* in the mercy of the Lord and the power of the Lord to *shield* you from the evils of the Devil..."

That suited Cade just fine. He didn't trust the Pastor further than he could piss, and he had a feeling it was mutual. They were using each other – or at the very least, not killing each other – but no more than that. Cade needed a base, and the Pastor needed some eyes. Everything else was window dressing.

Of course, that meant the Pastor figured he needed a pair of eyes that could take being staked down on the tarmac for three days and then get up and kill near seven feet of solid muscle without thinking twice. That was a hell of a pair of eyes.

Made a man wonder what might be waiting out there.

"Ain't the first."

The Pastor drew back, surprised and slightly confused. Cade looked at him, that look he took on when people didn't catch his meaning right away, and the light dawned on the Pastor's face. "Ah... no, I have sent men out before. I have to *know,* you see – what he's doing. But nobody ever comes back."

Cade shrugged. "Converts, maybe."

Folks not coming back didn't necessarily mean they were dying. Could be that they took one look at the hippie setup – which probably included decent fresh vegetables, books and a toy or two – and decided they'd just as soon stay there forever as head back to the Pastor. If Cade had been the kind of man to have a sense of humour, he'd have said they'd been tempted into the ways of sin.

Instead, he leaned back in his chair, studying the Pastor carefully. "Who's 'he'?"

The Pastor hissed, crunching the paper of the map in a bony fist. "The *Devil!* Devil among devils, prince of demons! How many souls did he *condemn,* oh Lord, how many souls did he send with his own hands into the eternal *fire?*"

Cade frowned. "Couldn't tell you. Who is he?"

"*Doctor* Leonard Clearly!" the Pastor spat the words, his eyes narrowing, the lines on his brow turning into deep, furrowed trenches. "A botanist and bio-chemist – *they* called him, the media, the liberal apologists. He wasn't anything but a pusher! A *dealer* who spoke with the forked and hissing tongue of *Satan!* The teacher of worldly pleasure! I knew the man, before the Lord brought his wrath upon this land. I... I *debated* him. In a lecture hall. A special event." He spat. "*Hah!* A setup by the *liberal elite!* They *ambushed* me with their questions, their *science!* As if their science knew better than the voice of *God!*" The Pastor turned his eyes to Cade's, and there was pain in them, all of a sudden

– an old humiliation. "He called me a *lunatic!* Can you imagine, Brother Cade? He said I should be taken to the booby hatch and locked away with the nuts – his exact words! Because I dared stand up and tell him that happiness came from your *soul!* From the *glory* of the Lord! Not a *pill-bottle!*"

The Pastor sank into his chair, releasing the map from his grip. He raised his hands to his head. Cade leaned forward a little. This was the first time he'd seen the Pastor rattled, and he couldn't help but get curious.

The Pastor exhaled a long, shaken breath. "They laughed at me. A whole roomful of young people. Students. Just young. They weren't real hippies then, you see. They weren't tools of the Devil. Not *then.*" He shook his head. "But they didn't *hear* me. Wouldn't listen to the holy word, no... and all the time, he was talking about – about *mind alteration.* And... *open sexuality.* We know what that means, don't we, Brother Cade? You can dress it up all you like, with your *words,* your fancy liberal *words,* but you can't hide from the *Lord* with words, no you can't, you cannot conceal your sins from His gaze..."

He raised his head, and there was pure hatred in those ice-grey eyes. "*Free love.*" He let out a harsh, barking laugh, bitter and poisoned. "We know where that leads! *Oh* yes! Freedom to love – *love,* they call it! There's only one love, yes indeed, and that's the love provided by the Lord! That's right, the Lord in his glory and his purity and his... his *chastity...*" The Pastor let out a sob, covering his eyes.

Cade didn't say anything. There wasn't much to say.

The Pastor swallowed. "Free love leads to sins that cannot be forgiven. Profane *lusts* – evil and heathen *perversions!* It's not me that says so, oh no! No *sir!* It's the *Bible!* Those crimes are outlined for all to see in the very written word of the *Lord!*" He pounded his fist into his palm. "They're crimes against nature and God, crimes that gotta be paid for, yes sir, paid for in *blood!* The blood of a *sinner!* You got to see that!" His tone changed suddenly, as he leant forward, his hands out in supplication. "You – you see that, don't you? You *gotta!* You do – you *do* see that? Don't you? Don't you see? Don't you see I was *right?*" He was almost begging.

Cade thought about the skeletons on the crosses. He just stared. He wasn't about to give the Pastor absolution – he didn't figure he could if he wanted to.

And he didn't much want to.

Some crimes can't be forgiven, all right.

Eventually, the Pastor stood, shaking his head. "Oh, he was a devil, that Doc Clearly. A *fiend!* He corrupted hundreds, *thousands,* yes he did... Too many to count! His words were a *poison* that blanketed this city and inflamed *sin* within all they fell on! He preached *Satan's* word! Condoned *psychedelics* to muddy the mind and doom the soul – why, he even *created* some! Things the law didn't cover! Drugs to chain the mind and heart so it might be brought quicker to the Devil's grip!" He slammed his hand down on the map, as if trying to crush the man he hated under his palm.

He stood like that a moment, shaking his head... then he sighed, and his body seemed to wilt a little, held up by his hand pressing on the map.

"Then the end came."

Cade just watched.

"The end came, and billions died, and *Doctor* Clearly... he wasn't one of them. No. The Lord... the Lord must *test* a man. Only the *worthy* can enter His kingdom. He sets us *challenges...*" He looked up suddenly and jabbed a bony finger at Cade. "*That's* why I put those iron spikes through your hands, you see? That wasn't *my* idea. *I* didn't think of that. It wasn't my test to give you. The *Lord* spoke in my ear, *whispered* it. He said to me that you could do *great service...*" He blinked, shaking his head – then reached into the desk, pulling out the knife, still coated with dried blood, and the length of chain. "So, then. Do great service *now,* Brother Cade. Bring me word of Doctor Clearly, or if you can, bring to me his *head* that I might offer it in *sacrament* to the Lord..."

Cade reached for them both, slotting them into their proper places. "Obliged. Now I just need my truck."

The Pastor smiled. "Our need is greater, Brother Cade. We have a use for your vehicle – it will be the chariot that will carry our... *gift.*" He chuckled like a dusty mirror cracking in a haunted castle. "Judgement as a gift. I like that. Walk south and west, Brother Cade – towards Alamo Square. Take Lombard Street and Divisadero... *don't* walk down Van Ness Avenue."

"Sure." Cade muttered, locking the padlock on the chain. Lombard and Divisadero was the direct route. He wasn't planning on walking Van Ness anyhow – that'd take him far out of his way, and there was no reason for it that Cade could see.

Except there was a reason the Pastor could see. Might prove interesting to see what that was.

The Pastor shook his head, as if to clear it, then brought the topic back where he'd left it. "Clearly... he's a persuasive Devil. He has a silver tongue. I don't think you'll be fooled *easy* by his words... but so many have been. So, so many. I don't know if you'll return to us."

"I will." murmured Cade. He stood, checking his gear. He'd be back soon enough, all right.

The Pastor grinned. "He *is* the burner, Brother Cade. The force of chaos. He's the one you're looking for, the one who took the torch to Sousalito, yes he is... the Devil is a man of *fire.*" He chuckled, like a knife dragged down a sheet of glass, then raised a bony hand to wipe the sweat from his brow. "Kill him, or find his weakness, and then we'll talk. The Lord is a powerful *friend*, Brother Cade. The Lord provides for many needs..."

Cade nodded, once, and walked out.

His hands still itched, and they shot fire every time he moved them. For a moment, as he walked through the supermarket, between the mattresses, listening to the soft singing and praying of the people there, he wondered if he was going to walk out and find a big crowd with railroad spikes in their hands... but when the doors opened, all there was was a parking lot and a sunny day.

In fact, it was the most beautiful morning Cade had seen in a while.

That's some eerie shit, dog. Fuckin' surreal is what it is.

"Don't have a need for you now, Fuel-Air." Cade said, walking past the thin figure in the utility gear, chewing dip and grinning that fuck-you grin of his. "Get lost."

You'll need me later. Guaren-fuckin'-tee it. And you got me now anyway.

He laughed, a caffeinated little giggle.

I'm gonna keep an eye on you, Cade.

Cade didn't bother to reply. When he looked back around, Fuel-Air was gone.

Cade scratched the back of his neck, mouth twitching a little as the pain in his hand bothered him, and then turned right, heading towards Van Ness Avenue.

The Pastor didn't want him to know what was down there, and Cade figured that was reason enough. He set to walking.

Van Ness was a walk, and then some – a couple of miles of straight road. But Cade didn't exactly mind. After what he'd been through the last couple of days, it felt good to just move – good to get one foot in front of the other. Good to just breathe. Even the garbage he was starting to see on the road was starting to look good.

Shit, man, what are you, some garbage con-o-sewer now? Fuck, that's some fucked-up American Beauty *shit...*

"Thought I told you to get the hell out." Cade wasn't in the mood for Fuel-Air right now. He had business to be getting on with, not to mention finding whatever the Pastor didn't want him to see on Van Ness Avenue. He was getting damn tired of being pestered by a ghost.

Fuck you, bitch. You're missing some elementary fuckin' shit here, you know? How come that garbage looks so damn good to your dumb ass?

It was a sign Cade was outside the Pastor's territory – away from all his religion, his rules and regulations, his damned crosses and the rest of his assorted bullshit. Every empty bag of corn chips blowing about the streets was like a dove with an olive branch in its mouth as far as Cade was concerned. A sign that things were getting halfway back towards normal. He didn't bother saying any of that out loud. Fuel-Air would pick it up anyhow, he figured.

Okay, so you're sentimental for the days people didn't bother picking up their shit, fine. Something's still missing, dog. Check it out.

Fuel-Air walked past him, humping his pack on his back, tin lid on his head. He pointed across the road. Cade looked – there was a converse trainer sitting on a step, another one a little further down the street.

"So?" Cade was trying to sound like he didn't see what Fuel-Air was trying to say, but he was getting a sinking feeling. He'd seen it the second Fuel-Air had pointed it out.

You got shoes over there, dog. Where the fuck are the feet?

Cade didn't say anything.

No corpses, you dumb motherfucker. You got nobody picking up the garbage and shit, but people are picking up the fuckin' bodies off the ground and burying them or some shit. Ain't a single one here. Means you got another faction operating, one the Rev didn't want to mention. You're in enemy fuckin' territory, dog. Better get your shit together.

Cade nodded. Much as he hated to admit it, Fuel-Air was right. He needed to get his shit together. He'd been making damn fool mistakes ever since he'd reached San Francisco. He'd lost the truck, damn near lost his hands and probably lost his damn mind if a stupid kid he'd seen get blown to pieces with his own eyes was dropping hints at him from six feet in the ground. He wasn't noticing things he needed to.

Hell, maybe this was the mythical Doctor Clearly at work. If the hippies were growing food, they'd need fertiliser...

That boat don't fuckin' float and you know *it, dog. Shit, man, where's your fuckin' head at?*

"Shut up, Fuel-Air." Cade snapped, raising his head. Then he froze.

Fuel-Air wasn't there.

Instead, Cade saw a boy of about eight or nine, with hair down to his shoulders, covered in dirt and dust. He was barefoot, wearing a ragged T-shirt and a cut-off pair of jeans that had both seen so much assorted crap that they'd lost any colour they might have once had. The boy was holding something in his hand – Cade couldn't work out what it was at first.

Then the boy grinned with a mouthful of rotting teeth, raised it up to his mouth and bit into it, tearing off a strip and chewing. Cade watched, eyes narrowed, looking at the thing the boy was biting on like it was a strip of beef jerky.

The thing was wearing an earring.

CHAPTER TWELVE

THE BOY

Cade looked at the boy.

The boy looked at Cade, and chewed his ear. His eyes were heavy-lidded, slow-looking, a cow's eyes. Cade knew you could go crazy pretty quickly from eating human meat – it caused lesions on the brain. Affected you a little like CJD.

There was a good chance he could get to the boy before the boy made a run for it.

Whether he could answer a question would be another matter.

Cade counted to three. Then he moved.

The boy moved too – breaking right, making a bolt towards Grove Street, heading east. He was quick – fast as a whippet. Cade was a good couple of heads taller than him, but he was having some trouble closing the gap. Probably still weak from before.

Should've taken a day off, dog. Got a couple nights sleep and shit. I know you hated that motherfucker but that didn't mean you couldn't eat his food and sleep on his fuckin' piss-stained mattresses until you got your strength back. Shit, you didn't even change that fuckin' shirt.

Cade spat. Goddamn Fuel-Air.

Fuck you too, bitch.

Cade was gaining slowly, but the boy didn't seem to tire. At this point Cade was wishing he had the truck – remembering how he'd dealt with the last crazy kid he'd found.

Youth of today, man. What the fuck you gonna do, dog? Kill 'em? Oh yeah, that's you all over. Fuckin' baby killer. Come on, catch that motherfucker, bitch.

Cade cursed under his breath. It was hard enough keeping up without Fuel-Air criticising his damned moral choices.

Shit, fuck you then, baby killer...

The boy gained another couple of feet on him. By now they were heading past Larkin Street, and Cade could see Market Street coming up. The boy was angling to the left. Where the hell was he running to...

Cade cursed again, and spat. He wasn't a film going man, but he'd seen enough of them in his time to know a cliché when he saw it. The little bastard was heading up Market Street, towards the Civic Centre. Towards the BART.

Cade put on a spurt as they rounded the corner, trying to catch him, but it was like trying to catch the hare at a greyhound race. He was in shape, but he wasn't a runner, and this kid obviously did a lot of running.

The hare at a greyhound race. Something about that made Cade uneasy. He slowed as the boy darted around the building, letting the dirt-coated kid get some distance and skitter down the steps into the darkness of the BART station. Cade slowed to a walk, catching his breath, walking carefully forward...

The hare at a greyhound race. That was a hell of a comparison. Because this kid did a lot of running. Like that was his job.

Cade could hear Fuel-Air laughing at him.

Because... the job of a mechanical hare at a greyhound race

wasn't just to move fast.

It was to get the dogs running after it.

It was bait.

The air filled with screaming.

"Hell." said Cade. There wasn't time to say much of anything else.

Out of the mouth of the Civic Centre BART Station came about two dozen men and women, all screaming their lungs out, covered in dirt and filth, teeth rotting, naked but for ragged jeans and cutoffs or torn business suit trousers and skirts, a couple of them not even having that. They had madness in their eyes, and they were fast as the boy – hell, they were faster.

And they were headed right for him.

Cade cursed out loud this time. Then he drew his knife out of his belt and swept it around in a wide arc, cutting into the first wave as they came for him. The lucky ones got their arms up in time, coming away with defence wounds as the blade glanced off the bones in their forearms. The unlucky ones reached up too late, grabbing hold of throats that were flapping open and gushing blood.

Cade only had time for the one swing before they were on him. These people made the Pastor's mob seem gentle – they slammed forward, not seeming to give a damn if they trampled over their own, pushing their dead to one side, a couple of the pack splitting off to drag the convulsing bodies away and tear into them with their rotten teeth. The mass of bodies hit Cade, one of them impaling themselves belly-first on his knife as their rotten breath washed over him. Cade couldn't tell if it was a man or a woman.

Their broken fingernails clawed at him, tearing at his ruined top and the wounds on his chest, the stench of their bodies hitting his nostrils hard enough to make the bile rise in the back of his throat. He flashed back to the corpses nailed to the crosses on the basketball court. It was like they'd come to life now, rotting flesh and all, to swarm over him and drag him down into the dark.

He hit out at best he could, feeling his fists slamming into jaws, breaking bones, sending rotting teeth tumbling onto the precinct as they fell from suppurating gums, feeling ribs snap and legs break, and none of it doing a damn bit of good. He could beat on them until sundown and they'd still keep coming. It was in their eyes – crazed, rolling orbs, swinging about in their sockets. It was in the sounds they made, not quite human any longer.

He could still beat them. If he could get free of the crowd, he could make a run for it, maybe get into one of the buildings –

Something slammed into the back of his head, blurring his vision and making him see stars. He hit out with an elbow, smashing in someone's nose, then turned his head, trying to see what'd hit him. He caught a glimpse of someone holding a human thighbone.

It had teeth marks on it.

Another bone slammed into his ribs. They were armed. Cade tried to fight his way free, swinging his fists and snarling like an animal whenever they made contact and he felt the pain slam up his arms, but the best he could do was block the bone clubs as they swung at him. He wasn't going to be able to break free of them. The knife was out of his reach – they were already eating the one who had the blade in his belly. Cade didn't rightly know why they weren't eating him.

But he knew they would soon enough.

He'd screwed this from beginning to end, since he first set foot in the city. He'd acted like he knew what the hell we was doing and he'd screwed up time and again, and now he'd screwed up for the last time. Now he was going to die for it. Cade wasn't someone who felt fear, exactly, but he felt something like it now. A cold certainty that sat like a frozen stone in the middle of his chest. He was going to die down there, in the dark. Maybe they figured they'd cook him first. Maybe they just wanted him out of the sun before they tore him to pieces and used his bones for tools.

He kept fighting even while they dragged him to that dark tunnel, the sheer weight of numbers forcing him down the steps, into the darkness, the pitch black, and there were even more of them there, a sea of monsters, human beings made less than human, running their ragged nails over him, scratching and clawing him, trying to tear his eyes out of his head.

Cade figured his eyes were probably a delicacy. That and the testicles.

The only light was coming from the street above, and that was mostly blocked by the crush of bodies, but Cade could make out piles of bones and skulls, sigils drawn in blood on the walls. They'd been eating the dead, those dead from the plague and anyone else they'd managed to catch since – eating their own when they had to. San Francisco was a big city. Cade wondered how many there were down there...

Fingers found their way into his mouth, nails scratching at his tongue, trying to yank it out. He bit down and his mouth filled with blood. They were going to tear him into pieces.

Cade felt a kind of calm wash over him. That was it. He figured they'd do him in quick. Too bad about the Duchess, but maybe Woody'd head north and get something from one of the small towns up that way. Hell, maybe they'd both move north and get out from under the jackpot that'd hit Sausalito.

Wasn't his problem anymore.

Cade relaxed, closed his eyes and waited for them to get it the hell over with.

"Let him go. I want to talk to this one."

The voice was deep and rich, in every sense of the word. It was a television voice, a radio voice, a money voice. A voice used to getting what it wanted.

The cannibals let Cade go. He nearly fell backwards before he steadied himself on his feet.

When he opened his eyes, he was damned near blinded – someone was shining a light right at him. The cannibals were creeping back, shielding their own eyes. Some of them slinked up to the surface, looking to join the ones who'd stayed up top to eat the fallen. Some crept towards the barriers, vaulting the turnstiles and disappearing deeper into the system. A handful stuck around to watch.

Cade spat out the severed fingers in his mouth, swallowing the blood. "You in charge?"

The voice chuckled. "Straight to the facts, light on tact. That's good. No place for small talk in a negotiation situation – shows weakness. In this frankly chronic economic climate crisis... you need to be strong. Trust me... I'm Strong." Cade narrowed his eyes. It sounded like the start of a TV show. He was pretty sure it was one.

The voice lowered his lamp, putting it on the ground. Cade blinked a couple of times and then took a look.

The man in front of him was about Cade's height, black, handsome, well-groomed – or as well-groomed as you could get living in a subway station. He had on a white suit that was pretty much untouched by the dirt, shiny black shoes and a gold watch. His gaze was steady – none of the eye rolling the others had. His teeth were clean and white, apart from one gold one, slightly off from the centre. It had a diamond embedded in it that glinted when he smiled. He was smiling now.

Put him in the middle of a Hollywood premiere, he might have looked a little shabby. Put him in the Pastor's supermarket, he would've looked like a prince. Down here, surrounded by human wreckage twitching and grunting and smearing their own waste on the walls, he looked like a God.

But his breath had the same stink of raw meat on it.

"Washington Strong. Your money-saving, flesh-craving host with the most – of any currency you name, I can put you to shame. Of course, stocks and shares don't have the same exponential potential that they once did." He grinned, and his tooth flashed. "These days... you could say I'm an investor in people."

Cade was trying to place the name. He'd seen the man on the TV in Muldoon's, with the sound down – taking up three minutes on the evening news some nights, an hour-long show at the weekends, pointing to graphs of plummeting shares, playing with props, taking phone calls from worried old folks who'd lost everything they had. It was coming back a little now.

Washington Strong, CNN's money maestro. Blue or white collar, he'd protect your dollar. News flash, here's where to put your cash. You could trust the man with the million-dollar smile.

Only it turned out you couldn't. Cade had a hard time remembering the news from before the bad times hit - financial meltdowns had a way of paling into insignificance when everybody you knew was dropping dead in the street – but he remembered the old woman in Tennessee who killed herself after putting her last thousand dollars into Washington Strong's Investment Success Superscheme™. He remembered the endless pre-trial hearings as Strong put off going to prison on a dozen counts of investment fraud, embezzlement and tax evasion. It would've been a hell of a trial, but the trial never came. The bad times turned up first, and suddenly nobody gave a damn about the man with the million-dollar smile.

Cade nodded. He figured he should say something. He'd never met a celebrity before.

"Nice smile."

"An affectation that befits my station." Strong grinned. "Can't have a king with no bling, a ruler without a jeweller. You want loyalty – be royalty. Down here, a man's leadership skills can be a matter of life and dinner."

Cade shrugged. He'd take the man's word for it.

Strong stepped towards Cade, looking down at the severed cannibal fingers and stepping neatly over them. "You fought back pretty hard, pard. A display that made my day. Moves with something to prove. Got a name, my hard-fighting, finger-biting brother?" He still talked like he was on his TV show. Combined with the wash of rotten meat coming off his breath and that never-ending diamond smile, it made the whole situation seem unreal.

"Cade," said Cade.

Strong put a hand on Cade's shoulder.

"You've made the grade, Cade, my bone-breaking, life-taking, widow-making buddy. You've got the greed you need to succeed. You're what you might call... hungry for success." He grinned, gesturing upwards at an imagined sky, his shadow making hideous clawing gestures on the wall. "I saw a lot of guys like you up in the towers, looking down on the ordinary joes, the pathetic shmoes... now we're under the ground looking up, but it's the same game, different name. We're sharks. We survive by taking lives. Once upon a time that meant taking every dime, but that was small time. If you've got real cohones, you take the meat from their bones..."

Cade was about ready to punch that diamond out of his face, but he figured this wasn't the best time for poetry criticism. He looked around him, at the crowds of half-human things down in the BART station. A hell of a lot of them were wearing the rotted remains of suits. One of them had a tie.

And those jeans had designer labels on them. No wonder they'd lasted so well.

Cade took another look at the walls, the symbols drawn in blood. Dollar signs. FTSE, scrawled on the wall like a magic word. DOW. Jagged lines, smeared in human fat, rising up, up, up.

Cade figured he knew what these people had been before the bad times had hit.

He never knew San Francisco had such a thriving banking community.

He turned back to Strong. "So?"

"So, my ultra-violent, practically silent friend, there are two types of people in this brave new world. The eaters and the eaten. I think you've got the power to devour, Cade. I think you've got a bone-crunching, human-munching predator inside you, just waiting to get out. I think... you need to decide which side of the food chain you're really on. Right now. Because the offer I proffer comes with a deadline, my time-costing, patience-exhausting brother. And this rolex I'm wearing is just a shade fast."

Cade got the message. Either join the program or join the menu.

"Sure." he said.

"Wise move. But I'd like a practical demonstration of your dentation, Cade. I'd like to know if you're serious about being deleterious." He paused, then smiled wider. "Eat someone for me."

Cade narrowed his eyes. "Told you I'd do it."

"I'm from Missouri. Show me."

"Who?"

Strong grinned, and looked over to the corner of the room. Cade followed his eyes, and saw the boy who he'd chased to get here. The one who'd got him into this. He looked at Strong.

"Him?"

Strong grinned. The diamond flashed.

"Him."

CHAPTER THIRTEEN

THE POLITICIAN

Cade looked back at the boy, sizing him up. The boy looked right back at him and snarled like a stray dog. He'd heard what Strong had said – didn't like it much. Cade figured this would probably be a test for the boy as much as for him. If Cade didn't kill the boy and get eating, the boy was going to try and kill him, and he'd probably have an even chance. He'd have killed already – if he was being used as bait to lure suckers or other cannibals in, he was most likely trained to kill fast if he had to. Cade had killed his first man at age eight. He knew how easy it was once you'd started, kid or no kid.

Even if Cade managed to put the kid down without killing him, he'd fail the test and the cannibals would come back for him, and Cade knew he wasn't going to be able to beat them all. This wasn't a crowd of normal folks – they were crazy as rabid dogs. They weren't going to hold back or try to avoid getting injured.

They were just going to bury him and then tear him to pieces.

That's unless he killed the kid. Cade wasn't comfortable killing children.

But Cade wasn't exactly in his comfort zone.

He looked around the BART station at the men and women in their stained, dust-covered clothing, their rotten teeth. He was right out of options – he wasn't getting through that crowd unless he turned cannibal himself.

He shot Strong a look.

"Got a question."

Strong grinned, and the diamond flashed. "You got a meal to eat, Mister Cade. Call it an hors d'ouvre that must be obeyed."

Cade didn't move. "Got a question. How come you're in charge?"

Strong looked at Cade for a moment, then at the boy. The boy hunched like an animal, readying himself to pounce, his teeth bared. Strong shook his head.

The boy backed down, slowly.

"That ain't the question you were suggestin', Mister Cade. What you want to ask ain't why am I in charge. It's why should I be in charge of *you* – if I'm a product that's safe to invest in." He smiled again. "Let me ease your mind. I'm in charge because I have what it takes, Mister Cade. When the plague hit, a whole lot of the survivors – the movers and shakers and money takers in my particular circle – they looked around and they panicked. They thought they weren't going to make it in this new economic scenario. No more TV, no more internet, no more phones, everything falling to pieces. The only way forward was to maximise your survival potential, and that's where I stepped in. Washington Strong, the man with the million-dollar smile. The man who can tell you just what to do."

Cade kept his eye on that flashing diamond. He figured if he looked at the boy, the boy might see it as a challenge. Better to keep Strong talking.

Cade figured Strong was going to.

Strong chuckled. "If they ever bring TV back, you should try getting on it, Cade. You don't have to know much... you just talk like you do. You got authority, you set the priority. When you tell people to jump, they don't ask why, they ask how high. They were used to following me, even after all the scandal. They wanted to put their money where my mouth was." The chuckle became a laugh, the light dancing as the lamp in his hand shook.

"So... people were panicking. A few people were looting, but a lot were just breaking what they could find, burning things, running wild... they needed someone to tell them what to do, and I happened to be there. I told them the truth. It's a dog eat dog world, Mister Cade, and there are luxuries you need to set aside to abide. All those things you don't need to feed... like a conscience. Morality. Laws. All the things that stop you just taking what you want. And it's easy to take what you want when you're up against weaklings who won't, Cade. People who don't go that extra mile to live in style. My people already knew that – hell, they'd been feeding off folks for years. They didn't take much convincing." He smirked, and that gold tooth of his sparkled. "All I'm doing now, my hesitating, procrastinating brother, is feeding off people literally instead of metaphorically. And if you're on my team, you can live the dream. Eat like a king, live like a predator, do all the things you always wanted to do but didn't want to get caught doing. There's nobody to catch you any more, Cade, nobody but you."

His smile vanished.

"So go ahead. Hold back. Make out you're better than us. It'll last just long enough for you to die. And then we'll forget you were ever anything but the main course."

Cade nodded.

"So. You're in charge 'cause you're the biggest bastard here."

"That's right." smiled Strong. "Now, you gonna eat the boy? Or is the boy gonna eat you?"

Cade shrugged.

"Neither."

Then he moved.

Strong was still smiling right up until the lamp crashed to the floor, lighting everything up like a horror movie and throwing dark shadows onto the walls. He tried to bring his hands up, but they weren't quick enough. Cade's teeth were already in his neck, biting into the jugular.

Cade snapped his head back. There was a tearing sound that made the people skulking by the walls lean forward, anticipating.

Strong couldn't quite believe it. He kept not believing it when Cade starting ripping chunks of flesh out his throat and chest with his fingers, using the switchblade in his pocket to carve. He died not believing it.

The last thing he saw was Cade chewing his own meat.

Cade swallowed. It didn't taste too good, but he figured he needed to eat plenty if he wanted to make an impression, so he cut off a little more. Strong hadn't expected that. He'd spent a little too long with folks who either took orders or died quick. He'd starting thinking he was as invulnerable as his own image. The man was a sucker for his own hype.

Bad mistake for a man to make.

Cade tossed a chunk of meat to the boy. "Eat up." The boy looked at him for a second, then tore into the scrap. Cade figured there was more where that came from if he needed it, and it'd stop the boy doing anything stupid for the minute. Right now he had other fish to fry.

He stood up and turned to look at the cannibals. There were more coming now – trickling in to see what the fuss was. Some of Strong's blood had got on the lamp, drenching Cade in red light. He tore into another strip of flesh with his teeth, and the hot iron taste of Strong's blood made his head swim. Hell of a thing.

Half of them were shrinking back against the wall, trying to take in what had happened. These had been people, and then they'd given Strong everything they had, right down to their humanity, just to survive. Cade figured they'd be easy work.

It was the others that he didn't like the looks of. The ones who were leaning forward, eyes narrowed, almost salivating. Animals had a habit of challenging the alpha male for pack dominance – or Cade had heard something like that on Discovery, anyhow. He figured if he wanted this lot on his side, he was going to need to apply a little carrot and stick.

He looked each of them in the eye, one by one. Then he growled, deep in his throat.

"I'm in charge now."

He kept looking, looking for the challenge, looking for the eye-fuck. There was a big one, long hair, biker tattoos, matted beard – he'd muscled his way to the front. His teeth weren't just rotten, they were black, most missing. This one hadn't come into it out of fear.

He'd come into it because he liked the idea.

This was going to be the one. Cade locked eyes, eye-fucking him right back, then spat. If the biker backed down now, he was a coward. Cade was hoping he wouldn't.

He needed some stick to go with his carrot.

The biker charged, lanching himself forward, letting out an animal roar. Cade stepped to the side, catching the biker's head in his hands and twisting. There was a loud crack, like a branch breaking, and the biker's body stumbled forward to crash onto the tile floor.

Cade looked back at the crowd. Some of the eager ones were leaning back, mistrustful, weighing it up. They knew that what happened to the biker was probably going to happen to them, and that was the lesson Cade wanted them to take away.

Time for lesson two.

He leant down, using his skull-handled switchblade to cut a fat strip of meat off the biker's calf. Then he tossed it to the furthest man forward. Then he did that again, carving up the biker, tossing scraps of meat to the crowd. The growls turned to mutters of satisfaction – occasionally even gratitude. Once or twice, Cade heard human words.

A couple of the cannibals still didn't get the message. Any time one of them got within a couple of feet, Cade slit him across the throat with the switchblade and then opened up his belly. Then he used their meat to feed the rest. The message was pretty simple. *I'm in charge. Act up, you die. Toe the line, you live and get fed.*

Cade might have been cynical about politics, but he was pretty good at it.

Eventually, the ragged people in the BART station all had meat in their hands and in their mouths, and Cade was a bloody mess, coated with clotting red. Occasionally he still chewed on a piece of Strong, just to keep the illusion up.

He was the leader now.

Time to lead.

"Okay. Round here's deserted. Nobody left to eat. You been following bullshit." He wasn't used to making speeches, but he didn't have to say much. They were already looking at him with heads cocked, curious, like dogs following the stick before you threw it.

"Head north – up Van Ness, up Franklin, towards Marina Boulevard. Big Safeway – that's where the meat is. Meat in cans –" There was a rumble of discontent, he was losing them – "Raw meat. On the hoof. Human meat. Weak meat. Use kids as bait, you'll starve. You got to hunt."

He stopped, and looked at them. They blinked back at him, unsure.

Cade growled. He'd drawn them a god-damned map. What the hell more did they need?

"*Git!*"

They got.

As the throng of barely-human, half-naked things scuttled and scuffled up the steps towards the failing light, Cade noticed Fuel-Air standing in the light, shaking his head. On an impulse, Cade put his hand on one of the cannibals – one who looked a little more like he knew what was going on.

"No women, no kids. Someone eats a woman or a kid, I kill ten of you for every one that falls." The cannibal looked at him, opening his rotted mouth. "I will do it. *Git.*"

The cannibal scurried into the shifting crowd, passing the word on in halting, broken English. Cade looked to Fuel-Air, but Fuel-Air was gone.

Cade wondered if he'd have thought of that on his own. He wondered if he'd have cared one way or another.

He looked at the marks on the wall and mused for a second

on just how people – human beings, bankers and stockbrokers, CEOs, educated folk – could fall so far in just a couple of years. Then he shook his head, figuring himself for a damn fool.

Hard part wasn't falling. Falling was easy as hell.

Hard part was standing up in the first place.

Pretty soon they were all gone and it was just Cade – and the boy, gnawing on a piece of tattooed skin, looking at him with narrowed eyes. Questioning. Cade turned to look at him.

No point in sending him out to die with the rest of them. The Pastor's men were going to take a hell of a hit, but they had at least a couple of sniping rifles and a hell of a lot of other weapons. Cade figured the cannibals were going to knock his cosy paradise for a loop, maybe shake the faithful up a little bit. Make things harder.

Then when Cade came back, the Pastor's paradise might just be open for a coup. Worth trying, anyhow.

Cade would've made a hell of a politician.

He nodded at the boy. "You. Go get me my knife. I think I left it in a fella out there."

The boy looked at him warily for a second, then vanished. He was back a couple of minutes later with Cade's knife.

Cade took it from him, slotted it into his belt, and saluted. "I'm abdicating. Rule wisely now."

The boy looked uncomprehendingly at him as he climbed the steps. Cade figured he was better off alone than he had been with the rest of them. And he was a hell of a lot safer in a deserted BART station with a couple of dead folks than he would've been with Cade.

What the fuck was that shit? A salute? You growing a sense of humour in your old age, dog?

Fuel-Air was sitting under a tree with a porno mag and an open can of coffee granules. Cade nodded to him, then set off down Market Street, heading for the intersection with Oak. "Sure."

About fuckin' time, man. Shit, you look like all ten fuckin' Jason movies. You planning on washing some of that shit off before you meet the fuckin' hippies? They're gonna think you're Charles Manson or some shit, dog... fuckin' helter skelter n' shit, right?

Cade narrowed his eyes for a second, wondering what Fuel-Air knew. There was something about Fuel-Air that Cade was starting to find troubling, beyond the fact that he was a sure sign Cade was going nuts.

Hell with it. He needed to wash off the blood and find a change of clothes. Fuel-Air was right about that, at least. Cade nodded towards him.

"You coming?"

Fuel-Air flashed his usual shit-eating grin. Cade noticed he'd gotten a gold tooth from somewhere. With a diamond lodged in it.

Thought you'd never ask, my meat chuckin', Pastor-fuckin' brother. Thought you'd never fuckin' ask.

Cade scowled, picking at the dried blood on his arm.

Goddamn Fuel-Air never could take anything seriously.

CHAPTER FOURTEEN

THE WAR

No dead on Oak Street.

Cade didn't know whether that was on account of the cannibals having eaten them, or whether he was in hippie territory and they'd picked them all up to use as fertiliser. Either way, he wasn't comfortable. He never thought he'd want to see a rotting corpse laying in the street, but now it came to it, he missed them. They were a sign people weren't around to screw things up.

Cade was missing the dead and resenting the living, and he figured that was more than a little fucked up. So when he saw the coffee shop after the intersection with Divisadero, he figured it was as good a place as any to wash up and rest for the night.

The taps weren't working, but there was an old cooler behind the counter with bottled water in it, and he managed to get a fair amount of the blood off his hands and face with it, although he had to get rid of his tank top. After that, he checked in the back room.

That was where he found Frank.

Cade didn't know it was Frank – all there was as far as he was concerned was a skeleton that stank to high heaven. He didn't know it was Frank's white t-shirt he found in the back of a closet, either. But he was pretty grateful to Frank anyway. Frank being there let him know the place hadn't been found yet. It meant he was as safe as he was going to be for a few hours. It meant he could get a little sleep, tend to his wounds, think about what he was going to do next.

Frank had a little whisky too, which Cade poured into the holes in his hands and over his chest, letting the alcohol burn into the cuts, saving a little for drinking purposes. It wasn't exactly standard medical practice, but he figured it was better than just letting the wounds fester, especially after his pierced hands had pulled a few bodies inside out. It was a miracle he hadn't come down with an infection already.

After he'd cleaned up and washed his wounds as best he could, there wasn't much else left to do but watch the street. The coffee shop had a second floor, and from there Cade had a good look at anybody who might be coming from Haight-Ashbury. Plus, sitting with a view to the west, he got a good look at the sun going down. Cade wasn't a man who had much appreciation for natural beauty, but he wasn't about to turn it away when it got handed to him on a plate.

And it was a hell of a sunset. Boiling pink clouds scudding across a sky filled with fire and brimstone, blood and copper. Cade hadn't seen a sight like it in forever.

Kind of reminds you of something, don't it, dog? Sky all on fire and shit.

Cade shook his head. He knew what Fuel-Air was getting at, and there wasn't any point thinking about it that he could see. That sunset wasn't anything like an artillery strike. And Cade wasn't going to think about the artillery strike anyway, so it didn't much matter if it was.

He looked up at Fuel-Air, who was sitting in a booth on the other side of the room, sipping a frappucino. Half his face was missing, and he only had one arm, plus his guts were hanging out on the table. So the frappucino was slurping out through his ruptured throat and what was left of his guts, pooling on the table and the floor.

He still had Strong's gold tooth shining out from what was left of his mouth, though. Goddamn fashion plate.

Shit, dog, sorry. I should get myself together. Bringin' back painful memories and shit, I bet.

Cade spat, and took another sip of whisky.

"Where'd you get the coffee?"

Ways and means, bitch. Fuel-Air grinned, flashing his new diamond. Cade hoped he got sick of that thing fast. It'd been irritating enough on Strong.

Say what you like about Strong, at least he knew enough to stay dead.

Cade could feel the memory pressing on the back of his mind. It wasn't going away any time soon, but he was damned if he was going to spend time reliving it. He was getting enough of Fuel-Air anyway without remembering the way his voice shook as he huddled next to the humvee.

Shit, dog, you reckon the Captain knows there ain't no motherfucker out there? Figure he's just getting his total up for the Commander – shit, is this dumb motherfucker actually in charge?

He didn't need to hear Sergeant A standing up for the chain of command the way he always did when there was a clusterfuck going on all around him.

There's a chain of command, Killer. It's there for a reason. If the Captain says artillery, we go with artillery. The Captain's the Captain and what he says is what... Jesus, Killer, what the fuck do you think you're doing? Sit down! Cade, I said sit down...

He sure as hell didn't need to remember the Captain barking into the radio set, laying down co-ordinates that were maybe a hundred and fifty metres from where they were sat, calling up an artillery strike on some bad intelligence, a damn phantom Chinese whisper that'd made its way up and down the comms. They were close enough to see with the naked eye that there wasn't any Republican Guard in that field, and even if there had been, Cade could have blown them away without breaking a sweat whether there'd been a squad of trained Marines to back him up or not. But Captain Chaos, in his infinite wisdom, was calling up an artillery strike. A hundred and fifty metres away from them.

Sir, I'm respectfully asking you to rethink this. It's danger close...

The Lieutenant. Nice guy, at least by Cade's reckoning. Named Hunter Cragg, if you can believe that. If Cade had seen that name in a movie, he'd have laughed. Hunter Cragg was a good man, though. Hunter Cragg had seen the elephant. He had one hell of a lot of combat experience. Ran his men right, gave them shit when they needed it, let it ride when they didn't, smart enough to know which was which. In another war – say, a war where the people running it had any kind of plan – Lt. Hunter Cragg would have been hailed and respected as the leader of men that he was. They'd have put a medal on him. They'd have made him Captain, maybe Commander. Maybe General. Hell, maybe President.

Cade figured as long as he was wishing, he'd like a pony.

Hunter Cragg had been stuck in the war he was stuck in, and in that war folks like Dollings got to be Captain and folks like Cragg had to suck it up and be Lieutenant and do what they were told. And if they were told to jump in the shit, they were meant to ask how deep.

Cade took another shot of whisky.

He hated thinking about the Captain most of all.

Danger close? You little pissant, danger close is coward talk! No such thing as danger close for a Marine!

Cragg's voice came again. Desperate. A strong man begging.

Sir, please, call off the strike... at least delay it while we pull back...

And then that barking, angry, ugly voice of the Captain. Captain Paul Dollings, known in the lower ranks as Captain Chaos, born in the great state of Texas, enjoying his first taste of combat and divorced from any kind of shared reality. A first-class, grade-A dumb-fuck son of a bitch, to put it mildly.

Captain Dollings had never seen real combat in his life. He'd never seen the elephant. And every word he said made that loud and clear.

Coward talk! You had best wake the fuck up, Lieutenant, because the only place you're headed after this kind of gross insubordination is a military tribunal! I'm going to tear that bar off you myself, do you hear me, you damned coward? You're finishing out what's left of this war as a grunt like... who the goddamned hell is that? Jesus! Put that gun down! This is treason! This is...

It wasn't a happy memory, all in all. But that moment when the Captain had seen Cade raising his assault rifle, had seen the barrel swinging towards him, had looked into Cade's eyes and read the unmistakeable truth in them - that Cade was going to wipe the Captain out like a stain right there and then, and not because of any personal dislike of the man, or hatred of country or Corps or government or God or any other reason that'd allow the Captain to die a hero...

...but simply because Captain Paul Dollings was a dumb son of a bitch who was in the way and needed to be taken out of it...

...to have the Captain look in his eyes and understand his own worthlessness in the seconds before he died...

...*that* was a happy memory.

In his booth, Fuel-Air grinned, raising his frappucino.

You the man, dog. The look on that motherfucker's face. Fuckin' Kodak, man.

Cade raised his whisky, and nearly smiled. That'd probably been the second-best moment of his life, right after his first kill. Then Fuel-Air ruined it.

Too bad you shot the wrong guy, huh?

Sure, thought Cade. Too bad.

Too bad the Lieutenant had to go and be a god-damned hero by hurling himself in front of the bullets. Cade had liked the Lieutenant. Hunter Cragg was a hell of a good man, and he treated his men right. He'd seen the elephant.

Cade didn't know why he'd step in front of the barrel like that. Just couldn't figure it.

But he had.

The bullets had pretty much torn Cragg into pieces, which was a hell of a shame for his wife and his little boy. Cragg'd probably have survived it if he'd let himself hold back for a second. He'd probably have killed Cade, but Cade had figured on dying anyway. Probably wouldn't have been such a loss.

A couple of the bullets managed to find their way through the Lieutenant and smack into the Captain – one in the gut, one in the shoulder and a couple in the leg. None of them hit an artery, but the gutshot would have killed him eventually. Of course, he might have gotten medical aid, and Cade couldn't have that. There was no way this son of a bitch was going to stay alive one more second if Cade could help it.

It wasn't just the artillery. It was all the grabbing of souvenirs from the dead and the dying. It was shouting on open comms about how vulnerable they were whenever they were vulnerable, which was often. Mostly, it was that time he shot a five-year old - accidentally on purpose – and then wouldn't medevac him. Just watched him die with a grin on his face, talking about how mistakes were often made in war.

The artillery was something of a last straw.

Cade took another gulp of whiskey and tried to remember what it'd been like before that moment, back when he'd given a damn whether he lived or he died. For the life of him, he couldn't. Maybe he'd never given a damn. Maybe he'd only pretended.

Maybe he'd only pretended he didn't want to remember this.

Cade poured more whiskey and thought back, remembering, picturing that look of cold fear in the Captain's eyes, hearing the way the bark in his voice had turned to the whimpering of a kicked dog.

You can't do this! I'm a Captain! You can't do this! Please! PLEASE!

All of a sudden, Paul Dollings had seen the elephant. He was staring the damned elephant right in its eyes.

And the elephant was going to walk right over him without even stopping to blink.

Cade had brought the butt of his weapon down between

Dollings' eyes hard enough to cave the skull in. He figured that was it for him too. Sergeant A had his sidearm drawn and was yelling something. He wasn't calling Cade 'Killer' anymore, and if Sergeant A stopped using a man's nickname it meant he was pretty mad.

Cade had raised his hands and turned. He saw Sergeant A yelling the words *chain of command,* over and over again, Fuel-Air behind him staring with his eyes almost popping out, the other men starting to run towards him, weapons drawn.

And then the strike had hit.

It was about a hundred and fifty metres off target. In their direction.

Danger close.

Cade didn't remember much after that. He remembered reaching with a hand covered in blood and dirt, nothing in his ears but ringing, turning over a body and seeing Fuel-Air with half his face gone and his guts hanging out. No diamond tooth, though, which looking back was a mercy.

After that, all he remembered was waking up in the hospital. He wasn't the only one out of his unit to survive, but the other survivors hadn't got a good enough look at what had happened with the Captain and Lieutenant Cragg, and the bodies had been torn into pieces by the shelling. Cade had been lucky to escape with shrapnel and broken bones.

Lucky motherfucker, grinned Fuel-Air. *You had guilty written all over you, dog.*

Which accounted for the year in the hole, the dishonourable discharge and the promise – delivered to him through unofficial channels – that if Cade ever showed his face again anywhere, he was a dead man. Which suited Cade fine.

All he wanted was somewhere quiet to lay his head. A trailer park in the middle of nowhere, near the coast. Somewhere where they didn't investigate violent deaths too good, in case he had any problems. Somewhere he could forget himself until he died.

You really thought I was gonna let you forget? Shit, you should be so lucky, bitch.

"Yeah." Cade was tired. He'd had enough memories, and he'd

had enough booze, and he hadn't seen a damn soul coming down that street. The sun had sank under the horizon, and all that was left now was the night and the dark. Time he got some sleep. He had a lot to do in the morning.

Big day tomorrow, dog. Those hippies sound like some Satan-worshipping motherfuckers, into all kinds of sacrifices and shit – least according to the Pastor. You ready for some shit like that, dog? You think you want to put yourself in the jackpot with some crazy acid-head freaks like that?

Cade shrugged, finishing his whisky and stretching out on the leather of his booth seat.

"Sure."

Then he slept.

CHAPTER FIFTEEN

THE GANG

Cade didn't dream.

It was after nine when he woke up. Cade was usually a dawn riser – he figured sleeping in like that was his body telling him it needed the rest. That and having something close to a real bed for the first time since he'd driven out from the trailer park.

Fuel-Air was gone. Cade figured he'd gotten what he wanted – Cade had had a chance to relax for an evening and he'd spent it reliving getting blown half to pieces because a damn fool figured his reputation was worth more than the lives of his men. And feeling bad about it, he realised, which was new. Cade hadn't been someone who felt guilt, or regretted things, in all the time he could remember.

Guilt was new.

Cade couldn't help wondering what Fuel-Air was up to.

There was no sense Cade could see in wasting any more time.

He cracked open another bottle of water to wash up, making use of Frank's toothbrush and paste to get some of the taste out of his mouth while he was at it. He made a note of the area – he didn't know what the rest of San Francisco looked like right now, and he'd probably want to come back here, or to another place like it nearby. So far, this looked to be a little oasis, untouched by any of the various factions he'd seen or any other looters who might have happened along – people like him, in other words.

Of course, he'd not met the hippies yet. Could be they just weren't too hung up on personal possessions, or maybe they had their own water supply fixed up and didn't feel the need to go looking for more. He might be deep in their territory and not know it – so far, he'd only met up with groups that'd been too far into their own craziness to sort out the basics of living, but it could be that they were the exceptions instead of the rule. After all, he didn't exactly know what big city life was like these days. It was something Cade would have to check for himself.

Cade figured the best thing to do right now would be to get onto Haight Street, by way of Divisadero. Then he'd just keep heading west. By the time he got to Haight-Ashbury, he'd have run into the hippies or they'd have run into him. Simple.

Nothing's simple in this world, dog. Just ask the Lieutenant.

Cade cursed under his breath. Fuel-Air was really starting to get on his last nerve now.

Fuck you, dog. I'm a motherfuckin' calming influence on your raging ass. Last time I left you alone for two minutes you took over a fuckin' cannibal cult and sent them to eat a man of God.

Cade gave him a stare and then stalked out of the front door of the coffee place and onto the street. The sun was already up – looked like another beautiful day.

Still, Fuel-Air had a point. He'd have to see how the situation with the Pastor and the cannibals had gone once he was all done with the hippies. It was starting to nag at him. What he was hoping was that the Pastor would deal with the cannibals and lose a lot of his own strength in the process – but if he was really lucky they'd have gotten themselves into a siege situation, something to wear both sides down a little and keep them occupied while he did what he needed to. He'd probably got as much as he could expect to get out of it just by staying alive, but a man could hope.

Of course, a worst case scenario would be the cannibals wiping the Pastor's people out. Eating the children. Tearing the babies from the wombs of their mothers and ripping them open, eating up the tiny organs like popcorn. And that all being Cade's fault.

That would be the worst case scenario.

He wondered why he cared all of a sudden. Still, it was a matter for another day.

Today was hippies.

Cade checked the time – about ten. He kept his eyes open crossing the street and heading down Divisadero, looking for anything that might smack of company. He'd heard a hell of a lot about the hippies, and while he doubted any of it was true, he didn't exactly want them to get the drop on him either.

He was crossing the intersection with Haight Street when he heard the engine.

It was a low growl in the distance – rumbling, chugging along. A van, by the sound, probably pretty old, coming from the east – from cannibal country. Cade ducked behind a bus shelter on the corner and drew his knife. Then he waited.

Eventually, the van trundled into view. It was a VW van – Cade was a little surprised it was still running, but it proved a lot of things. For one thing, the hippies had it together enough to drive, which expanded their territory some, and meant they had enough mechanical skill to keep cars in repair, or at least hot-wire them as needed. Still, that didn't mean much. You could say the same about him, and he was just one man.

What was interesting was how the van was painted. It was a bright, livid blue with a wide green stripe, dotted with pink and yellow flowers. Scrawled on one side in self-consciously 'psychedelic' writing were the words CONUNDRUM CAR.

Cade watched the van crawl past him, then stop in the middle of the intersection.

Looks like they're looking for you, dog.

Cade nodded. Fuel-Air was sitting cross-legged on top of the bus shelter, wearing a caftan, love beads and long hair. He still had half his face missing, though.

Fuel-Air was a hell of a comedian now he was dead.

Cade waited, and watched. He could hear voices from inside the van – young voices, not more than twenty – and then the back door opened and a couple of them got out.

Cade noticed the kid in the green oversized t-shirt first. Brown hair, scruffy up top, not too long, with a barely-grown goatee hanging off his chin. No muscles to speak of – Cade thought he had a kind of malnourished look to him. Half-starved, lean as a greyhound. He flopped about as he moved, like his arms and legs didn't have the co-ordination to propel him along.

Along with him, there was a brunette girl, short and dumpy, in an orange pullover that looked too big for her, and a pair of granny glasses with thick lenses. Cade wondered if she'd had a better pair before, but they'd gotten broken and she'd needed to scavenge for new ones. It was possible.

Neither of the kids looked like any kind of threat. Cade didn't peg them for Satanists, or killers, or the kind of people who'd burn a city to the ground. They just looked like the kind of hipster kids Cade had always seen on any trips he'd made to San Francisco, only a little thinner, a little dirtier, maybe a little bit more thrift-store than they had been. There was something else about them, too.

A kind of glassy-eyed look.

Right then, Cade was focussed on the dog. The dog was going to be the problem.

A Great Dane – a big one, big and brown, maybe half the height of the skinny kid. There wasn't much flab on the dog either, but what there was was muscle. Cade had a feeling that dog could probably cause him some trouble if they told it to attack. It could probably cause him some trouble if they didn't – it was already sniffing the air, catching his scent.

Cade listened, his knife tight in his grip, working out what his next move was.

"Are you sure you saw somebody here, Scruffy? I don't see anybody out here now!" The girl rubbed her chin, looking around the intersection.

"M-m-maybe he was a g-g-*ghost!*" mewled the boy. He had a voice like a surfer – probably spent most of his time down on the beach before the bad times.

"Well. Jeepers, this certainly is a way-out mystery!" chirped the girl, scratching the back of her head with a serious look on her face. "I mean, there sure weren't any cannibals over on the east side at all! It's like they've just vanished into thin air!"

Cade's eyes narrowed. He glanced up at Fuel-Air, who raised his remaining eyebrow.

Seriously, dog. 'Jeepers?' 'Way out?' What the fuck, man?

"It's, like, a spooky happening, Thelma! Like, what if they came this way? Or what if they got scared by a really big monster that's, like, waiting for us right now?" The skinny kid's voice trembled as he said it, and then he went into a bizarre pantomime of fear, clattering his teeth together and knocking his knees before finishing up with a theatrical gulp. Cade had never seen anything quite like it – he figured maybe it was some kind of drug paranoia. The kid seemed to be afraid of just about everything, looking at the buildings as though they were about to come to life and start coming for him. Cade figured that was probably why he had the dog.

If that was why he had the dog, then the dog was going to be trained to kill. Admittedly, the dog didn't look like much – if anything, he looked kind of goofy – but Cade knew better than to judge a book by its cover.

He just needed to let it get a little closer, and then he could take care of it. He took another look at the van, narrowing his eyes. The van was starting to rock – shifting to and fro in a regular rhythm. That was a little weird.

Maybe they had some kind of generator ticking over in there.

Cade shook his head, and concentrated on the two hippies and their dog. That was the important thing.

The dog looked in his direction, and sniffed the air again.

Cade held his breath.

"Like, what do you think, Doob?" said the skinny kid in that stupid-scared surfer voice of his. Cade's eyes narrowed as the dog reared up on his haunches and waggled its paws, giving a kind of shrug, lips pulling back from the jaws in a weird parody of a smile, before it barked twice – *rruhhuhh rro* – and fell back on all fours.

Dude, did that fuckin' dog just answer the question?

Cade doubted it. But that dog was definitely trained to perform a couple of tricks, and if the skinny kid had taught it to get up and do a little dance when it got asked a question, it was probably trained to disarm or disable an opponent. If they were regularly checking on the cannibals, the dog would need to be able to defend them. That was just common sense.

The dog sniffed the air again, then started padding in his direction.

"Well, it looks like Doobie's got the scent of something!" said the short girl. The dog was sniffing and walking in Cade's direction. He gripped the knife tight.

"Yeah, like, he's got the munchies, right Doob? Maybe somebody, like, made a sandwich nearby!" The boy licked his lips, leading with his face, throat exposed. Cade let them get a little closer.

The girl wagged a finger at them. "Well, don't get too far off, you two! There have been some spooky goings-on around here and –"

Cade moved. The dog had to go first – that was obvious. He rolled out of cover and grabbed the mutt in a headlock, bringing the blade of the knife down near the base of the skull, between the second and third vertebrae, neatly severing the spine as it buried in the dog's neck. The dog gave a strangled bark and went limp as the skinny kid jerked back.

"It's a g-g-ghost! Like, run, Doob!" He jumped up like a jack in the box, turning pale, then turned and ran towards the van, hurling himself underneath it. The brunette didn't seem to blink.

"Don't be silly, Scruffy! That's no ghost – it must be the owner of the Ben & Jerry's! I'll bet he just dressed up as a ghost to warn people away from some buried treasure, that's all!" she smiled, still with the same wide, glassy eyes.

Cade looked at her for a second, then let the dog drop to the ground, sheathing the knife in his belt. He had a feeling maybe he'd read the situation wrong somewhere. He walked forward slowly, keeping an eye on them. As an afterthought, he hooked a hand through the dog's collar and dragged it behind him.

"You've got to excuse Scruffy, Mister! He sees ghosts just about everywhere ever since... well, ever since 'you-know-what'!" She did finger-quotes. "Don't worry, though, it's never actually ghosts. It's just people in masks. Scary masks. That's all." She grew thoughtful, looking at the dog's twitching corpse. "See, there's no such thing as ghosts. When you see things that couldn't possibly exist, it's most likely to be a man with a hidden movie projector or someone dressed up to scare people away from hidden treasure. Or a smuggling operation!" She beamed up at him, then looked at him suspiciously. "Is that your real face, or a mask?"

Cade blinked, then tried to get the conversation back on track. "Doc Clearly?"

The brunette smiled. "He's kind of the king around here. He's the one who gives us mysteries to solve! Well, more little tasks to take care of. Errands that need running, like checking on whether the cannibals are spreading into our territory." She pointed at the dead dog. "That's pretty realistic. Are you doing that with a hidden camera?"

"Sure." said Cade. He figured it was probably easier to go along with that for the second – at least until he met Doc Clearly. Besides, he kind of regretted killing the dog now – it was pretty clear these kids could barely train themselves to function, never mind a dog. Still, better safe than sorry. He cleared his throat.

"Got some questions. Hoping Doc Clearly could answer them. I'd be obliged."

The brunette brightened up. "Oh, Doc Clearly can answer all sorts of questions! You know, I'll bet he'll clear up an awful lot of things for you!" She smiled, brightly, and then opened up the back door of the van.

Cade blinked.

There were two more kids in the back – a big blond fella and a red-haired girl. The blond fella had a red neckerchief on, the redhead was wearing a purple hairband. Neither of them were wearing anything else. The girl was bent over, doggy-style, and the fella was slamming into her like there wasn't a complete stranger looking at the pair of them. The brunette smiled brightly.

"Company, guys! Mister... hey, what's your name?"

"Cade." said Cade.

"Mister Cade was wanting a ride to see Doctor Clearly! I thought he could come back with us!" the brunette didn't seem to mind what was happening in front of her. Cade didn't feel right pointing it out.

"Pleasure – *nnf* – to meet you, Sir!" said the blond kid with a sunny smile. The girl panted and nodded. Cade was glad they didn't offer to shake hands. He got gingerly into the back of the van as the brunette went around to the driving seat.

The girl lifted her head. "Ahhh... hey, what happened to Doobie-Doo?"

Cade swallowed. Didn't seem much point in denying it. "Killed him. Sorry."

Fuckin' heartfelt apology there, man. Shit, you'll kill just about anything, won't you? Kids, pets – you really are a brutal son of a bitch and you don't give a fuck who knows it, know what I'm saying? You feel me?

"Sorry." Cade muttered again. He didn't know where the hell to look.

"Don't apologise. I'm sure you..." – the blond fella inhaled sharply – "... had your reasons..." He grimaced, freezing in place, then brought his hand down on the girl's backside with a hard *smack*. In turn, she closed her eyes and bucked her hips hard, squealing out through clenched teeth. Cade still didn't really know where to look. He wasn't used to being invited into these situations and he didn't want to offend anybody.

Then again, he had just killed their dog for pretty much no reason. If they were okay about that, he figured they were fine with him getting an eyeful.

The brunette buckled her seatbelt and put the van into gear, then stepped onto the accelerator. There was a strangled scream from underneath, cut off by a loud *crack*, then a crunch, as the back wheels of the van bucked upwards.

"Oh gosh! I forgot Scruffy was underneath the Conundrum Car! Jeepers! I killed him! Oh, Doc Clearly's going to be so cross!" The brunette put her hand to her mouth, continuing to drive the van as the blond kid shook his head with a lopsided grin.

Cade leant back against the wall of the van. Opposite him, Fuel-Air was shaking his head, blame in his one remaining eye.

It was going to be a long trip.

CHAPTER SIXTEEN

THE DOC

"See, what I'm trying to say is that the motivating force in the universe is Love. It's that simple. Everything is defined by its capability to feel Love, and it follows that Love is the highest emotion because it's the thing that defines us as a species. And it follows from that that it's our duty, *as* a species, to rise *to* that highest definition and become a species motivated by Love. So we should be judged on how much we Love one another. It's like Doc Clearly says – within each of us lies the potential to become the balance of the universe. You get what I mean, Mister Cade?" The blond kid paused, sucking on the reefer he'd lit a minute ago.

Cade nodded, then looked at Fuel-Air. Fuel-Air grinned and shook his head slowly. He was back in his utilities, holding a reefer like the blond kid – Ted, Cade thought he was called. Cade raised an eyebrow, wondering what Fuel-Air made of all this talk. He'd been a similar age to these kids when he'd died. Maybe he'd talked like that once.

Shit, dog, I'd have said anything if there was a blowjob involved.

The redhead lifted her head – Cade had to wonder if it was a reaction to what Fuel-Air had said – cradling Ted absently while she spoke. "It's not just a sexual thing either, although I do resent the implication made by the previous society that sex for mutual pleasure has to be somehow inferior to sex that's been labelled as something 'deeper' –" Ted's balls flopped down in their sac as she made the finger quotes. "– anyway, what we've achieved is Love shared by an entire community, and offered to anyone who comes to us, as well as the natural world around us that was neglected so badly by the previous society." Having made her point, she went back to what she'd been doing before, taking Ted in her mouth and bobbing her head slowly up and down, her fingers squeezing lightly. Cade looked back at Fuel-Air for want of anywhere else to look. He still hadn't quite figured out what the etiquette was for this, and while they'd forgiven him for killing the dog – and by extension the skinny kid – he didn't want to ruffle any feathers. He still felt a little guilty, which was odd for Cade.

Fuel-Air just grinned.

The brunette – Thelma, was it? – chimed in from the driver's seat. "We even Love the cannibals and that weird religious sect up to the north, although obviously we have to love them from a distance, seeing as they're, um... well, they don't exactly Love us, if you see what I mean. But any who come by, we welcome with open arms. We've had a couple from the north, and once they saw how nice things were for us, they stuck around. I think they were maybe a little repressed. The cannibals, though – Jeepers! They're the opposite!"

"The cannibals are the ultimate 'me-first-and-screw-the-other-guy' society. They have no inhibitions, but they also have no sense of anything beyond themselves. It's like Doctor Clearly says – you need a balance between yourself and the world. See, the cannibals just don't care about other people. You can't be part of their culture and have any kind of relationship with another human being. It's no wonder they're dying off." With that, Ted closed his eyes, taking a drag on the reefer, idly putting a hand into the redhead's hair. Daisy, that was her name.

"And Scruffy?" Cade said, despite himself. Now wasn't the time to start an argument, but there was something about the way they'd just driven over the fella that didn't strike Cade as being right.

Didn't you drive right over someone a while back? You want to get judgemental, dog, you best take a look in the mirror.

Cade frowned and shot Fuel-Air a look. That was different.

Daisy raised her head. "That was an accident. Thelma – well, she's, uh..." She looked up, then raised her eyebrows, mouthing the words *not right*.

Thelma hissed. "There's nothing wrong with me! When we find the Pastor and take his mask off – well, you'll see! It'll all turn out to be a smuggling operation! You know he's going to get away with it, too, if we don't do something! Besides, Scruffy probably isn't dead. He's just hiding in a vase. What we felt was probably just projected by a movie camera..." She lapsed into silence. The van was moving a lot slower than it had been – Cade figured they were moving through a crowd. The kids were probably taking him directly to Clearly. That was fine – he wasn't in a hurry to end the conversation just yet.

Ted blew out a cloud of marijuana smoke. "I'm sorry about what happened to Doobie and Scruffy, but it's like Doc Clearly says... their individual egos are merged with the universe now. There's no point feeling bad about it. Sooner or later, we're going to make that trip too. I mean, even today... people still die all the time – even voluntarily, sometimes. If the end of your life comes from a decision that's been made, we have to respect that decision. I can understand that. It's hard to function sometimes. At least since 'you-know-what'." Finger quotes again.

Cade wondered if Doc Clearly did finger quotes too, or talked in such a roundabout way about a man killing himself. Most likely.

Still, this answered a couple of questions. Cade figured the hippies were dealing with the bad times pretty much the same way as the Pastor's were – putting their faith in an afterlife and following the nearest authority figure. Clearly was going to have a hell of a long way to go to be worse than the Pastor, but Cade wasn't convinced yet. Ted and Daisy seemed relatively normal, despite the fact that they hadn't stopped screwing since Cade had met them, but Thelma shouldn't have been driving that damned van. Cade was slightly surprised they hadn't killed anybody else on the way.

There was something else, too. Cade wasn't a prude by any means, but at first he'd instinctively avoided looking at Ted and Daisy – the etiquette thing. But now he was getting a close look at them, he'd noticed something weird.

There were a hell of a lot of bruises on both both them. Some fresh, some old. And scratch marks as well – again, a couple fresh, most of them old. Like these kids got into a lot of fights.

Might be coincidence, though. Cade figured there was a lot of hard work involved in the hippie way of life, and if you were doing errands and lugging crap around the whole day there were ways to get a little banged up.

Fuel-Air snorted. *Face it, bitch, you're only cutting these weird-ass motherfuckers some slack because you don't want to have to kill another bajillion people. Sex monkey and his girlfriend are fucked up, and the crazy freak-girl with the Choose Your Own Adventure fixation is super-duper ultra fucked up and you fuckin' know it, bitch. I give you until midnight before you break some poor motherfucker's neck over this shit.*

Cade checked the clock on the dashboard. It was only about a quarter to twelve. Twelve hours without killing someone. Cade figured it could be done. "You're on."

"On what?" said Ted – then he stiffened, letting out a strangled grunt, at the same moment Thelma stopped the van.

"We're here, Mister Cade. Just open the door and hop out. Daisy, do you want to park the van when you're done? Then I can take Mister Cade to see the Doc."

"Mmmhmmm." nodded Daisy. Cade turned away and opened up the back door without wishing them goodbye.

The smell of dope hit him the second he stepped out of the van. They'd gone past the Haight-Ashbury and the van had pulled up outside the entrace to Golden Gate Park – and the park was full of people.

Cade hadn't seen that many people in one place since the bad times - it made the Pastor's couple of hundred seem like a small group. Cade could see at least five hundred people here – stretched out on rugs, kissing underneath trees, sitting cross-legged and meditating, playing guitars and shaking tambourines, most just walking and talking. A couple of them were naked – Cade noticed a livid bruise on one girl's thigh – some were decorated with body and face paint or home-made jewellery. The rest dressed in simple, comfortable clothing that covered the arms and legs.

There was a paper sign thumbtacked to a tree, reading 'SOFTBALL GAME AT KEZAR STADIUM TODAY 2PM ALL WELCOME' in brightly-coloured marker. Cade wandered up to it, running his fingers over the letters. He wondered if the game was still going on.

Shit, bitch, you gonna cry?

Fuel-Air was sitting with a couple on a tartan rug, smoking the same joint he'd had in the van. The couple were eating a picnic of some kind - the man had a fresh tomato, the woman was eating some canned spam with a fork. Tomato plants at least – probably other produce. There was a botanical garden near here that'd be perfect for that. And a food distribution system that worked.

Shit, you are gonna cry. You motherfuckin' pussy.

Cade shook his head. "Been a while. That's all."

A thought struck him. Why did he have to take the insulin back to the trailer park? Why couldn't he just bring the Duchess here? If the population was as big as Cade figured it was, they'd have diabetics, and they could care for them. The Duchess and Woody could both move here – if Woody could drag himself away from his mother's. The cannibals were going to be a problem, but they'd do what he told them – and even if they didn't, by now they'd worn themselves down against the Pastor's people. As for the Pastor – hell, Cade could deal with him easy enough. There were ways and means.

His eyes went to the man sitting on the rug. He was wearing a white polo-neck, and Cade could see the edge of a fresh cut on his neck, that the polo-neck was hiding. He turned, smiling at Cade, and Cade noticed he had one black eye.

The people here certainly did seem accident prone, all right.

Fuel-Air was laughing. Cade looked at him, and almost flinched. Sitting next to the young couple was Fuel-Air as he was now – a rotting, decomposing skeleton, covered in writhing maggots. And laughing.

Listen to yourself, you dumb motherfucker. Shit, you're so fuckin' stupid I'm gonna let you find out for yourself, you fuckin' empty-headed shit. You motherfuckin' hippie-ass Alice B Toklas fuckin' bitch...

Cade looked away, back at the sign on the tree. He kept his eyes on the sign until he couldn't hear Fuel-Air laughing any more.

"Mister Cade?"

Cade turned – it was Thelma. She was smiling nervously. Behind her, there was a man of about fifty, with grey-brown curly hair and a drooping moustache, dressed in a light brown suit and a pink shirt. He smoked a pipe. He had a trustworthy air about him, like a college professor, which Cade figured was probably because he was one.

"You Clearly?" Cade's voice sounded wary in his own ears. He was waiting for the other shoe. Waiting for Fuel-Air to be proven right.

Thelma smiled, and then went back to the van, which still hadn't moved. Clearly stuck out his hand. Despite himself, Cade took it. Clearly smiled, taking the pipe from his mouth. "You must be Cade. Is that a first name or a last name?"

Cade narrowed his eyes. "You in charge of this place?"

Clearly chuckled. "Not one for small talk. All right. Yes, I am the head of the community, I suppose, if you want to make that kind of distinction. But I do a lot of delegation. We're run according to principles I set out, but a lot of the actual work – agriculture, food distribution, manufacture and supply of the essentials for living, entertainment and so forth – I leave to other hands. I just sort of keep an eye on the whole shebang, so to speak." He smiled, genially, his eyes dropping to the knife at Cade's belt, and the bloodstain on the white T-shirt. "Thelma told me how you, ah, met the gang."

Cade swallowed, feeling like a damned fool. "Sorry about the dog. And the boy. I should've said something when we got in the van without him."

Clearly shook his head. "Well, we'll talk about the dog. But..." He sighed. "Scruffy... he can't be laid at your door. I've been sending the gang on errands, mostly checking on the cannibals and the religious fanatics up north – trying to instil a sense of responsibility into them. But those are troubled kids – more than most who survived the plague. I'm of the opinion that they had serious problems even before they lost everyone they knew and loved. As I'm sure you've noticed, Thelma and Scruffy live – well, lived – in a fantasy world, and Ted and Daisy... well, they have fun all the live-long day, I suppose you could say. Not that a lot of the people here aren't the same. In fact, being the, ah, spiritual guru around here doesn't preclude me from enjoying myself occasionally." He chuckled, paternally, as he looked over at a group of nudists passing a ball to one another. Cade saw a red bite mark on a man's shoulder, and one of the women had a deep scratch down her side. "Responsibly, of course. We're not short of birth control, or any other drugs we might need. Recreational or, uh, or otherwise." He looked off into the distance for a moment, as if debating whether or not he should continue the sentence.

Cade missed the cue. He had other things on his mind.

"Insulin?" he asked, scanning the man's eyes. He didn't seem like a liar. But you never could tell. There was definitely something not quite right about this whole set-up, though Cade couldn't put his finger on what that was exactly.

On the edge of his hearing, Fuel-Air was still laughing.

"Oh, we have a stockpile of that, as well as other... well, anyway. We've got a number of diabetics among us – a legacy of the days when we ate processed sugar instead of growing our own food – and there's enough to last them a good few years. Also..." he smiled, almost bashfully. After his slight stumble earlier, his confidence was coming back in force. "I am, as you may have heard, a noted drug pusher. Which brings us, in a roundabout way, back to the dog. You're a violent man, Cade, a lot more violent than we're used to around here. Did you come from the Pastor's camp?"

"Passed through it." Cade nodded.

"But you didn't start off there."

"No."

The Doctor nodded, taking a long draw on his pipe. "Hmm. Judging from the state of your palms, I knew you'd fallen foul of the Pastor at some point." Cade reflectively clenched and unclenched his fists, feeling the wave of agony sweep up his arms. He'd almost forgotten about the constant throbbing of his palms since he'd cleaned out the cuts with whisky, but that didn't mean he shouldn't get them looked at properly sometime soon. Maybe now.

Clearly noted the gesture, nodded slowly, and then continued. "I would say... and feel free to correct me if I'm wrong... that you came into the city from the north and found yourself in the Pastor's territory, and you – being a man with a violent nature – presumably made some trouble for him. Well, that or your sexuality didn't meet his approval."

Cade nodded. "Along those lines."

Clearly smiled. "I can't help noticing you've got a lot of scratch-marks and bites on you too. You wouldn't have been given any, ah... black and white..." He paused, rethinking the sentence. "I mean, is there anything I should know about, ah, concerning that?"

"Had a run-in with the cannibals." Clearly was sharp, but Cade didn't see the need to tell him any more than he had to. Doc Clearly nodded, and smiled wide, sucking on his pipe. Cade was taking a liking to the man, but there was still something there that made Cade uneasy.

He could still hear Fuel-Air laughing at him.

The Doctor nodded. "Okay. So let's recap. Your first reaction when you came across the gang was to kill their dog. There's no two ways around that, Cade. You're a man to whom violence is second nature, and from the moment you came here – to San Francisco, I mean – you've been immersed in constant violence, which seems to have made you... well, jumpy." He shook his head. "But I don't think a reaction like that is healthy, Cade, and I doubt you do either. So I want to ask you, man to man – is that the normal way you'd react in that situation? To just kill without thinking? Without a second of hesitation?"

Cade looked into the Doc's eyes. He was serious. Cade had an inkling that if he got this question wrong, he'd be shown the door. Clearly probably wouldn't get violent about it – it'd be very polite – but it'd leave him without any answers to speak of, not to mention without any insulin either.

Cade needed to mingle with these folks a bit. Find out what their deal was. He figured he'd better tell Clearly what he wanted to hear.

"No. No, it ain't." lied Cade.

He could hear Fuel-Air laughing.

Doc Clearly breathed a sigh of relief. "Well, that's good. That's excellent, Cade. You see, I don't think violence should be unending. I think there should be a balance between a man's baser instincts, and the baser instincts of a society, and their higher selves. I believe that you can acknowledge all the awful things that have happened, and still build a community despite them. That's what I'm trying to do here. I'm trying to build a community, and... well, Cade, I think it'd be in your best interests to be a part of it."

Cade's eyebrow twitched.

Clearly smiled reassuringly, shaking his head. "Trust me, this isn't leading where you think it is. I know you've probably been given a recruitment speech a lot like that by the Pastor, most likely before he nailed you up, and I'm not going to follow down that route and tell you to join me or else. It's your decision. If you don't think we've got anything here you want, you can leave right now." His face grew serious, and he put a hand on Cade's shoulder. "What I'm offering you, though, is a chance to breathe. A chance to live – a chance to... to work through the violence that's become your life, and... well, come out the other side. Stay for the night, Cade. You might find you belong here. I won't deny we can use a man who's handy with a weapon – so long as he can put it down occasionally." He smiled, patting Cade's shoulder gently. Cade could see his thumb joint was badly bruised, as if it had been wrenched recently. He didn't pay much heed to it.

Accidents happened.

"Give us a try. See what you think." smiled the Doc.

Cade almost smiled back. "A test drive?"

Clearly chuckled – a warm, fatherly sound. "Sure, why not. Give us a test drive, Cade. I'll let you wander around rather than give you a tour – let you take it all in without my input – but you can ask me any questions that come to mind, and I'll send someone to find you if there's something I want you to see, or experience, or... well." He grew contemplative for a moment. "What I'm trying to say is... I really don't want you to join our community unless you want to. If you feel like it, you can walk out of here tomorrow – right now – and head back where you came from or keep moving south, find somewhere that fits you. But what I do want you to do, at least for the time you're here, is try to be happy. Because I really don't think you're a happy man. Am I wrong?"

Cade didn't say anything. Cade was a lot of things, but happy wasn't one of them. In fact, even content would be pushing it.

Clearly waited for a response, then smiled, gently lifting his hand off Cade's shoulder. "Well, I'm rambling. But... do you think you can do that, Cade? I'd consider it a personal favour. Just... let yourself be happy for a little while."

Cade looked at Clearly for a long time. Then he nodded.

"I can do that."

And out of the corner of his eye, Cade saw Fuel-Air, laughing fit to burst as the maggots crawled over his shrivelled skin and in and out of empty eye-sockets. Laughing like he knew the biggest joke in the world. And maybe he did at that.

Fuel-Air knew it was Cade's second lie of the day.

CHAPTER SEVENTEEN

THE RITUAL

Cade ended up going to the ballgame.

Kezar Stadium wasn't one of the bigger stadiums in the state, but for all that it was a pretty impressive place to have a softball game. The stands could have held a good eight or nine thousand, even with the wear and tear of the bad times, but they were all but empty. Most people watching the game sat around or even inside the diamond itself, laughing as the foam ball sailed over their heads, cheering and catcalling as a grinning, joking Castro Street refugee, all muscle and tan and chewing gum, pitched a lazy, easy shot to an older woman in granny glasses and tight jeans and bad co-ordination, who swung her bat gamely but missed the ball all the same, face flushed with laughter. There was no competition to it – just folks having fun on a sunny day. The clowning kid had already struck a couple of batters out, and Cade guessed he was feeling bad about it – shooting that cocky grin one more time, he tossed the ball to someone in the crowd, flashed peace signs and sauntered off to hit on one of the batters. He was replaced by a burly type, a biker, all frayed denim and unwashed hair, who high-fived him on the way to the pitcher's mound to the cheers of the crowd. There weren't really teams as such as far as Cade could see – just people wanting to play.

Then again, Cade guessed that they hadn't really put a baseball league together just yet. That was the kind of thing Cade would term a luxury. He sat back and watched the game, shaking his head slightly. By now the biker was pitching some harder balls – hard as a foam ball could travel, anyway – and the laughing woman in glasses swung her plastic bat, full breasts bouncing in time with the swing, almost toppling over. The ball sailed past the bat – strike two.

Cade felt light-headed, like he was dreaming. It was surreal. It was like he'd fallen asleep in that van and everything since he'd stepped out of it had been an illusion. It was like the Wonderful Land Of Oz. Like being in Technicolor.

The woman in the tight jeans struck out for the third time, and Cade felt his eye drawn to her ass as she bounced off the diamond to the good-natured claps and wolf-whistles of the crowd. She laughed and shook a finger at one of the crowd. Cade wondered how easy it'd be to get hold of her for a drink later. If they drank here at all.

Fuck, dog, how come everybody here's a hottie? What's up with that?

Cade sighed. He didn't look round.

I'm serious, dog. Nobody older than mid-forties, mostly young folks but no kids to get in the way, no fatties, even... Shit, this is fuckapalooza right here, bitch. It's fuckin' poon paradise. Come on, don't tell me you weren't thinking of bouncing a quarter off that ass. I'd bounce my life fuckin' savings off that.

Cade shook his head, watching a man in taped glasses with close-cropped hair and a T-Shirt reading I BRAKE FOR CHRIST pick up the bat and stride out purposefully to the plate. One of the Pastor's people, maybe. One of the converts to Doc Clearly's way of thinking.

Shit, what's up with you? This is valuable information here, bitch. Valuable motherfuckin' information about the amount of poon-tang you could get, dog. Pay fuckin' attention.

"Ain't in the mood." said Cade. He wasn't. He felt tired, suddenly – a tiredness that crept through his muscles and sat in his bones and refused to go away. All of a sudden he didn't know what the hell he'd been doing. He could have come straight here at the beginning of it, right after the bad times, taken the Duchess and Woody and set up here where they all belonged, with people who smiled and laughed and played softball and ate good and all the rest. He wasn't fool enough to ever think he could be a part of this, not the way he was. But he could find a place on the outskirts, like he had in Muir Beach. Things could be like they were before the bad times.

Fuckin' pussy. You want a white picket fence too? That the reward for a dog-killer these days?

Cade lowered his head. There was a part of him that was right there with Fuel-Air, part of him that knew right in his tired bones that things wouldn't ever be like they had been again and maybe he didn't deserve them to be, and there wasn't any sense wishing otherwise. Part of him that felt sick to his bones.

Cade hadn't been a man who felt things like that before Fuel-Air had shown up.

Damn, but he was tired.

"Is this seat taken?"

Cade looked to his left, half-expecting to see Fuel-Air, maggots and all. Instead there was a blonde girl of about seventeen wearing a contrite smile and some kind of poncho – it was hand-woven, with a poorly-rendered caricature of Deputy Dawg. Cade figured she'd made it herself. She was looking down at his shirt, and Cade was suddenly glad he'd taken the time to pick a fresh one up – there'd been a box of them, free to all comers, and he'd grabbed one at random.

It was white, with the words HUG ME – I HAD A HARD DAY and some kind of cabbage patch kid staring winsomely out from the region of his right nipple.

Cade wasn't a man troubled overmuch by fashion.

"Sorry. Bad joke." she smiled, looking down at the ground. "You looked kind of, um, lonely. Well, I guess you would because you're sitting up here on your own, but, um – I mean you looked kind of down as well. I thought I'd say hi. See if you needed anything." She blushed. "Doc Clearly said you might need something, not that he sent me to..." She shook her head, giggling. "I'm making a real mess of this, aren't I?"

"It's okay. Just figuring things." said Cade, half-shrugging. He didn't much want to talk about it, but he didn't much want to make her feel bad either. She was already worried he was thinking she'd been pimped out to him by the Doc, by the sound of it. Wasn't any mileage in making her feel any more embarrassed.

"Um, my name's Cassie, by the way. Short of Cassiopeia – like the star? My dad was kind of into astronomy and Mom figured it'd be a good name. Sorry. Don't know why I'm telling you that." She laughed, a little bashful.

"Cade." said Cade. He didn't figure there was much he needed to add on top of that. There wasn't any sense in making small talk – asking where her folks were now or if she had any other family. If she had any other family, they were dead. Where her folks were now was in the ground pushing up tomato plants, or laying on some street corner, or in the belly of a cannibal. Wasn't any getting around that.

Small talk wasn't Cade's thing anyway.

She smiled, and looked at his palms, starting at the wounds. "Oh gosh. Are your hands okay? God, nobody here did that, did they?"

Cade looked at her, wondering if she'd been told about the Pastor. He guessed there was no reason why she would've been – it wasn't going to make anyone sleep any better.

Every time someone mentioned the wounds in his hands, he was reminded of them – he was trying not to think too hard about them, himself. They were itching like crazy still – a constant, painful throb that was never far from the back of his mind. He shook his head, opening and closing them slowly, feeling the brutal rush of fire crackling through his nerves to the base of his skull.

She blinked. "Wow, you're kind of intense. You know what? You should definitely come to the happening later. After the TV show, I mean. The Doc was totally right. It'd really help you." She smiled, looking out at the softball game, and Cade noticed she had a livid scratch running down the back of one hand.

The batting team had stolen a couple of bases while they'd been talking – Cade noted without real surprise that the Castro refugee from before was now running from second to third base. He wondered how they even knew if any team had won or lost. Maybe there was no winning and losing here. Maybe Doc Clearly didn't believe in it.

Cade felt that dreamlike, light-headed feeling again. There wasn't a cloud in the sky. He turned to look at the girl, wondering if he'd heard right before. "TV show?" Maybe they'd rigged up a generator with some old DVDs.

"Well, it's not real TV." she said, looking down, embarrassed. "I mean, we've got electricity, but it's kind of precious. We need it for important stuff, like the hydroponics and the Doc's lab. But we kind of get together and, uh..." She shrugged, suddenly embarrassed, and clammed up.

Cade wasn't a man who felt much sympathy for people or for beasts, but he did feel a twinge of something for this girl. She was reaching out, as best she could, trying to bring him into the community. Probably out of a request from Doc Clearly, but still. He figured he should do better than he was doing.

Plus maybe then you can nail her, right, dog? Shit, fuck her for my sake, man. I ain't getting none lookin' like this.

Cade winced, but didn't acknowledge Fuel-Air – didn't even look at him. Instead, he looked over at the girl and nodded. "I'm listening."

She smiled sheepishly. "We get together and act out the old shows. Mostly comedy shows. Last week was *Frasier*." She giggled. "Oh wow! 'I'm listening.' You'd make a really wild Frasier, you know? You'd be like the most intense Frasier ever." She had the giggles now, and it took her a minute to calm them down. "'I'm listening'. I can totally see it! You should talk to Rob and see if he's got a part for you."

Cade blinked. He didn't have much to say to that, either. Amateur dramatics weren't really his line.

Over their heads, the sun shone down, warm and kind. Down on the baseball diamond, the kid from Castro street had stolen home and into the arms of the guy he'd been hitting on. The woman in the tight jeans was sharing a flask of coffee or tea with a bearded man roughly her age, flirting and joking. Cade remembered the kids in the van, describing Love. A love shared by a whole community.

Cade was a fool to think there would be teams. He glanced over at the girl, who was looking shyly at him, evaluating him. He hoped she was just being friendly. It wasn't like he'd made the Duchess any promises – Cade wasn't the promising type – but she was too young for his tastes by a good twenty years.

Fuckin' MILF hunter. Shit, you got no taste at all, motherfucker.

Almost as if she'd heard Fuel-Air speak, she flushed, and her eyes darted away from Cade's to the softball game. She didn't speak for a few long seconds, and Cade could see her turning her thoughts over. "You know, I think it's better that way. The TV shows. Doing them like a play, I mean, with us. I think if we hooked up a, a..." She groped for the word. "DVD player. I don't think I could take that. Seeing how it used to be, I mean."

Cade didn't speak.

"But when people are acting it out... it's different. Like an escape. Does that make sense?" She smiled, blushing again, and looking down at her bare feet, twisting them together and rubbing one on top of the other. Her big toenail was bruised black. "You don't talk much, do you?"

Cade shook his head, and the girl laughed. "I can't work out if you like me or not. Are you coming tonight? It's at the old movie house on Haight Street – everybody's going to go."

Cade twitched an eyebrow. "Everybody?"

The girl nodded. "All of us. Everybody crams in. There's even people on the street outside, so make sure you get there early if you want a seat. I mean, I'll save you a seat. If you want." She blushed again, fidgeted, then stood. "You'll be there?"

Hell with it, thought Cade, and nodded. The girl beamed, and walked off, turning and waving at him.

Cade turned and looked at the seat on the other side. Fuel-Air was there, rotting and flyblown, grinning his skeleton grin. *Didn't know you had it in you, dog.*

Cade shook his head and shrugged. Below, the ball game was starting to drift apart, with only a few die-hards still playing until they, too, gave up on it. There'd been no whistle, no signal, but everyone had decided that it was time to stop. Eventually, only the Castro boy and his new friend were left, kissing lazily under the stands.

Cade stood up. That feeling of unreality was stronger, now that the initial shock of seeing people even halfway normal had worn off. It was starting to occur to him that he didn't know the rules around here. These people had found their own rhythm, and their own system, and it didn't include him. Not yet. Maybe it never would.

Cade made his way down from the stands, figuring he'd slip out without disturbing the two kids. Castro Street broke off long enough to shout to him. "Hey, man! You going to the show later? It's *Rules Of Engagement* tonight!"

Cade turned. On the one hand, he needed to get to know these people. On the other hand, it was *Rules Of Engagement* that night. He thought about it.

"Might be busy."

The young kid laughed, disbelieving. He had a shallow cut on his forehead that Cade hadn't seen from up in the stands. "Busy doing *what?* The whole com*mun*ity's gonna be there. You've *gotta* be there. Nobody's *not* going to be there. What, you want to miss your treats?" He snickered.

Cade narrowed his eyes. The batter spoke up. "He's right, bud. Gotta be there. You new?"

Cade nodded, and the batter gave a dry chuckle. "Seriously, you never been before? Aw, man, no spoilers, but you need to be at this thing. Trust me, man. You will *love* it." he grinned, showing a gap where two of his front teeth had once been, then went back to frenching the Castro Street kid. Cade stared for a second, then went on his way.

He figured he could sit through an episode of *Rules Of Engagement* if he had to.

"Too bad. It must be, uh, really hard." said the girl on the stage, lowering her eyes as if willing herself to remember the lines.

It was a girl of about twenty-three, with dark hair, and she looked quite a lot like the original actress – Cade figured that must have been why she got the part. But the delivery was stilted and wooden, even by the standards of a crappy sitcom, and Cade got the feeling that most of the audience were laughing from sympathy. Cade had never watched more than about ten minutes of this show – he didn't have much time for the tube at the best of times, and by all accounts this'd been a failure even by the low standards of the idiot box. Cade wondered why they'd decided to bring it back this way. Maybe there was something about it that people related to, even after the bad times. Or maybe anything better would just remind folks about what they'd lost.

"That's what she would've said," sighed a man of about forty, the one actor in the bunch, although he looked nothing like David Spade had – he had short hair, glasses and a heavy paunch. Nevertheless, Cassie started giggling on Cade's left and wouldn't stop, and the whole of the movie house erupted into a long burst of applause.

Easily pleased, Cade figured.

The place was packed – in a lot of the seats, people were sitting on each other's laps. The aisles were filled with people sitting cross-legged – even the sides of the stage had people sitting on them, occasionally getting in the way of the actors as they made their way on and off. Cade suddenly wondered if it was true, if everybody in the whole damned community liked old sitcoms so much that they'd come in here.

He scanned the crowd. There was nobody there Cade could have called old – the oldest person he'd met in the town was Clearly himself, and he wasn't yet fifty. And no kids. Not a single one.

He'd seen about a dozen in the Pastor's territory. The law of averages said he should be seeing the same here. It nagged him.

"Wasn't that *awesome?*"

Cade turned to look at Cassie and shrugged. There wasn't much more to say. He made a move to get up from his seat and she put a hand on his shoulder, gently. "Don't get up yet, silly. It's time for Doctor Clearly to hand out the treats."

Cade's eyes narrowed. The kid from Castro street had mentioned *treats*.

People were passing plastic bags filled with pills along the aisles – black pills and white pills. Everybody took two, one of each colour, then passed the bag along. Cassie took her two, smiling brightly, then passed the bag expectantly along to Cade. Cade met her eyes for a second, then gingerly reached out. To his right, a rail-thin man in a cheap suit and tie growled "Don't bogart 'em, mac, pass 'em down the line."

Cade hesitated, then took a black pill and a white pill, palming them. Slowly, the rustling plastic bags made their way through the audience, then vanished back into whatever storage they'd emerged from.

As Doc Clearly took the stage, there was muted applause – people could only clap so hard without dropping the precious pills.

"Everyone got a black pill and a white pill?" he smiled, holding up his own. Cade looked at him, eyes narrowed. He hadn't mentioned this during their brief talk. Cade wondered if that was just absent-mindedness. "Remember, take them both together - otherwise they don't work." He smiled. "I hope everyone's got something to say to God tonight." There was a ripple of laughter in the audience.

Cade straightened in his chair. He hadn't signed up for a suicide cult and he figured it was probably time to get out of there – either quietly or by force. Cassie noticed his sudden shift of posture and smiled, placing her hand on his shoulder again. "It's okay," she whispered. "We do this every night. The pills help us to see God, you know? We get to meet him."

Cade turned to the man on his right. "Yeah?"

The man played with his pills, almost nervously. "Sure. We see God, all right. You should try it."

"He's wonderful – a kindly old guy with a beard and big sad eyes. And he created us all." she sighed, her hand squeezing Cade's shoulder in a way that made him vaguely uncomfortable. She didn't give him the impression of someone totally in control of herself. Cade wasn't a man who got nervous exactly, but the way she'd attached herself to him in the past few hours made him a mite uneasy – restless, even. He didn't see it ending well. Not to mention all this God talk.

He'd had enough of that from the Pastor.

"I love God!" Cassie breathed, looking out into the middle distance, then downing her pills suddenly, almost furtively. Immediately she slumped in her seat, eyes rolling back.

The man on Cade's right grinned. "Comes on quick. Hey, y'know what God told me once? He made us, but he didn't make the world, or the bad times. That was someone else – Simon or Simeon or some shit. Satan figure, I guess. He said he was sorry, but there was nothing he could do." The man chuckled, light glinting off his oily skin. "Isn't that wild? Sorry. Don't that beat all?" He chuckled again, then swallowed the two pills and slumped down.

Cade looked around at the rest of the audience – without a word, they were all slumping, one by one, as the pills hit their systems, keeling over where they sat, heading into dreamland. Cade looked at the stage, and his eyes met Doc Clearly's – those kind, wise, infinitely patient eyes.

"Mister Cade. I guess I should have told you. Kept you informed. This is probably quite a shock to you." The Doc smiled, taking a seat in a prop chair, fiddling with the pills in his hand.

"Sure." said Cade, head cocked a little to the side, sizing the man up, Deciding if he was going to need to kill him.

He still seemed trustworthy.

"Our little... well, ritual seems strong. Our communal trip, put it that way." He smiled, genially. "It's one of the things we keep the generators for – running my laboratory. It's where I synthesise this stuff. My compound. It really does make you see God, you know. I think that's important these days – something people need. Faith, but without the evils of religion. Faith in pill form." He shrugged, then looked about him. "Does wonders for these people. A nightly escape from the horrors of the world... the terrible losses... every night, we can visit our Creator and get some answers, or shout at him, or hit him, or tell him about our day. God confesses to you, or you confess to God." He chuckled. "It's kind of theraputic. Even for me."

"You see God?" Cade raised an eyrbrow, leaning back in his seat. He was still evaluating. Wondering if he was going to need to do any killing.

Wondering if he should take the pills.

The Doc shrugged. "Or it's a drug trip. So sue me. The point is, this is what keeps these people sane. You can join in, or not. It's up to you. You sound like you've made your peace with the world as it is. You probably don't strictly need to take it. But I recommend you do. It really is something." He smiled, popping the pills into his mouth. "Try it, if only the once. I'll see you on the other side, Cade." He swallowed, and settled back, closing his eyes.

Cade was alone. All around him, he could hear the heavy breathing of the sleepers, lost in their drug dreams.

He looked at the pills in his hand, one black, one white. They felt heavy.

It was too damned risky, he figured. He wasn't about to take a drug – hell, two drugs, drugs he didn't know the first damned thing about – on the say-so of somebody he'd only just met, even if they did have a perfect community, even if everybody there was happier than anyone he'd met since the bad times, or before. It was too big a risk to swallow his damned pills even if God was at the other end of them.

Cade wondered what God would have to say.

It was a good sell Doc Clearly made.

Cade made up his mind. Slowly, he put the pills in his mouth. They tasted metallic on his tongue, and he found that the black one was sour, like aniseed. He felt his head get light.

He could still spit them out, he knew that. Instead, he swallowed, slowly.

And closed his eyes.

CHAPTER EIGHTEEN

I AM AS I AM

Drrr-rrrr-rrrrrrrr goes the alarm. It's not really an alarm, but it's the alarm function on a cheap mobile phone and it does the job well enough. It vibrates against the makeshift bedside table that I put together out of boxes of old CDs, waiting against the day I go to IKEA and get a proper one. I still haven't gotten around to that. Eventually I will.

The phone chirps sadistically while it vibrates and for a moment I don't know where I am. I try to open my eyes and there's a stabbing pain in my eyeballs, and I need to keep them shut and rub at them for a minute, feeling involuntary tears course down my cheeks. Clearly I didn't get enough sleep last night.

The phone's still chirping away, practically dancing about on the cardboard lid of the CD box. *Drrrrr. Drrrrrr. Drrrrrrr.* I need to find a more soothing way to wake up.

Drrrrrrrrr-drrr-drrrrr, right through my head until I reach out blindly, fumbling for the thing, fingers poking at my glasses and an empty can of something from the night before, finally knocking the phone off the boxes and down the side of the bed, reaching and gripping and finally managing to get the damned thing to shut up.

Then I set it to go off an hour later, put it back and go back to sleep.

What's the point in getting up?

Eventually I have to. There's work to be done and it's already after ten. I always hope that the morning will magically give me the will to carry on, and then once the morning finishes I hope for some renewed vigour in the afternoon. It never comes.

After the glasses go on, I rummage through drawers and pull on the first clothes I see. Nothing special – a drab maroon pullover – sweatshirt thing, black trousers, my jacket to keep out the cold. I don't need to make much of an effort today. I'm not seeing anybody, the flat's empty, everyone's gone. I've got the place to myself. Nobody's going to care how I dress, least of all me.

The face in the bathroom mirror is tired, eyes baggy, beard scraggy, face set in a dispirited scowl. I drag a flannel over it for the sake of habit, brush my teeth, look at the dark patches under the bloodshot, bleary eyes. I feel as bad as I look. I wasn't even drinking last night – I just didn't sleep. Too much news. Too depressed to sleep.

There's some leftover pizza that'll work well enough as breakfast. There are anchovies on it, and anchovies are the secret to eating cold pizza. An anchovy doesn't care if its hot or cold, it'll taste just the same and overpower anything else into the bargain. I highly recommend anchovies.

Of course, now I have to get myself into a world where there aren't any anchovies, and there isn't any pizza – not delivered, anyway, and certainly not the way we're used to, ordered online and perfectly customised for the ultimate leisure experience. This perfect community of Doc Clearly's probably makes pizza, albeit the old-fashioned way, like they used to in old Italy. I wonder what that is – I should look it up. I suppose the way things are going we'll all be finding out soon.

I made the mistake yesterday of looking at the financial news and the environmental news – I couldn't work for an hour after that, just listlessly trawled for some sign of hope, but there wasn't one. We're long past the stage where the naysayers can make me feel any better, and the doomers seem more and more credible all the time. It's no wonder everything's tanking – money's just a shared illusion, and the scales are methodically falling from our eyes as things get worse and worse. We're not going to need a pandemic.

I remember the last time I had to write a post-apocalyptic world. In the first draft I never bothered to explain how things got to be post-apocalyptic – the apocalypse was inevitable. Just extrapolate from now.

If anything, the world of Afterblight is too optimistic.

This line of thinking isn't going to help me write. I crack open the laptop and set things into motion, listening to the grind of the processors as they turn over.

The laptop's new, or relatively new – an HP monstrosity that gets very hot very quickly, probably a sign it's using too much power. I'm worried it'll burn out faster than another computer might, start acting up, developing minor glitches that turn into larger and larger problems until finally I'm trying hopelessly to get five hundred words out of the thing between grinding, shuddering crashes. The day is coming. Everything degrades. Everything falls apart.

I got a Samsung TV last year, and it didn't last the week. Neither did the replacement. The second replacement lasted quite a while but recently fell over and died in exactly the same way. According to the web, they use cheap components that have a problem with power surges in certain areas. That warranty's paying off, I'll tell you that much. It's the way the world is these days – things built to perform, but not necessarily to last. Not much thought about the future.

The word processor opens and I'm looking at a blank page.

And the blank page looks back at me.

I push the 'hibernate' button and the screen goes black. I've just remembered I've got a contract from some script work that needs to be sent out if I'm going to get paid, and I need to get stamps and envelopes.

Best get that done now, before I start writing anything.

I'm not procrastinating, you understand. This is very practical behaviour.

I pull on socks, shoes and a coat – it's midwinter and the air's bitter – then quickly check the mirror. A scruffy, bearded man looks back at me, scowling with tired eyes. It'll have to do.

I'm not likely to be making any first impressions on people, with any luck. I'm just going to get stamps. It's not like I'm going to the pub or anything.

Just a quick errand and then back to work.

The envelope rack in the post office is right next to the magazine rack, and while I'm there I pick up a copy of a games magazine on impulse. I don't play that many computer games these days, but I've got a soft spot for a few of them and there are some coming out this year I'm really looking forward to.

It won't do any harm to stop off for a sandwich somewhere while I read this. Maybe a lunchtime pint, too.

Just to get the juices flowing. I'm not going to have more than one.

There's work waiting at home, after all.

York isn't so much a city as a town with pretensions. It's got walls separating the city centre from the suburban sprawl, and a cathedral to cement its city status, but at the end of the day you can walk across it in fifteen minutes without breathing hard. Inside that fifteen-minute radius there are several dozen different pubs, maybe as many as a hundred. The city as a whole – apparently – has a pub for every single day of the year.

With so many pubs, there's something for every kind of drinker and every kind of drink. If you're a real ale snob, visit the Three-Legged Mare. If you fancy a fight, the Lowther on a Saturday night is a good place to make an enemy, although you probably won't be able to start anything until you're down the street. If you want to feel cramped, try the Maltings. Personally,

I like nooks – quiet spots where I can either read a book or talk without shouting. The Golden Slipper's good for that.

They're not serving food, so I just get a pint of Worthy's and some peanuts. I've still got plenty of that pizza in my belly.

Besides, a drink might help.

I'm definitely not going to have more than one.

The magazine's full of news about the new Sims game. You'll have heard of that – little computer people you can play around with, control their lives. This one's promising to make the little computer people even more human with even more human personalities. You can tailor the personalities how you want them and then turn them loose on each other and watch the soap opera unfold, or dive in and tweak it in the directions you want to go.

A virtual world of self-creating stories, set in motion by a god-like player. I like games like that.

There's an upcoming superhero MMORPG where you can create your hero and an arch-nemesis and set them out in a virtual world to be admired. I'm definitely getting that.

The irony hasn't escaped me. Even when I'm avoiding work, I'm still working. I'm just not getting paid.

About halfway through the pint, the door opens and he walks in. I don't see him at first – the little nook I'm reading my magazine in is blocked off from the door – but I hear the conversation in the room stop.

I only notice him when he's looming over my table. The shadow falls across the magazine and I find myself looking up, right into his grey eyes.

He's six feet, shorter than me, but he looks so much taller. He's standing and I'm sitting, of course. I'm sure that's what it is.

He's got the face Mark gave him on the cover, and the clothes – the black tank top and chains - but instead of the close-cut mohican he's got a shock of black hair, like Bluto in Popeye. Mountain man hair. Just like I pictured him, in fact.

It could be a coincidence, just someone who looks the same.

But it's not.

It's him.

He doesn't speak. He just looks at me, eyes heavy-lidded, no expression on that face. Staring. Maybe he's got nothing to say.

When you think about it, there isn't much that can be said.

He breathes in, bunching one hand into a fist, then breathes out. The hand opens. The puncture wound running right through the palm bleeds a little. I still can't read the look in his eyes.

I'm very conscious of my own sweat. It's hard to swallow but I manage it anyway.

He had a pair of railroad spikes knocked through his hands. I'm not sure why I did that – there was some symbolic value, and I wanted to show the hero enduring in a hopeless situation. To an extent, I thought myself into that situation, at least in his place and with the inhuman power to survive I'd given him. But I wasn't in that situation, of course.

He was, though.

Because of me.

I look up at his eyes, opening my mouth to say something, and think better of it. My mouth is bone dry, but I don't dare lift my pint.

I still can't read the look in his eyes.

Is he angry?

I wasn't the one who killed his world. It was like that when I got there. Someone else built the whole thing and started the dominos toppling, I just came along after the fact and used it as a handy backdrop.

He clenches his fist again.

That isn't quite true. I might not have thought up the setting, but I killed off his town, his friends – no, I made it so he couldn't have friends. I killed everyone he knew. I described the end of the world for him in loving detail. I made everything as horrific as it could possibly get, and then for good measure I made sure his past was horrific as well.

I stripped most of his human feelings from him, only allowing him the occasional hint, because I thought that'd make for a better protagonist.

And now this person – this damaged psychopath – is standing in front of me, flexing his ruined hands.

Idly, I wonder what the barmaid thinks of all this. I look over at her – she's looking suspiciously over at me, muttering something to the landlord. I look back at his eyes, those grey, unreadable eyes, to see if he's registered it.

Suddenly, his head drops slightly. He looks at the games magazine, at the half-finished pint. Then he looks back in my eyes.

He doesn't look angry. He never did.

He looks sad.

"I'm sorry." I mutter, cheeks flushing. He doesn't respond.

There isn't anything to say.

After a second, he walks out. I feel guilty, and angry at him for making me feel guilty. I listlessly finish the pint in a couple of swift gulps, then walk out, the accusing eyes of the barmaid following me. I won't be able to go back there for a while, I suppose.

I stop off at the Mason's Arms for another and get some food with it, and finish the rest of the magazine. I'm really interested in this game. You can actually reach into the game world and move their things about, even enlarge or shrink their houses while they're walking around in them. Change and edit their lives between moments.

I wonder if they notice?

I have another pint – coke, this time – over some sausage and mash, which takes me into the afternoon. The day's a write-off, frankly, but it's not too late for me to get a couple of thousand words down – I ask the barman if he'll let me have a can of Red Bull without opening it. He doesn't have a problem.

By the time I get back into the flat, it's become obvious that the bloke in the pub was just some random nutter. He looked a bit like... well, like *him,* but he was probably just some goth or a local Hell's Angel or something. I probably just took his chair while he was out having a fag in the street and he wanted to stare me out of it.

Or something. I don't know.

The laptop is still sitting open, screen black. I crack open the can and sip it, letting it wake me up a little and counteract the booze. The stuff makes me jittery, but it helps with the writing, especially on a deadline. It's past time I got some work done.

I'd left him in the theatre, and now I want to jump forward in time a little to that big orgy, and what happens after that... yes, with Cassie.

Right.

The machine judders back into life and I'm confronted by a loading screen and then the stark whiteness of the blank page. This time it doesn't seem so intimidating. My fingers find the keys.

'CHAPTER NINETEEN.' I type.

'Cade opened his eyes, and the sky was a livid red'... no. Bloody red.

No, not that either.

'Cade opened his eyes, and the sky was on fire, burning orange with streaks of blood red that ran from horizon to horizon. He could feel Cassie...' No. No. Doesn't work.

'He could feel someone's fingers brushing through the hair on his chest.'

Better.

Fingers tap and words appear. I smile, happy to be back in the zone, back writing. The envelopes and the stamps are sitting forgotten in the bedroom, and I know I won't get around to posting off the contract until tomorrow, maybe not until the day after, but that doesn't matter. It took me a while to get into it today, but I'm in it now.

I reach out and take another sip of the Red Bull, and then settle down to making Cade's life worse.

CHAPTER NINETEEN

THE HELTER SKELTER

Cade opened his eyes, and the sky was on fire, burning orange with streaks of blood red that ran from horizon to horizon. He could feel someone's fingers brushing through the hair on his chest.

It took him a second or two to realise he was naked.

The fingers played over the fresh scabs on his chest, the cross that was cut there, then reached down to play slowly over his belly, and then Cassie's face filled his vision and before he knew what was going on, her lips were on his and her tongue was diving and darting against his own.

Cade figured he should be shocked at that, or at least surprised, but it felt like the most natural damned thing in all the world. He realised his hands were on her bottom, squeezing, fingertips rolling up the small of her back and into her hair, but he couldn't quite remember telling them to do that.

It didn't much matter, he figured.

Nothing much mattered.

In the back of his mind, he was finding it a mite strange, through – Cade wasn't a man to let his guard down lightly and Cassie, though she was sweet and pert and all the rest of it, wasn't Cade's type at all. Cade liked women with a good twenty or thirty years on them, and like as not a few years on him into the bargain. That was how come he got on so well with the Duchess.

Cade blinked, feeling her young, slim fingers taking a hold of him and half-stroking, half-tugging, in an inexpert sort of a way that was exactly the reason why he usually fooled around with older women. This time he didn't mind – as a matter of fact, it felt pretty damned good. Cade let his head drop onto the grass, and he felt each cool blade brush softly against his fingertips, and the muscles in his face twitched into something that anybody who'd ever known him long wouldn't recognise.

Cade smiled.

He was out in the park, then – Golden Gate park – and in the arms of a girl of no more than eighteen, maybe seventeen, which at any other time might raise a moral complication, but not now. Not during the zero hour.

Cade blinked, wondering where the hell that had come from, and then Cassie's lips were on his again and she was clambering onto him, and then he was in her. All around him, he could hear people together, in twos and sometimes threes and fours, laughing and sighing, tumbling over each other and intertwining like coiling snakes, some quiet as a whisper, some shouting out with every stroke. Cade lay back and let it all wash over him.

He turned his head to the left, and he saw the woman in the well-fitting jeans from the ball game – only now she was in nothing but an unbuttoned shirt, nuzzling with another girl about the same age and the actor from the TV show, or stage play or whatever the hell it was. The three of them were writhing and rubbing, not doing anything in particular but enjoying the contact of skin on skin. Cade guessed there was an element of polymorphous perversity to it. Then again, the same could be said of him.

He pulled Cassie close, breathing in the scent of her neck, and gave it some thought. That in itself was a feat for Cade – the thoughts in his head seemed like quicksilver, slippery and impossible to get any kind of a hold of. He'd been drugged, he knew that – or rather, he'd taken the damn drug himself. He'd forgotten why he'd ever been tempted to, although in the back of his mind he could remember meeting a fat, depressed-looking fella... the thought left him as soon as he latched on it, and was gone. They were all under the influence of whatever this was, and it was pretty good at that. Cade hadn't felt quite so free in a while.

Still, there was something wrong, he knew that.

Something in the way the shadows were lengthening across the park, spreading out like a black pool of contaminating liquid.

The sun was going down.

Cassie leaned in again, breathing him, her giggle filling his ear. He could hear something over that, and the sighs and the laughter.

He could hear screaming

It was the kind of screaming animals did, enraged, snarling beasts, and it was coming from the shadows – from those parts of the park where the shadows fell. Cade turned his head, and saw that the shadows were starting to fall over the park. Only natural.

The sun was going down.

He blinked, wondering why he didn't care, and then remembered the drugs. He'd taken a white pill and a black pill, and they were working together on him. He had an idea that it was the white pill that was making him so mellow and easily pleased, so ready to let Cassie do what she wanted and to do what he felt in return. He wondered, idly, what it was the black pill did.

The screaming was louder now.

And the sun was going down.

The shadows slowly crept towards him, flowing over the actor and the woman who filled her jeans while she wore them, and the other girl between them, and they changed. It was such a sudden change that Cade almost couldn't see it – it was as though it was just one more kind of lovemaking. But their faces were twisted now, masks of rage and hate and pure menace, the actor flexing his arms and smashing out, backhanding the unknown girl across the face and sending her tumbling, while the woman who'd filled her jeans so well reached out fingernails like long talons for his face, laughing cruelly as they plunged down for his face, raking down the cheeks and drawing blood.

"Helter skelter!" she screamed, or maybe it was him, it was hard to say. Their mingled voices rose up as she clawed at him, and he struck out wildly at her, the girl out cold beside them with her nose bloody. Naked people clawing at each other and shrieking, maddened: "Helter skelter! Helter skelter! *Helter skelter!*"

And the whole park seemed to be shrieking it as the shadows lengthened and caught more people in their grip. Cade felt cold, suddenly, but didn't feel anything else but good, even though that wave of violence was spreading closer to him and Cassie.

She was in his arms, and her lips were on his neck, and somehow that was all that mattered. His hands slid up her back, taking hold of her shoulders, and he turned his head to kiss her, deep and long.

And then the shadow hit him.

At first, it was like nothing had changed, and it took him a second to work out what had. Only the sun had gone, after all.

Cade was now in a world with no sun.

It seemed as if there had always been an inferno at the front of his skull, burning and crisping his frontal lobes, sending white-hot needles of pure agony scorching down his spine and back up again, setting his blood alight and pumping it around his body. It seemed like he'd always been angry.

There'd never been a time he hadn't wanted to kill anything that moved.

Above him, the girl thing screeched and clawed, raking her nails over his chest, opening up the wounds. The pain hit him, but became lost in the red roaring flames that burnt and scorched his mind. It seemed that that heat – that burning, hateful rage and pain – had always been there and always would be. The girl-thing was screaming at him – "Helter skelter! Helter skelter!", over and over. He realised, without being surprised, that he was bellowing it as well.

Hell with it. It was how he felt, he might as well say it.

Helter skelter. Helter skelter.

Over and over.

The air was full of screams and snarls as fights and scuffles broke out all around – here and there Cade could see people scratching and clawing at themselves, unable to reach anyone else to hurt but needing to hurt something. Once people were unconscious, they were ignored – Cade realised he had to force himself to see them, as if now that they didn't pose him any threat his brain felt free to just pass over them and move on to something else.

Cade was rationalising, and he knew it – fighting the drug. That was no damn good. That just made it hurt more. What he needed was to take that hurt out on somebody. The girl-thing brought her fist down at his lip, splitting it, and all his attention was suddenly on her. She'd do as well as anybody.

His fist snapped up, slamming into her jaw and cracking it, skinning a knuckle in the process. That familiar blast of agony rolled down from his mutilated hand, but it was a weak thing now compared to the fire in his brain and he paid it no heed.

He couldn't remember her name.

All he knew was that she was moving around, rolling on the grass, hissing and clutching at her face, and every time she moved it caused another wave of flaming pain in his mind. He needed to do something about that.

Through the fire and the fog in his mind, it came to him that everyone was lashing out almost randomly – they must be feeling the same pain that he was, the same rage and hate, but they weren't focussing. Cade guessed they'd never learned how to focus past pain, or maybe they just weren't of his mind. Maybe they just didn't feel as strongly about it as he did. They damn sure weren't going to do much in the way of damage in that state, although Cade figured he knew where all those little injuries he'd seen had come from now.

But Cade could damage them. Cade could damage them a hell of a lot.

And he would.

He reached down and grabbed the girl-thing by the throat, closing his screaming hands and twisting. Her spine went with a sickening crack of sound, but he kept squeezing, not realising that his teeth were gritted and his eyes were bulging right along with hers until after she'd gone still. Only then did his fingers relax, and once she'd flopped onto the ground, cold and heavy and without life, he simply forgot she'd ever been there.

The actor was swinging out wildly, not doing much more than bruising the woman he was fighting. Cade went for him next. He wished he had his knife, or his knuckledusters, or anything at all – maybe he left them in the movie theatre. He'd go there soon and find what he needed, but in the meantime he had work to do. The fire in his head wasn't going away.

It was all rational for Cade. It was the most natural, rational thing in the world to grab the actor's head in his hands and twist it round with one motion until it sat backwards on the neck, the flesh twisted and the vertebrae snapped apart, the man's bladder and bowels voiding on the grass. Cade kept kicking him as he shuddered and convulsed, the nerve endings sending their last signals to the dying body. Finally he went still, and vanished from Cade's head.

Cade moved on to the next one.

And the next.

And the next.

It was a long night, and there were a lot of people in that park, maybe fifty in all, maybe more – Cade went through them one by one, breaking necks for the most part, but occasionally getting in something closer to a real fight, trading brutal punches again and again until they crashed to the floor with nothing but a red smear where their face had been – whoever they were.

The only thing in Cade's head was pain, but he kept moving, cracking spines and snapping necks, choking and killing, while all the folks around him just fell to the dirt and hollered and shrieked, repeating their nonsense phrase over and over. Somehow, he managed to gain a kind of calm from it – a balm in his blazing, burning brain. He was a man reduced to one function, and that function was death,

And death had no mercy.

Eventually, there was nobody left to kill, and Cade slowed, and stopped, falling to his knees, a clockwork man with a stopped key. He would have broke his own neck or carved himself open like a turkey on a farm, but somehow he couldn't raise his hands anymore, so there he knelt until the dawn.

By the time the rays of the sun started to wash over the park, and the blood and the corpses on the ground, the pain in Cade's mind was almost faded anyway. The drug had worn off after a few hours, and the first light of dawn washed it out entirely.

Cade felt washed out right along with it.

He lifted his head, and saw someone walking towards him from the gates of the park. A man wearing a good suit, looking at the carnage Cade had caused. He looked horrified, stumbling through the dawn like a man who'd released some terrible virus, some contagion upon the world, without considering what it might do.

Like a biochemist, maybe.

Cade nodded. "Doc." His voice sounded ragged in his ears. He cleared his throat and spat the taste from his mouth.

Doc Clearly looked back at him. His face was white as ash. "...Cade."

He looked around at the piled corpses. He reached out with the toe of one immaculate shoe and prodded the thing that had once been Cassie, raising a buzzing cloud of flies from her stiffened body. He swallowed hard, shaking his head. Then he looked back at Cade.

"I think... I think we'd better talk."

CHAPTER TWENTY

THE CONFESSION

"It was all about balance, you see. Balance and release."

Doc Clearly sighed, scratching his head, before leaning down quickly to check the pulse of one of the more recent kills, then standing slowly, sighing and shaking his head. He was dead, of course – a young man in his early twenties. Cade couldn't remember seeing his face, but there was nobody else who could've twisted his head around like that.

Doc Clearly seemed to read his thoughts. "It's possible not all of these were you. We do have fatalities sometimes. It's... it's the nature of it." He pinched the bridge of his nose, as if warding off a developing headache. "I'm sorry, Cade. I expect you're wanting to know why."

Cade nodded. "I'd be obliged."

Clearly sighed. "Why I dose them with it... the compound. Why they keep taking it, night after night, despite... well, despite this."

He shook his head. "I should have warned you. I should have given you some kind of indication what to expect, or... well, or told Cassiopeia not to bother bringing you." He looked up, angry. "Damn it, Cade, you told me you didn't have this in you!"

Cade stared back, not moving. The Doc looked at him for a moment, then the anger dropped out of him and he just looked depressed. "Sorry... Sorry." he sighed, rubbing his brow. "Cassiopeia was someone... well, I liked her a lot." He shook his head, slowly, and turned away from Cade. Cade got the impression Clearly didn't want to look at him. He couldn't blame him for that.

He could sure as hell blame him for slipping him something that turned him into a killing machine, though. "Why didn't you tell me?"

Clearly sighed. "You killed the dog because you thought it was a threat. I didn't know how you'd react to hearing about the compound, whether you'd... oh, I don't know. Whether you'd think we were just like what you'd been through up north. I thought it would be safer to just introduce you to it – let you see for yourself. Experience how good it could be." He sighed. "Not one of my better ideas."

They were at the gate of the park now, and Cade could see a few of the love children staggering through the streets, bruised and sore, covered with bites and scratches, looking for their clothes. They looked tired, but there was something healthy about them all the same, as if the watches of the long night had drained some boil. They were standing straight and proud, despite their nakedness. A couple of them waved to the Doc.

"The park's off limits for now, everyone. I'll need a work party in an hour or two – about twenty, and they'd best be prepared for some ugly work. Oh, and we'll need someone to take census. Spread it around." The waving people nodded and went back to what they were doing. Satisfied, the Doctor walked on grimly, heading back towards Haight Street and the movie theatre. Cade followed. He was more aware of his own nudity now – the way the other folk didn't seem to give a damn about theirs seemed to have that effect on him. He shook his head, waiting for the Doc to carry on.

Eventually, he did.

"Most people just pick up afterwards and carry on, as you saw. Like I said, we have fatalities sometimes, but generally it's just bites, scratches, the occasional black eye... things have calmed down a lot from how they were. Most people... they still hold back, you see. From doing anything permanent. Even in the grip of it, we hold back." He looked at Cade. "I really should have known when you killed the dog, Cade. You don't hold back. Do you?"

Cade shook his head. He wasn't a man to hold back much when it came to killing, it had to be said. He looked up at the Doc, eyes narrowed. "Got some questions."

Clearly scratched the back of his head again, his moustache seeming to droop further. "Of course you have. We all have. Why do we do this to ourselves? Why do we take this terrible substance and put ourselves through a night of hell? What do we gain?" He looked down, at a man lying on the sidewalk, the left side of his face beaten raw, one eyelid puffy and closed. He was smiling serenely, looking up through his good eye at the clouds overhead. "You okay, Ed?"

Ed grinned, revealing missing teeth. "Just fine, Doc. Just fine."

They carried on walking in silence for a moment before turning the corner onto Haight Street. They were starting to see some people wearing clothes now – long-sleeved shirts, polo-necks and ponchos were popular, pulled down over the arms to hide the bruises and scratches, shades hiding black eyes. They smiled, and waved, and one girl walked up and threw her arms around the Doc and hugged him, then leant in to kiss Cade's cheek. Then she moved on, leaving her gesture to do the talking.

"You won't be so popular when they find out what you've done. That many dead... it's hard for the community to absorb. I'll need to decide what to do about that – whether you'll be staying. Whether I can trust you with any more of the compound. Punishment... I don't know. I don't think I can let you have any more."

Cade blinked, looking at Clearly out of the corner of his eye. "More?" Once was enough, he figured. That damned drug had sent him halfway to hell and turned his hand to the murder of maybe fifty men and women. He didn't like to think about what might have happened if there'd been kids and old folks there.

What it implied that there weren't any.

Clearly turned to look at him as they approached the livid red façade of the old movie theatre. "People always want more, Cade. But we're back to the 'why' of it." He closed his eyes, shaking his head. Suddenly he looked tired to Cade, bending over as if there was an infinitely heavy weight pressing down on his back, one that he didn't admit he wore for the most part, but one that was there all the same. "Cade... can I ask you a personal question? Tell me, how did you *feel* when things fell apart? When people were dying?"

Cade fell silent. After a moment or two, he spoke slowly, like he was admitting to a crime or guessing the answer to a quiz question. His eyes were guarded.

"Didn't."

Doc Clearly raised one sad eyebrow. "You didn't feel anything?"

Cade felt guilty all of a sudden, looking away. "There were things needed doing. Not much time to sit around." He shrugged.

Clearly smiled humourlessly. "Huh. I've never met a sociopath before." Then he winced, catching himself. "I'm sorry. That's... quite a value judgement, considering the kind of things people have been up to here. Even me, with my special pills, mixing up horror every night... God. I didn't set out to do things this way, Cade. Believe me." He sighed, leading the way inside the building.

"When you lose everything – everyone – in a matter of days... I know I'm asking a lot, but put yourself in that place. You have a wife and children, a family, or at the very least friends. And if not friends, then structures – institutions, social conventions, things that are fixed. Even the lowest of the low, the loneliest of the lonely, know that when they turn on the television someone will be there. When they leave their hovel, people will be walking the streets. Aeroplanes will fly in the sky. There is a world and they are a part of it, no matter how large a part they might be."

They walked through the foyer, passing a smiling couple. The man was buttoning his shirt, covering up a criss-cross of scratches, a forest of them, some days old. A girl huddled into him, nuzzling like a cat, looking perfectly content. There was still blood under her nails, and a bruise was developing on her cheek. Doc Clearly half-waved to them, then turned back to Cade.

"There is a world, and then it goes – and what you're left with is flyblown corpses and filth in the streets and the complete dissolution of any structure or system you relied on. You understand, Cade? You could adapt – you have, for better or worse, a unique outlook that makes you perfectly adapted to these times. I imagine you didn't function all that well in the old world, did you?"

Cade shook his head. He had to admit that he'd not exactly distinguished himself.

Doc Clearly smiled. "You picked a good time to arrive yesterday. People had picked themselves up from the night, so you wandered in when things were at their best. You saw how normal everything was – especially in contrast with your ride in with the Gang. Not like anywhere else you've been, is it? The Pastor and his religious fanatics, the cannibals..."

Cade frowned, then spat. "Bunch of folks following blind after authority. After a fella says he's got the answers."

It was a long speech, and Cade meant every word.

Clearly looked at the carpet for a moment. "Well, I deserve that, I guess. Come on, I think your clothes are in here."

He led the way into the theatre they'd been in, and Cade saw his clothes – the T-shirt with HUG ME on it, the blood-spattered jeans, his chains, his knives, even the knuckledusters – laying in a heap where he'd sat, along with a few other piles of clothing here and there. It looked like everyone had stripped there and then, probably once they'd come out of that vision or whatever the hell it was – something about a bar, Cade remembered. It looked as if most of the clothes had been picked up and put back on by now, though.

Cade pulled on the T-shirt first, then tugged on the jeans – he'd fallen into the habit of going commando – while the Doc carried on talking behind him.

"There's a price for that normality, Cade. Trauma like the death of a world full of people... nobody living has ever been through something like that, nobody in history. The Black Death, the Spanish Influenza – chickenfeed." He shook his head. "Nobody's normal after that. Nobody's sane. The hate and the anger and the terror, the trauma, it builds up in you. The compound... well, it's like draining pus from a wound. It's cleansing. People let out their demons. Usually... usually nobody gets hurt, not badly. I try and make sure they're kept in check..."

Cade nodded, lacing up his boots. "That's your drug. Being in charge. Spiritual guru." He breathed in, disliking the necessity of talk, but some things had to be said. His eyes were cold as steel. "You burn Sausalito?"

Doc Clearly opened his mouth, then closed it.

Cade looked him in the eye. "Helter Skelter. That you?"

The Doc opened his mouth again... then hung his head, turning and walking up to the back of the theatre, away from the people who were trickling in to reclaim their clothes and shoes. There he sat, and waited for Cade to join him.

Cade took his time, fastening the chains about himself, locking them to biceps and waist, then checking his knives. It was a damned good thing he'd followed everyone else in stripping down – if he'd had his knives with him, he'd have killed everybody in the city.

Maybe he still would.

Slowly, he walked up to the Doc, who sat like a man in a confession booth. Cade didn't bother making anything out of that – he just sat, and waited.

After a minute, Clearly spoke.

"I developed the compound two months before the end came. Simple to manufacture – all I needed was a large quantity of raw materials and I could cook it up on a camping stove." For a moment he seemed like he was going to laugh. "Almost like it was meant to be. The high... well, you experienced that. Meetings with the divine – all the firing of certain chemicals in the brain, of course, but the experience seems quite real for all that. Then the charging of the libido, the mind becoming lost in a sea of pleasure, love, togetherness... and all completely legal." He chuckled, unable to help himself. "All I had to do was get rid of the after-effect of the black pill. If the light receptors weren't kept stimulated at a certain level – if it got dark – the compound brought on the other symptoms. The blazing anger, the hatred, the neural pain, the violence – barely controllable. In your case it was totally unrestrained..."

Cade nodded. He figured he knew where this was going, but he had time. Might as well hear it.

"The end came, and... well, at first there was just chaos. We managed to get a community together, but those were nightmarish days. I don't know why I suggested using the drug – maybe I thought the end would come more easily if we were stupefied." He put his head in his hands, suddenly. "No, no, that isn't it at all, is it? I handed it out at night – at night, you see? I knew what it would do. I knew what it *needed* to do..."

He swallowed, and Cade could see the disgust at himself written on his face. "I said it was like draining pus from a wound. But the pus builds up, and the horror builds up, and there was so much of it in us then... you have to understand, they were *eating people*. Some capitalist TV personality had actually got citizens to eat each other. The Pastor and his men, they took torches to Castro Street, grabbed people and dragged them away, and they were never heard from again. God, I heard those poor kids were crucified – I heard the Pastor actually nailed them up." He was shaking his head, and his whole body was trembling with the effort of remembering. "We were caught between all that. Trapped. We were angry and we were scared. And... well, with my compound in us..."

He stared ahead, into the middle distance. "I remember my brain was alight, and there were hundreds of us – there were several thousand survivors at that stage, although that number dropped fast – and I'd made so much of the compound we could all have some. And we went on the hunt – it seemed to last days, that first time. The Pastor's territory was to the north of Golden Gate Park –"

Cade nodded. "The Presidio."

Doc Clearly shuddered. "He called it the Garden of Eden. We burnt it. We drove him out and we smashed everything we could lay our hands on, and we burnt the ruins. And we weren't done. We ran up the highway, screaming like banshees, and the light of day couldn't dim it then. There was too much pain to be vented, you see? We kept running and running, up Highway 1, smashing the cars, grabbing fuel cans, killing anyone we found on those roads..."

"Then you hit Sausalito." Cade nodded.

There was some satisfaction in solving that one at last.

"We burned Sausalito to the ground. We murdered anyone we found and burned everything we could. Marin City too. We'd have demolished every building and laid it all flat if we could. Dear God, I still remember..." He shook his head, and raised a knuckle to his eye, wiping away the tears that were forming.

Cade didn't speak.

Doc Clearly was silent for a minute or two, then spoke, low and soft. "Eventually, the madness faded, enough to come home at least. There were some scavengers on our territory – a few of the Pastor's people, the occasional cannibal, although by then they'd already found their home in the BART tunnels and established their pattern of hunting for people who strayed too far east." He shrugged. "We killed them. We made it clear that Haight Street was ours, and we went to work clearing the bodies and setting it up so we could live there. We'd exorcised our pain, you see? We were refreshed, purified, ready to work. And work we did."

He sighed. "Eventually, we fell into the pattern – we'd work through the day, then take the pills in the evening, meet God – all very theraputic – have sex, and then... when the sun went down, we'd march, laughing and screaming, to somewhere we didn't own, and we'd put it to the torch. If you go below 17th Street... well, there is no below 17th Street. There are a few spots still standing around 24th, since the cannibals were protecting it, but... we smashed and burned everything we could. It's no

Sausalito, but there are very few places left in the south of the city to live in, which had the side effect of mobilising most of the survivors who were living down there to join either us, if we kidnapped them, or the Pastor if we beat them and left them to die."

Cade looked at him. Clearly looked back.

"I'm not proud of those times."

Cade didn't speak. Eventually, Clearly shook his head and continued speaking. "The pain grew less with every use of the drug, until finally we'd exhausted it. The pain, I mean. Not the compound. Never the compound... we were happy, is what I'm trying to say. Content. Where the Pastor's bunch are still shell-shocked from the end of the world, we have shrugged off the culture shock and rebuilt thanks to the power of chemistry. Yes, every night we kick, and we bite, and we pummel each other, and occasionally people still die, but... there wasn't another way to get through it. I'm convinced there wasn't." He bowed his head. "I'm not looking for absolution, Cade. I don't think there's any to be had, and... well, I should know, shouldn't I?" He laughed, another humourless little chuckle. "I met God."

Cade turned his head, curious. "What'd he say?"

Doc Clearly smiled, wryly. "He told me I'd turned out a better person than he'd created me to be. Nonsense, of course. My guilty conscience speaking."

Cade shrugged. "Must count for something." He thought about how the Pastor'd almost broke down that time, begging to be told he was right. He'd believed in something, at least, even if it was crazy as a rattlesnake. Clearly didn't seem to believe in anything except keeping his people going, even if that meant killing a whole bunch of other folks. Cade didn't know if that made him any better than the Pastor. Maybe it made him worse, on account of how the Pastor at least had crazy for an excuse.

Made him dangerous, though.

Too dangerous.

Cade turned, looking Clearly in the eye. "Got some questions. There insulin here?" His eyes narrowed. "Your folks didn't burn it?"

Clearly shook his head. "No. We looted what we could find. There were things we burned, but I don't think we'd destroy something we're so dependent on. I do have a supply of insulin like that, but... well, I can't let you take any." He swallowed, looking nervous for the first time. "I can't, Cade. People depend on it."

"You use it to make your pills?"

"No!" the Doc looked offended. "We use it to treat *diabetes!* Nothing goes into the pills that we'd need for basic survival, although it could be argued those pills *are* our survival. Maybe in five or ten years we can cope without them – not now." He looked away, flushing, angry with himself as much as Cade. "We're addicts, I suppose. But the pills keep us alive... anyway, I'm not letting you have the insulin. We need it."

Cade nodded. He figured there'd be another supply somewhere – buried in a wrecked depot, maybe. He could go find it, if he had to.

If he had to.

"Your folks don't burn things any longer?"

There was a pause. Doc Clearly seemed to be contemplating his shoes. Finally he spoke.

"They were working out their pain, Mister Cade. That's what the rampages were all about. The better life got in the community, the less pain there was to work through in those night rampages – although there's always some. Life is about pain, even if you do build a paradise. That's what I meant earlier, about balance."

He lifted his head, still not looking at Cade.

"You left fifty corpses in that park, Mister Cade. I don't know what's going to happen when people find them. They've probably found them already – my word's only good for so much, it's not a police barricade. These corpses..." He shook his head. "These *people* are lovers, friends, workmates. People who've come to replace lost loves and lost family – you understand? I imagine for you, death is just part of your day... sorry, that came out wrong..."

Cade shrugged. Didn't seem so wrong as far as he was concerned.

"I don't know what kind of impact this is going to have. They're going to want to lynch you, and they're going to feel hurt and betrayed, and then when they take the compound – and they will want and need the compound tonight, Mister Cade, I very much doubt we'll be going through the ritual of performing a pre-pill show when my community needs to mourn fifty dead – when they take the compound, all that will come out."

He shook his head.

"And it's my fault. My fault entirely. I can't believe I thought you'd just... fall in line. Not after the dog." He stared straight ahead for a moment. "Perhaps I saw the opportunity to break a stalemate. Maybe we'll go after the Pastor tonight. Or maybe... maybe we'll just rage. Maybe that was what I was looking for." He sighed, his voice bitter. "Maybe that's the sort of spiritual guru I want to be. A Manson."

He shook his head, his voice breaking as the tears flowed. "Or maybe I just made a mistake. Maybe there isn't any psychology to it. Maybe I'm just a stupid man who let things get out of hand. I'm sorry, Cade. I wish things could have worked out for you here." He put his head in his hands. "I wish they could have worked out for all of us. Get lost, Cade. Go away and don't come back. Please, for your own sake, don't come back here."

Cade stood, looking down at the weeping man.

"I won't."

It was the third lie he told to Doc Clearly.

And the last.

CHAPTER TWENTY-ONE

THE SEIGE

Cade left the theatre and took the first turning north, up to Oak Street. He figured he had a lot of ground to cover if he wanted to get back to the Pastor's compound by nightfall.

He didn't look at the people he was walking past, but he could see their faces out of the corner of his eye. Some of them looked drained, some looked disbelieving. Some were openly weeping, asking over and over again whether it was true, if it could really be true... Cade thought back to what Doc Clearly had said. Lovers, friends, co-workers.

Damn it to hell.

Everybody was walking towards the park except him – he was walking against the tide. Running from the scene of the crime, in other words. A couple of folks were starting to put two and two together and they turned towards him, eyes narrowed and stabbing daggers, lips curled to a scowl, the accusation boiling towards the surface even as Cade marched past them and away. Word spread fast in a small community, and it was starting to spread about the massacre in the park.

His massacre.

Fifty-odd people, dead from his own two hands. Cade spat. Hell with it, anyway. He wasn't to blame. If that god-damned fool hadn't decided to drug him without even –

Can't kid a kidder, dog.

Cade didn't break step, but he turned his head and saw Fuel-Air, as whole and hearty as he'd been in life, marching alongside him like it was a parade ground. Doc Clearly's moustache bristled above his upper lip, looking out of place on his young face. He was grinning.

You were the one who lied, man. If you'd told the truth, he'd have told it to you. Shit, don't get me wrong, these people are fucked up – I mean, this is some Wicker Man *meets fuckin' Age Of Aquarius shit right here, dog – but they were getting their sadomasochistic freak on just fine right up until you showed up. They were the most fuckin' self-regulating motherfuckers in this fuckin' town, dude, and then you blew in and killed them like fuckin' cockroaches because you couldn't handle something they were taking every night. And now, what, you want to cry like a bitch because you were all fucked up on their shit? It ain't the drug, dog, and you know it. If it was, those assholes would've killed each other inside of a day, first time they took it. It's you, dog. All the Doc's super shit did was break out what was already there.*

Cade stared for a long moment. It wasn't nearly that simple, but that didn't help him. He wondered if that was what Fuel-Air was going to be doing from now on. Pulling him up short when he bullshitted himself.

Fuel-Air smirked. *Fuck yeah, murder boy. Better get used to seeing my dead ass around.*

Cade frowned, turning east on Oak, hurrying past the people staring and whispering. Right or wrong, he didn't have much time for Fuel-Air right now. He needed to get out of Clearly's territory before somebody decided to take him on. People were starting to call out to him, asking where the hell he thought he was going. He didn't want to end up getting into a fight.

Cade only fought to kill. And he'd killed enough of these folks for his taste.

Yeah? You think? 'Cause I think it's never enough, motherfucker, not for you. I don't think there's a body count big enough for you in the world, the way you been handling shit. You could've had a pretty good life here, you know? But you fucked it up for just about everybody, and now these assholes are going to go 28 Days Later *on your ass and anybody else they come across. Here comes the motherfuckin' night, bitch. Hope you're willing to take some responsibility for that.*

"Shut up, Fuel Air." Cade muttered the words as he turned up Masonic. He tried to remember the layout of the city – if he kept on this street, he'd run into the University. For all he knew, that was Clearly's manufacturing base – at the very least, it'd be a haven for students, intellectuals, Clearly's people, the people he wanted to avoid.

East on Grove, then. He figured by the time he got to Divisadero he'd be well out of Clearly's reach – that was the road the Pastor'd wanted him to take originally, if he recalled right. He could follow that one up all the way to Lombard.

Already the people were starting to thin out. The few still on the street looked at him a little funny, but Cade could tell they hadn't heard the news yet. They would soon, though. They were heading down towards the park, where their friends and neighbours were gathered to count and carry the dead and spend the day thinking over their revenge, and when they got there, they'd know all about it.

Night was on the way.

When it came – when they'd taken their pills and the sun was going down and they started to burn with rage and hate – then they'd remember he'd gone in this direction. They'd know where he was headed. They'd come for him, and they'd come for the Pastor, and after that... well, after that they wouldn't stop. Clearly had made that plain. He'd scarred them, and any battle with the Pastor's people would scar them more.

And they took their scars out on the world in blood.

They'd come for Muir Beach, eventually. They'd get revenge on anything he might have touched – torch the whole damned woods, most likely. Maybe if he hadn't been so damn curious, if he hadn't taken the drug, if he'd gone through the night sober – but no.

That was the hell of it. He knew himself, and the second they'd started coming at him he'd have killed them where they stood, even if they were holding back on him. It was the same as with the dog – he wouldn't have risked it. He'd have killed them in their dozens.

Cade guessed you couldn't kid a kidder at that.

Hell with it, anyway. Nothing he could do about it now. He kept walking, along the empty street.

Not a soul to be seen. Nobody to see him go. He'd about made it.

Yeah, dog. You got away with murder.

And the sound of a slow handclap from behind him.

Cade didn't turn to look. He ignored the voice and kept walking. He had a hell of a lot of ground to cover, and he was on the clock, no doubt about it. He didn't have much in the way of time, and he had a hell of a lot of things to get done.

The killing hadn't stopped for the day, he knew.

Far from it.

By the time he'd gotten most of the way down Lombard Street, it was not quite eleven o'clock and Cade was starting to notice things.

Bodies, for the most part.

There was a trail of four cannibals, hair matted, bodies filthy, flies buzzing, laying on the road, dead as hell. A couple of metres in front of them was a hunting rifle, and a pretty good one too, as far as Cade could see, laying broken on the ground. Cade glanced up quickly, and saw a man hanging half out of a window. Strips of meat had been torn from his head and body, and one arm was hanging by dangling line of gristle – the other one was plain gone. The man was a ruin. A charnel house of one.

Hell of a way to go.

Cade figured him for one of the Pastor's snipers – he must've seen the cannibals swarming up from the south, started shooting... either he was slow reloading or he plain ran out of bullets. Either way, they tore into his hole like a tidal wave and pulled him apart with their bare hands.

It wasn't a good omen for the Pastor's people, Cade figured.

Damn, dog, you're a fast-working motherfucker. Shit, I'll bet you managed to ruin two perfectly good little communities right about the same time. Regular man with no fuckin' name.

"Nothing good about this place," muttered Cade. Fuel-Air cantered up beside him – he was maggot-ridden again, eyeballs staring out of his festering skull, wearing Cassie's hand-woven poncho, with the addition of a cowboy hat and a lit cigar. It was the skeleton horse he was riding that pissed Cade off – that was overkill, pure and simple. "The Pastor set hell up on these damn streets and you know it."

He shook his head. Wasn't a good idea to start making speeches to Fuel-Air. It wasn't like he was about to listen to a damn word.

Fuel-Air grinned his skeleton grin, the bare hooves of the horse clip-clopping on the roadway. *Bullshit, dude. Kids didn't have toys. Boo fuckin' hoo. They got to eat, they got a roof over their heads, they got to live. That's the bottom fuckin' line right there, bitch. Only suddenly you decide in your role as king of the fuckin' zombies that you're gonna set a wave of fuckin' face-eatin' cannibals up their ass. Smooth fuckin' move, bitch. Hope they saved some kid stew, because I'm a hungry motherfucker and so is my horse, dog...*

Cade shook his head and kept walking. Another three dead cannibals on his right, next to a smashed-in door. Wouldn't be a prize for guessing what he'd find if he went in. For a second he thought about heading in there, retrieving the rifle from the cold dead fingers of the man who'd been using it – then decided against it. There probably weren't bullets for it, and he didn't want to be stuck with something that jammed or misfired or ran dry when he was in a tight spot.

Cade didn't like guns. Never had.

There were a couple more cannibals laying in the road as he walked east, along with a couple of the Pastor's people – wrinkled, lardy bodies draped in approved extra-large T-shirts. There'd been a running battle, and these were the ones who'd fell behind. Cade was trying to piece it together – had the snipers passed the word before they'd died? Had the Pastor sent an exploratory party to see what the hell was going on, or were these just luckless citizens on litter duty, or taking water for their sniping brethren in the Lord? Cade shook his head – no sense in playing detective. Whatever had happened, he'd find out soon enough.

Fillmore Street was a nightmare.

There had to be a hundred and eighty, maybe a couple of hundred corpses in the street outside the Moscone Recreation Centre – the Pastor's place of crucifixion. Cade could still tell the cannibals from the regular folk, although there were some with clothes torn, coated head to foot in blood, that could be either – he wasn't about to pick them over one at a time and check. It wasn't a football game, and Cade didn't exactly need a score.

Although there were a hell of a lot more of the Pastor's flock dead than the cannibals. He could see that much.

The tarmac was sticky with blood, and in the heat of the morning sun Cade could breathe it in, taste the hot metal of it in his mouth. It almost made him dizzy, the slick abattoir smell of it washing through him like wet paint.

Cade wasn't a man to get upset at blood, hot, cold or running, but there was something unsettling about seeing all those dead – reading them like a tracker might read the spoor of some big animal passing that way. There'd been some kind of gathering at the Recreation Centre, he figured – maybe another crucifixion, maybe some of Clearly's scouts caught on the Pastor's territory. Cade hadn't seen the Conundrum Car anyplace, but it was possible Thelma and what was left of the Gang had been sent off on an errand that way. Probably not, though – more likely it was just some hobo wandering in from the north, or nobody at all.

Could be they just wanted to smell the corpses awhile.

Whatever they'd been doing, the cannibals had caught up to them in the middle of it – no, first they'd have got the word something was happening on Lombard Street, send a posse to check it out. The posse'd come back with the crowd of cannibals snapping at their heels, and the battle had started.

Cade took another look at the slumped, stiffening bodies in the street. No women, no children. Not enough bodies fallen to make up the whole of the Pastor's people, which meant the rest of them had fled, and the cannibals with them.

He heard a sound to his right, and turned.

There was a cannibal picking through the bodies, peeling at the skin and trying to rip the muscles out of one of them. Cade got a closer look now – it was one of the Pastor's bodyguards, the aluminium bay laying by his side. There was a fair amount of meat on him still.

The cannibal saw Cade, and straightened. Cade wondered if he was one of the ones who'd seen him, or if he'd just gotten the word and followed along behind the rest of them. It was hard to tell – all the cannibals looked about the same to Cade, skin so coated with grease and grime that individual features were hard to pick out, faces lost beneath a scrubland of beard and ratty long hair. This one seemed to recognise him. He grinned, revealing his rotting teeth.

Cade wondered when he'd lost the ability to speak.

The cannibal looked at Cade's knife, then tugged at the exposed muscle, snarling like an animal. It was pretty obvious what he wanted – some help cutting the meat off the bone. Absently, Cade drew the knife, and the cannibal grinned, making a kind of grunting noise halfways between a dog and a monkey and clapping his hands.

Cade wondered how much he'd made a year. He wondered if Strong had told him when he started eating meat that he'd end up braindead and rotting. If he'd cared.

The cannibal was still making that dog-monkey grunting sound when Cade drove the knife through his belly and tore upwards, spilling his offal out onto the ground before the sharp blade split his heart. The cannibal made one last sound, a kind of shrill whine, as his eyes bulged and rolled back in his skull.

Then he flopped down on top of the other bodies.

Cade wiped his hands on his T-Shirt, adding to the fresh splash of blood that now covered HUG ME. Ruining perfectly good shirts was getting to be a habit with Cade.

It was one less loose end to take care of, anyhow.

The cannibals weren't capable of speech, so far as he knew, but on the other hand he didn't want to take a chance that one of them had brain enough still in his head to tell the Pastor what he'd been up to. Besides, Cade figured even one still alive might be dangerous later on, after he'd solved the problem of the Pastor and Clearly. Last thing he wanted was one leaping out at him on a dark night while he was trying to find insulin.

Better to take care of it now.

There were more bodies up Bay Street, and at the corner where it met Buchanan, the stink of sweet roasted pork and stinking gasoline made Cade's eyes water.

There was a gas station on the corner of Bay and Buchanan, *was* being the right word. Someone had taken a torch to it during the battle and now it was a smoking, smouldering ruin, littered with charred, blackened bodies and body parts. Cade figured they'd drained most of the gasoline from it a long time before, but they'd left enough in to make a big bang if they had to, and from the look of it, they'd had to.

It was mostly cannibals in the ruins, although there were a couple of dead men in their Jesus shirts. A couple more of the Pastor's bodyguards. A lot of the bodies were too charred to be recognisable.

Judging by the ways the bodies had fallen, Cade figured the forecourt of the place had been soaked down with what gas was left, and then someone had struck a match when the cannibals were charging it. After that, the fire would've ignited whatever gas fumes were left in the pumps.

A trap, then.

Self-sacrifice.

Something they'd set up for the occasion, maybe? Something planned, or a lucky inspiration that they'd found time for while the battle was raging outside the Centre?

Cade shook his head. There was no way of telling. He figured there were maybe fifty or sixty charred cannibal corpses, and the Pastor's fallen were in the single figures, so whatever it was, it'd worked.

Only maybe it hadn't worked enough.

The trail of dead led north, up Buchanan. Cade wasn't surprised. That was where the supermarket was. The Pastor's place of safety – that was where they'd have made the final stand.

The cannibals must have still outnumbered the Pastor's faithful – otherwise they'd have stayed and fought. At least, that was the way Cade figured it. To tell the truth, he was a little surprised how many cannibals there were dead on those streets – more than a hundred. Maybe two hundred, even – hard to say.

He hadn't figured on the cannibal lifestyle being healthy enough to keep that number of people alive any length of time. He'd figured he was just sending two or three dozen crazies to give the Pastor a headache. Instead, he'd called down an Armageddon upon them – a wave of screaming, blood-soaked freaks from George Romero's worst goddamned nightmare that outnumbered the Pastor's flock. And they'd had the strength and ferocity of madness on their side.

Cade was starting to wonder if there'd be anyone left alive in the supermarket at all.

Don't feel too bad if there is, dog. You tried your best.

Then that caffeinated snicker Cade was really coming to hate.

Goddamn Fuel-Air.

Cade turned the corner and found another bloodbath waiting for him in the supermarket's parking lot. By this time, he was used to the stink of blood, not to mention the piss and shit from bladders and bowels that'd let go, but there was a quality to this one that was a little different.

He took a deep breath, listening to the buzzing of flies as they landed on the older corpses. There were a good two dozen faithful, scattered and bloody, but for the most part the dead were cannibals – filthy bodies twisted in the positions they'd fallen. Cade blinked, narrowing his eyes, and stared for a moment. That didn't seem right, somehow. Most of the Pastor's people had died in front of the Recreation Centre, apart from the ones who'd blown up the gas station. Hand to hand, the cannibals should've torn what few of the Pastor's people remained to pieces, just through sheer weight of numbers.

The Pastor and his flock just didn't have what it took in a straight fight. Cade knew that from experience.

He took another look. Maybe fifty, maybe a hundred cannibals. Then Cade saw what he was missing. The common factor that'd killed all the cannibals in the parking lot.

Gunshot wounds.

From automatic weapons, if Cade was any judge.

Some had been shot in the front, brains blown out as they'd charged, some mown down in retreat, shot in the back. A couple had been hit in the legs and had bled out while crawling, leaving a trail of slick red the length of the lot. A few had been blown away while dragging their wounded brethren towards shelter – although whether that was out of some vestigial sense of right and wrong or because they didn't want to waste good food, Cade couldn't say. But they'd died, and died by gunfire, every damned one of them.

The Pastor had had a stash of guns and ammunition that Cade hadn't known about. Machine pistols, definitely. Mac-10s or Uzis. Hell, maybe even an M16 or two.

Cade could see some of the corpses were a little fresher than others – less maggots, less flies. So the cannibals hadn't died all at once – they'd made more than one attempt to break the siege. Was that out of revenge for the ones who'd already died? Or were they following Cade's orders to the last man?

Cade hoped they had.

That would mean they were another problem solved. They wouldn't be something for Cade to worry about any longer. Because Cade had to face facts – if they weren't all dead, if they hadn't followed his orders to the grave, he'd have to deal with those few that'd survived. As in eliminate them.

As in genocide.

Which was strong meat even for Cade. He'd rather someone else handled it.

Also, if the Pastor had had a cache of ammunition, wiping out the cannibals would mean it was running seriously low by now – maybe all gone. Which would be two bits of good news in one.

One fucking strategic motherfucker. You should'a been a General, dog. You're real fuckin' good at it.

Cade shook his head. There was movement out on the far side of the parking lot.

One of the cannibals, skin coated with filth, hair matted, looking shaky and feverish, huddling in the relative shelter of a parked car that'd already been riddled with bullets. He had a bullet wound in the meat of his thigh – a ricochet, or it would've torn right through and taken most of the femoral artery with it. As it was, he'd managed to bandage it with a strip of cloth. He was about five feet and eight inches, with a lean, wiry build. He looked young, under the dirt, and Cade wondered what he'd been – an intern at a big office, maybe, or even middle management, one eye on the prize and one eye on the door, a dog eating dogs in the world of suits and ties and fake smiles.

Cade looked in the cannibal kid's eyes, and it was pretty clear the boy didn't have a damned idea how he'd come to this. He stood, shakily, limping forward, wincing, tears rolling from his eyes at the pain, then pitched forward as his bum leg gave way, his fall broken by the flyblown body of one of the first to die. Looking straight at Cade, the boy opened his toothless, rotting mouth. Cade couldn't tell what he was trying to say.

Was the kid going to curse him?

Ask for more orders, General, Sir?

Or just take a bite?

There was a gunshot from one of the broken windows of the supermarket, and the boy's head jerked, the body lifting up as the force of the bullet pushed his brains out through the shattered skull, then lay still.

Cade figured that this would probably be a good time to feel

something. Anything. Remorse, maybe. Guilt. Triumph.
Something.

But Cade was sick and tired of feeling things.

And at the end of the day, he didn't give a damn about the kid,
just like he didn't give a damn about anybody else laying dead
in that lot. They'd made the decision to be laying there, one way
or another. All Cade had done was give them a push.

When he was in the mood for it, Cade could be a real stone
cold son of a bitch.

He looked up at the sound of the supermarket door opening, the
creak of old metal on metal. The Pastor walked out, a smoking
revolver in one hand and a bible in the other, eyes hooded and
scowling as he shuffled towards Cade, feet twitching and shifting
on the concrete like a snake's tail. He was flanked on either side
by his bodyguards in black tees. They weren't carrying baseball
bats this time. This time, they had Uzis.

"Brother Cade," hissed the Pastor, and his eyes were like stones
in black well-water, ice cold and unreadable.

"Welcome home."

CHAPTER TWENTY-TWO

THE PRODIGAL SON

The Pastor didn't say much for a while after that. He just stared, looking Cade up and down. He clicked his tongue once as his eyes lingered over HUG ME – I HAD A HARD DAY, but whether that was because of the seventies imagery or the fresh, wet bloodstain, Cade couldn't tell.

Cade didn't say much either. He was bone tired, and there wasn't much to be said.

The bodyguards didn't break the silence. They stared straight ahead, a pair of tin soldiers waiting for a little boy to pick them up and clash them together. Cade figured right off they weren't much on thinking – they'd wait for the Pastor to make the move, if there was a move to be made.

Cade figured he was waiting for that as well.

He didn't figure he could outdraw a pair of machine pistols with a bowie knife, but if that's the way the Pastor wanted to handle this then Cade was damned if he wasn't going to give it a damn good try anyhow. The two had a lot of muscle on them, but there was fast muscle and slow muscle, muscle that was built to move like lightning in a jar and muscle that was built for showroom purposes, for looking the part of a badass. The difference between them was obvious as the difference between a greyhound at a racetrack and one at a dog show with a ribbon in its tail.

Cade was the one, and these two were the other. He figured the Uzis made it just about even, assuming they had any bullets in them.

He kept his eyes on the Pastor and the Pastor kept his eyes on him in turn, those cold grey ice-chip eyes boring into him and ferreting out his secrets. Cade stared back like a block of stone in the place of a man – he figured there was a good chance the Pastor knew he'd brought the cannibals down on them, either because he was an intuitive little snake when he wanted to be or because one of them had remembered how to talk in words instead of growls. If he did, that'd make it tough for Cade to get any more use out of him. Might even lead to Cade getting a bullet in his back inside the next twelve hours.

Of course, we wouldn't know for sure until that bullet hit him.

The Pastor reared back, swaying in place like a cobra. His eyes were narrow slits, and his lip curled softly, the cracked lines of his face splintering up one side as he did. It was almost a sneer, but there was a look of appraisal there, too. A look of judgement.

"Praise be to thee, oh Lord, oh Lord..." hissed the Pastor, almost beneath his breath. "For thou, in thy holy *wisdom*... have delivered thy soldier *back* unto his flock. Praise be unto the Lord of Hosts!"

He let the words hang a moment. Then he smiled, a sinister little grin, teeth bared like a dog's.

Cade still didn't know what the hell the Pastor was thinking, but he knew better than to start something now. For all he knew, they had a dozen guns trained on him in there, and he needed to know just what they had and how many people they had left.

Cade didn't have much of a plan concerning the bigger picture at this point, but what little he had depended on the two remaining sides, the Pastor's and Clearly's, being pretty much evenly matched – enough to smash them together and whittle them down to something he could manage or control, or at least something that wouldn't bother Muir Beach in the future. It wasn't much of a plan, and Cade wasn't much of a planner, but it'd have to do. Trouble was, it looked like the Pastor'd taken a bigger hit than Cade had figured on. Unless a hell of a lot more of the flock were breathing than Cade figured, they'd be wiped out to the last man, woman or child before the night had passed, and Clearly's love children would barrel right on to Muir Beach without stopping for breath.

Which meant the best thing right now, near as he could figure it, was to throw his weight behind the Pastor, if the Pastor didn't decide to kill him. If he didn't, maybe they could take down Clearly's whole community of psychopaths.

You're a dead man, dog. Nice knowin' ya.

Cade didn't twitch a muscle, but he scowled. Damn Fuel-Air anyway. He was going to have to do something about that boy if he didn't shut up.

The Pastor turned and began to shuffle towards the doors of the supermarket, and Cade followed, with the guards behind him. He didn't need to turn his head to know that their hands were on their guns and those guns were probably pointed at his back.

Time to get a few things straight, Cade figured.

"What the hell happened here?" he said, though he knew damn well.

The Pastor chuckled, a laugh like jackboots wading through broken glass. "Cannibals, brother. Heathens and degenerates, lusters..." He hissed the word like a python. "I say, *lusters* after the foul stink of Mammon, most wretched and vile of all Satan's demons. Their thirty pieces of silver has become a pound of flesh, brother. Their craven need for money has become a thirst for blood..." The Pastor turned his head, fixing Cade with a long stare. "I can't help but *wonder*, Brother *Cade*, why Washington

Strong would be so... aggressive. Do *you* know why, Brother Cade? Did he happen to mention? Hmm?"

"Who?" Cade looked puzzled. He was a little surprised the Pastor was trying such a simple trap, and more surprised that he knew that Strong had been the one in charge of the cannibals before Cade had come along. Cade was coming to the conclusion that he'd walked into a regular damned soap opera, where all the players knew each other but him.

The Pastor fell silent.

They walked through the doors and into the supermarket - not much had changed, at least as far as Cade could see. There was still that near-silent atmosphere, that reverential quality. Everyone still looked distant, almost brain-damaged, and where the kids had been quiet before they seemed shell-shocked now.

Nice work, dog, said Fuel-Air. This time he was harder to take than before – morphed horrifically into a ten-year-old's body, scampering between the huddling children with a yo-yo and a Snoopy t-shirt, but the same rotting, maggot-ridden face, the same flashing gold tooth. Cade winced. Every time he saw Fuel-Air, he was looking worse, and this one really took the prize.

Nice fucking work. This ain't no way for a kid to grow up, says Big Bad Cade, the Social Worker That Time Forgot, I'm gonna be fuckin' Santa and make sure every little dickens has a toy. A regular Miracle On Fucked-Up Street, fuckin' yes, Virginia, there is a Cade, and he's gonna get any father figure you managed to pick up since the shit went down eaten by motherfuckin' cannibals and turn whatever fuckin' life you had left into a river of fuckin' ⸢ *shit, why don't you fuckin' LOOK AT ME you fuckin' asshole, look me square in my fuckin' empty eyes because I'm every damn crime you're ever gonna commit you god-damned motherfuckin'...*

Cade shook his head and squeezed his eyes tight shut for a moment, trying to focus past that incessant caffeinated whisper. Hadn't Fuel-Air been on his side once? A helping hand, helping him see things he'd missed?

What did it say that he wasn't on Cade's side any more?

What did it say that the thing Fuel-Air wanted him to see was his own body count?

Hell with it. Cade wasn't one for metaphysics and he wasn't one for psychology either, least of all his own. Best to ignore that gibbering thing scampering down between the legs of the trembling, ashen-faced women, caught up in horror beyond anything they'd imagined, horror that he'd brought down on them like a damned...

Hell with it.

Fuel-Air was right about one thing, though. Cade's cannibal army had taken a hell of a toll.

He'd been right to think the Pastor's force was broken. There were a few left – twitching, huddling shells of men cowering in corners, injured men cradling broken arms and open wounds, and those few who could still hold a gun and walk – about six or seven, by Cade's count. Cade figured the women had probably helped out with the ammunition, and maybe even fired a couple of guns themselves if the Pastor had allowed it.

He checked what ordinance they had left – a couple more hunting rifles, slow loaders, three shotguns, a glock and the two Uzis the guards had. Not to mention the police special the Pastor was holding. There were a few more police specials laying on the ground, among the shell casings.

Cade could put two and two together. If those guns were any use, they'd be in somebody's hand. That meant ammo was scarce, maybe gone altogether. If a gun was in somebody's hand, Cade had to assume there were bullets in it, and the fella with the hunting rifle could probably scavenge a little from his dead friends on Lombard if he had a mind to, but everything else had been pumped into the mountain of fresh corpses in the parking lot.

The Pastor had spent all his strength on that battle. Now he needed Cade's information – if Clearly attacked in force, with the kind of raging, blazing, burning anger that he'd apparently unleashed back in the day, the Pastor needed to move out or die. That was one theory, anyway.

Of course, if the Pastor thought that was the case, he'd have started packing up already, so Cade figured he had something in reserve. The plot thickened. Cade figured he'd try and nudge the Pastor into showing his cards.

"Looking short of ammo." He kicked a shotgun shell casing with the toe of his boot, and it skittered across the floor, banging into a couple of nine-millimetre casings as it went.

The Pastor looked at him out of the corner of one eye, the cracks on his face shifting as he searched for an expression. Finally he smiled again. "Tell me, Brother Cade, what did you see during your pilgrimage to the land of the Devil? Anything I should know about?" He let the question dangle without any of his usual flourishes.

Cade weighed it up. The Pastor could probably order him killed right there. Now ordering a man like Cade killed and actually killing him were two different things, and Cade didn't doubt that if need be he could make sure a lot of folks died in his place, but even for him there was a danger in facing down a pair of Uzis as well as a loaded shotgun or two.

Might as well be honest.

"I killed about fifty of Clearly's people. They were on something – me too. They ain't happy. Probably saw where I was going." He shrugged. "Coming tonight." Cade hoped that'd satisfy the Pastor. He'd gone over every detail at some length.

The Pastor raised an eyebrow. "You bearded the Devil in his lair and killed his demons..." He stared for long moments into Cade's eyes. "*Is* it true, Brother Cade?"

Cade wasn't used to being called a liar. It pissed him off something fierce, and the Pastor seemed to take note of that. He smiled wider. "You impress me, Brother Cade, with your dedication to the service of our Lord... so *many* have gone to the Devil and not returned, *tempted* and *twisted* by his potions and his powers and the *lies* spilling from his forked and hissing *tongue!* Oh *yes,* Brother, you stepped into the mouth of the *dragon,* the many-headed *Beast* of *Revelations* and breathed his poison *breath...* and found it in you to come back! And *join* the worshippers of the mighty and glorious Lord once again!" He reached, gripping Cade's shoulders for a moment with withered hands. "Lord *bless* you, Brother Cade! Lord *keep* you!" He chuckled, shattered glass raining down on slate, while his gimlet eyes fixed Cade's.

Cade frowned. There wasn't any mileage in this sort of bullshit as far as he was concerned. "Got a plan?"

After a moment of loaded silence, the Pastor turned again, shuffling towards the back of the store. Cade followed, shooting a quick glance at the handful of armed men still facing out of the window – all that was left of the Pastor's army, unless you counted the broken, sobbing heaps trying to burrow into the floor-tiles like moles, or the ashen-faced women the Pastor'd stupefied and brainwashed, or the kids, shell-shocked and malnourished. And Cade didn't.

Clearly's people were going to be as bad as the cannibals – maybe worse, since the cannibals were brain-damaged savages. The love children were going to turn into hate-crazed savages the second the sun went down, but right up until then they were keeping fit, drinking fruit juices and fresh water, probably getting any guns or knives they had ready into the bargain. Cade could picture the Doc looking on with his sad eyes as his followers raided kitchen drawers and police precincts, finding anything they could to kill folks with while he stood back and told himself that it'd all be worth it to make them whole again.

Cade wasn't exactly on the Pastor's side, but the kids didn't deserve to be torn to pieces by a bunch of feral junkies and he sure as hell wasn't going to let Muir Beach fall that way. Cade was hoping the Pastor had something to even up the score a little bit.

He wasn't disappointed.

The Pastor removed a bunch of jangling keys from his pocket, swinging them around on a bony finger, and then shuffled towards one of the double doors at the back of the store that led through to the storage area. Cade had figured this was where he'd kept his weapons cache up until now.

The turning of the key in the lock made a sound like a skeleton rattling undead bones in a cellar in the dead of night. Cade felt a sudden stab of instinct deep in his gut, and looked around for a sign of Fuel-Air. He'd vanished back to wherever he came from.

That made Cade uneasy, somehow.

Then the doors swung open, and Cade saw it.

It was squat and black, a huge ebon egg sitting on a wooden trestle. The metallic casing of the thing reflected the lights above in a dull sheen, and towards the back of it there were fins and an opened container that had once held a parachute, now cannibalised for cloth. Bolted to the side was some kind of improvised detonator system, an electronic hotch-potch that had replaced the original detonator. Somebody had done a lot of work to make sure this could be delivered by land instead of by air, but the purpose was still the same. Cade didn't have to read the word THERMOBARIC, stencilled with military precision on the old, scratched casing, to know what it was.

He didn't have to look too closely at the face on the front of the bomb either. The grotesque warping of metal into flesh that only he could see, grinning a grin with a diamond in it.

He knew exactly what it was.

It was a Fuel-Air Bomb.

Howdy, Fuel-Air said, and winked one black metal eye. *How you like me now, bitch?*

Cade took a deep breath. Under the circumstances, there was one question that needed to be asked first.

"Everybody else see that?"

The Pastor looked at him quizzically, eyes narrowing. "A thermobaric explosive, Brother Cade. Doubtless the noble men of the FBI would have swooped down with all their fury on the terrorist cell who were planning to detonate it, had they not died of the Lord's displeasure, and the terrorists too. Leaving only their weapon behind, to be found by one who will put it to more righteous use."

Al Qaeda, dog. The bomb pouted, mock-stern. *You stop fightin' those fuckers over there, they come over here, like Rush said all along. Chain of command, bitch. Shoulda listened, you fuckin' socialist.*

"Al Qaeda?" said Cade. That sense of surreality was washing over him again.

The Pastor shook his head. "Domestic terrorists." He grinned, pointing to a blood-red slogan painted on the side of the bomb: SIC SEMPER TYRANNIS. WE SURROUND YOU. "Of my faith, in fact, which explains how they were taken to the glory of the Lord all the sooner. Or perhaps He thought their way was too merciful for the liberals and the deviants, compared with mine." He chuckled, a chain mail fist crushing a wineglass.

Damn. My bad. Guess I'm just politically incorrect or some shit. Fuck it, dude, let's go bombing. The bomb winked again and grinned, waggling its tailfins. Cade turned his back on it, looking the Pastor dead in the eye.

"You didn't use that earlier?"

The Pastor's smile faded. "He turned many of my flock with his lies. If such a device was driven into Clearly's territory and the chosen faithful failed to set it off... if they were *corrupted*... then *Satan* would hold this power. I... I could not risk even the most *pure* of my brethren..." He turned away, looking into the distance, as though trying to grasp some awful theological dilemma that had plagued him for years.

In other words, he was too much of a fuckin' pussy to do it himself. Jesus motherfuckin' Christ, can't a weapon of fuckin' giant-ass destruction get some respect around here?

Cade ignored the voice behind him. Fuel-Air's voice was grating and metallic now, and interspersed with little electronic blips and whines. Cade wasn't a man who got the creeps as such, but that voice was definitely driving him close. Not to mention pissing him off.

"So why now?"

The Pastor's head snapped towards Cade's, fixing him with those eyes again. They burned, and the face beneath them snarled like a cornered rat, or maybe – hell, why not – a rattlesnake, swaying in place the instant before it struck.

"Because now is the endgame, Cade. Now is where the battle between good and evil, between the Lord and the Devil, comes to it's final end... oh, my brother, I tell you *now,* I give you the *word* that before the dawn rises, either I or the demon Doctor Clearly will be *dead...*"

His eyes narrowed, and the words hissed from cracked lips like steam.

"And San Francisco, that Satan City, will die alongside us!"

CHAPTER TWENTY-THREE

THE CONSCIENCE

Not much to say to a thing like that.

Cade just stared for a second, then looked back at the bomb. Fuel-Air looked pretty confused as well. Cade grunted, then turned back to the Pastor.

"This won't do that."

A bomb that size wasn't going to destroy San Francisco – a nuke might, but not this.

Cade didn't know what the hell the Pastor was getting at.

The Pastor looked at the floor for a second. "It's... it's enough to destroy Clearly's territory. Golden Gate Park." He muttered the words, suddenly looking smaller, like a boy caught out in a lie. Then he looked back up at Cade, defiant, his old self again. "With that Devil, that *Satan* gone, San Francisco, the city of sin, of filth, of *pre*-version, well, *that* city will no longer exist. You see?" He smiled, but his eyes twitched left and right. It wasn't a lie he'd been caught in, exactly – it was a vision. A vision of the apocalypse, an apocalypse he could bring on at his whim.

Now he was having to face up to the reality, which was that after his damned bomb went off, he was going to have to pick up the pieces and carry on, most likely.

"I... haven't decided on a new name for this city, but it *will* be one that reflects the glory of the Lord..." the Pastor tailed off, shuffling in place for a moment, then turned to the silent guards. "Brother Josiah, Brother Ezekiel, you go on and help Brother Cade load the bomb onto the truck. I... I will be praying..." He shuffled away, looking lost.

Cade wondered what kind of chink he'd just seen in the man's armour. The Pastor was on the verge of winning the war he'd set himself, or losing it decisively and for good, and in the face of that he seemed to have lost some of his fire. It left Cade wondering just how much of the Pastor was tied up in Clearly and his supposed evils, how much the Pastor needed an enemy, a Satan to battle. If he lived through what was coming, who'd he pick next?

Cade figured he knew the answer. Once his enemies to the south were all dead, the Pastor would start looking north.

To Muir Beach.

Unless the Pastor happened to be sitting on top of the bomb when it went off, mind. Cade filed that thought away for later.

Right now, he needed to be practical. He needed what was left of the Pastor's forces if he wanted to put a stop to what Clearly's love children were going to do to San Francisco and all points north. And he needed that bomb. No doubt about that.

Something occurred to him as he put his hands on the wheeled trestle and began to push it slowly and gently towards the doors. The Pastor had mentioned a truck. "My truck?"

Ezekiel – or it might have been Josiah – nodded, almost grunting the reply at him through lips that barely parted. "Ayuh. Red pickup. S'yours." He snorted and then spat mucus on the floor, as if the effort required to speak had clogged his sinuses. Cade frowned. On the one hand, it was nice to meet a fella who had the same attitude to talking as he did. On the other hand...

Damn, dog. Woody's going to be fucking pissed if you blow up his momma's pickup. Better get an excuse ready.

For a bomb, Fuel-Air had a point. Woody wasn't going to take this one too kindly.

The children watched the bomb rolling past them with wide eyes, faces lost in a kind of religious awe – *man, this is some Ark of the Fuckin' Covenant Indiana Jones shit,* said the bomb – while the womenfolk busied themselves clearing the old urine-soaked mattresses and other detritus out of the way of its path, fearfully, as if any sudden bump in the bomb's way might wake it to destructive life. Cade wondered how much jostling the bomb would be able to take. The last thing he wanted was for the damned thing to go off right there, or in the truck on the way over, although at least he wouldn't know too much about it if it did.

I'll make it quick, dog. Promise.

"Shut up, Fuel-Air," muttered Cade. One of the children gave him a strange look.

The truck was waiting for them outside. A couple of the men had gone to fetch it from where the Pastor had hidden it, and now they stood next to it, waiting to help load the bomb onto the back and then lash it down with straps and duct tape. It was a slow operation, and a delicate one, but it was done by the time one o'clock rolled around.

Cade wasn't too happy about that. Things were moving a mite too fast. If what he had in mind was going to work, the Pastor and his men needed to get a little less efficient.

He slowed things down some by making a couple of unworkable suggestions – for about a half hour they tried to fit six men onto the back of the truck, clambering gingerly over the damn bomb like it was the world's most dangerous climbing frame – but eventually the Pastor took matters into his own hands and suggested Josiah and Ezekiel ride on the truck and the other men follow on behind.

That suited Cade fine. It'd keep them at a walking pace.

By two, they were ready to set out. The sun was still high in the sky, a little too high for Cade's liking, and he thought a little on what he could do about that as he gunned the engine and peeled out, driving the truck out of the parking lot and turning down Laguna.

In the passenger seat, the Pastor clicked his tongue once, then peeled his lips back from his teeth. "Brother Cade..." He almost spat the words, like the bitter peel of some poison fruit. "Brother Cade..."

He was silent for a moment, as if weighing his words. Cade didn't speak. The truck rolled down Laguna, the few men left in the Pastor's force tramping behind, armed and ready.

Slowly, the Pastor ran his tongue over dry, cracked lips, his head slowly turning to face Cade as the scenery trundled lazily past them. "Brother Cade... I do not *lightly* treat what the Lord provides with *suspicion,* for my God is a God who provides *much,* and *mysterious,* oh yes, mysterious and *terrible* are his ways... *but.*" The sentence was cut off with clicking teeth, and there was a long pregnant pause before the soft, hissing voice resumed. "I know you hate me, Brother Cade. I know it, you need not hide the fact. You despise me and all I stand for, all of my works. All of my... *judgements.*" His slim fingers crept towards his revolver.

Cade watched out of the corner of one eye.

The truck rolled on.

"You need not hide it and you *don't,* Brother Cade, it flows out of you in waves of *disdain...* and *bile...*" He chucked, his fingers stroking the butt of the gun. "And you could no more *hide* your true nature from the Lord above, no, nor his *servant,* than you could hide a crow amongst pure white doves..." He chuckled. Ice chips cascading onto a steel coffin-lid. "As I said, I do not *question* what the Lord provides, even when He brings me a wild beast such as *you.* For His wisdom is infinite and ineffable, yes it *is,* and *not* to be questioned by fallible men. But... curiosity *compels* me." He licked his lips again, before they dragged back in that awful cracked-paper smile. "*Why* join with us, Brother Cade? Why lend your strength in the service of the Lord when your *hate* for His *glor*-ious presence is writ in you so *very* deep?"

Hell of a question.

Cade figured honesty was his best policy, or something near enough to it. Didn't change the fact he was going to have to make yet another damned speech. Cade figured he'd said more since coming into this city than in his whole life before, and it was starting to wear on him some. He was looking forward to some peace and quiet, even if it was in a grave.

"Clearly's dangerous. You ain't." He shrugged, then figured he'd best elaborate. "You ain't gonna hurt me and mine." He looked down at the Pastor's revolver, then into the Pastor's eyes, then back on the road. "Clearly will. Needs fixing."

Cade's speeches were getting a little more to the point.

The Pastor chuckled, glass knives rattling on a surgeon's tray. "A practical man. A worldly man too, oh Lord. Forgive him his great hubris." He looked over at Cade again, fingers brushing slowly over the police special, as if savouring it. "What makes you think I'll allow you to *leave*, Brother Cade?"

Cade frowned, then shrugged. "Don't try it. You've still got men living."

The Pastor stared at Cade for a moment, then nodded, bringing his fingers up to tap against one another. "But not many. The cannibals saw to that. I saw men *burn*, Brother Cade... burn for the Lord's glory, set themselves *ablaze* that we might *show* those heathens, those seekers of wealth and blood and worldly treasure and the *flesh* of men, that we might show them the *power* and the *strength* of *faith*... yes, oh Brother, of faith in the *Lord above*, the sweet Lord whose guidance and grace are *upon* us now..." He was working himself up again – he shook like a leaf on a tree, his whole body trembling for a long moment, before he flopped back in the seat and shook his head slowly, as if bringing himself out of some fugue. "Strange they should attack in force like that. They never did before." He smiled, and there was no humour in it. "Coincidence, Brother Cade?"

Cade shot the Pastor another look. He was getting sick of this. "Try. Or don't. Your call."

The Pastor raised an eyebrow, then smiled that humourless smile of his. "Why, Brother Cade, are we not *allies* in the service of the Lord?" He lapsed into silence, idly fingering the butt of the gun for a moment before crossing his arms and staring out of the window at the moving scenery.

Cade let it rest there. No sense forcing a confrontation – he was still going to need the Pastor's men, or at least need them not to start shooting just at present.

He checked his watch. Almost three, and they were just passing Post Street. Sun wouldn't be going down for another four hours, maybe five. And if they went much further they'd be in Clearly's territory, and then the shooting would start.

Hell with it.

He slammed on the brakes of the truck and turned off the engine, letting it sputter and die. The Pastor sat up straight in his seat, his hand stealing for the pistol. "Brother *Cade...*"

"Guard the truck." muttered Cade, opening the driver's side door and swinging himself out. "No cannibals left, but look out for a blue-green van. Clearly's people." He started walking, heading down to the corner where Laguna met Geary Boulevard. He turned, calling back over his shoulder at the blinking Pastor. "Gonna scout. Dangerous here. I'll fix any surprises."

The Pastor looked back suspiciously at Cade. "Be sure you do, Brother Cade." He licked his lips again, eyes flicking to the side of the road, then back. "You wouldn't be thinking of *warning* the Devil of our approach, *Brother* Cade?"

Cade shook his head, not looking back. "They'd kill me." He felt those icy eyes on his back, and wondered whether the Pastor was going to try anything. But no bullet came. He turned the corner, out of the Pastor's sight, heading down Geary.

Cade was telling the truth. Warning Clearly wouldn't do any good anyway – they'd only shoot the messenger. The love children were primed to kill him, and they'd do their damnedest to, drugs or no. What Cade needed to do right now was stall for time a little, give the sun some time to crawl across the sky. He kept one eye out for somewhere to hole up for a while, like a coffee place. His attention was nearly caught by something on the other side of the street – HALLOWEEN STORE – but then he noticed there was a coffee place a little way down and in he went. Cade figured he'd stick with what he knew.

The front window of the place was shattered, and it'd been picked clean a long time ago, but there was a clock on the wall, still keeping time. Battery powered, Cade figured. That was important – he wouldn't be able to keep an eye on the sun's position without being out in the open, and he wanted to be off the street in case the Pastor decided to send some goon to check up on him.

Wouldn't do to be caught sitting around.

Lazy-ass motherfucker.

Cade looked up, and there was Fuel-Air, dressed up in his utilities, flashing his gold tooth. His skin was black and metallic now, gleaming like the casing of a bomb. Every time Cade saw him, he was looking more malevolent, and now it was like he'd absorbed all the black metal evil of the bomb. Almost like everything bad Cade stuck his hand into was retched back up at him by Fuel-Air, grinning, chuckling, swearing, shouting Fuel-Air.

Cade wasn't a man who worried about his actions too much – at least not before he came to San Francisco. What was done was done, and there wasn't any mileage in fretting over it. But more and more, Fuel-Air was acting like...

Cade searched for the word.

... like a conscience.

Cade sure as hell didn't need one of those.

Escpecially considering what he was about to do.

Damn right you don't, asswipe. You need to be one cold, calculating motherfucker for what you got planned. You need to be the motherfuckin' Terminator. Shit, don't let all those fuckin' innocent people you're gonna wipe out...

"Not innocent," muttered Cade. And they weren't. Clearly's people took a drug every night that cut them off from any kind of moral reality, and it wasn't a coincidence that there weren't any children or old men there. They'd killed the children and the elderly and burned everything they could find to the ground, no matter how peaceful they'd been since. Their crimes were still there, waiting to come out again, and tonight they were going to walk the night like monsters. No, Clearly's people weren't innocent. No such thing as innocent in San Francisco.

Wasn't any point getting into a debate with Fuel-Air, he knew. The son of a bitch knew everything he was thinking already. But he had to say something. "They're on drugs..."

Fuckin' Nancy Reagan! Just say no, motherfuckers! Shit, you ever think not everybody in this world is fucked up the way you are? You caused this shit, dog. You walked in on a fuckin' stalemate that your new buddy, Pastor Nail-You-To-A-Fuckin'-Piece-Of-Wood, was happy to let carry on forever and a day, 'cause he didn't have fuck all else to do with himself! Shit, this place was a regular fuckin' ecosystem until you came to fuck things up...

Cade shook his head. "Wasn't like that."

Fuck it wasn't. You make things worse, dog. That's what you do. You come into a situation and make it as bloody and fiery as it's gonna get. You're a fuckin' catalyst for all the shit-fire in the fuckin' world, and you like it that way, 'cause it means you get to kill folks and call it necessity when all it is is your own fuckin' disease taking root. And you been that way ever since the day you were fuckin' born. He grinned, and belched fuel and flames from his bomb-mouth. *Shit, don't tell me you don't remember your first kill?*

Cade's mouth twitched, nearly smiling. "Sure. Bastard needed it."

Fuel-Air sneered. *You don't remember shit, dog. That wasn't your first kill, you stupid son of a bitch.*

Cade stiffened. He saw what Fuel-Air was getting at, and he didn't like it much.

Fuel-Air grinned, teeth gleaming like wires, black metal eyes narrowed.

Told you you didn't remember. He laughed, a high whine that sounded like something falling from an aeroplane.

What kind of asshole don't even remember his own mother?

CHAPTER TWENTY-FOUR

THE FIRST KILL

Cade's mother died in childbirth, of course.

She was a slight woman, thin and frail, anaemic-looking, sickly and washed out. It was a difficult birth, and though the doctors did everything they possibly could, Cade's mother passed away shortly after delivering the boy.

Cade's father was never the same after that. His name was Tobias and he worked in construction, and by all accounts he was a man possessed of both uncommon strength and uncommon gentleness, who smiled readily and often. This Cade only found out at his funeral, as Tobias had never displayed such qualities during Cade's life.

When his wife died, something broke inside Tobias, some essential part of the mechanism that ran him. Some inner gear slipped and snapped, the jagged metal teeth of it tearing at the workings of his soul, damaging them beyond any repair. He began to drink, where he never had before – beer by the case at first, and then when that failed to quiet his demons, rotgut whisky. To begin with, his sister cared for the boy while Tobias went on his benders, and she was one of the few who could calm the man when he came crashing through the door, howling and yelling, hitting out with fists as strong as brick at anyone unlucky enough to get within ten feet of him.

Cade was thus spared more than an occasional beating from his father, although perhaps it was a blow to the head, delivered at full strength, which landed him a month's stay in a hospital – and this before his first birthday – that accounted for what he became later in life. More likely, he simply absorbed the atmosphere of that first home, a trailer on the edge of a small town near El Paso.

He grew up quiet – so quiet that most thought him retarded – and serious, a little boy who said nothing but observed much.

After he'd turned six, his father's sister died. There were some, mostly those few friends she'd kept after moving in with her brother, who said Tobias had worried her into her grave with his drinking and his rages and with the strain of looking after his boy, who surely suffered from autism if not worse – although most treated it as an unavoidable tragedy. Tobias laid the blame elsewhere. On returning from the funeral, tears rolling down his cheeks and a bottle of rotgut in his hand, he had told the boy that he'd murdered twice now, that he was born a killer and a killer he'd remain. Then he beat his hide black and blue with a leather belt.

Despite this, Tobias remained popular with the construction crew. His drinking was limited to after hours, and he gave little hint of any problems at home, making sure his boy wore long sleeves and hid the bruises when he came around to the site after school. His job was never in danger – in fact, before much time had passed, he found himself promoted to foreman. Success in his career didn't limit his drinking – in fact, it only made him drink more, because there was more to spend on it. Somehow, he always managed to drag himself to work every morning and put in a full day.

It was as if the time spent beating his only child gave him strength.

The boy was hospitalised four times over the next two years, but nothing was said. If a doctor did suspect that the broken bones and contusions were caused by something other than a fall down the stairs – despite the fact that there were no stairs in the trailer – he either kept his own counsel on the matter or was unable to break through the twin walls of Tobias' denial and Cade's deep silence to find the truth.

It was clear, in other words, that this was a problem Cade would have to solve himself, despite being all of eight years old.

Time passed, and every day after school Cade would wander down to the site to watch his father work, waiting for Tobias to finish working so they could go home, where the drink and the belt waited. Sometimes he skipped school, so as to watch his father and the construction crew work through the whole day. There was no punishment for playing truant beyond what his father already did to him.

The men enjoyed the strange, silent boy's company – they ruffled his hair and joked amongst themselves about how the boy was touched. His father joked with them, keeping his anger for later.

Cade just watched.

He especially liked to watch when they got the big tarmac spreader, and spread the hot black tarmac over the foundations to make a parking lot or a driveway, and then rolled the big steamroller over it to make it flat. He watched that very carefully. He had very good eyes, for a boy of eight years old.

Then, one by one, the men would leave, and only his father would be left, checking through paperwork and time cards and then locking the site up for the day. He'd either take Cade with him to the bar, where the drunks and the rummies would ruffle his hair and say how the boy was touched while his father drank himself stupid on rye, or he'd just drag the boy back to the trailer and beat the shit out of him before going to the bar.

Either way, Cade could count on at least a few cracks of the leather belt, and probably a hard kicking with a steel toed work boot into the bargain.

This he tolerated until one day at the end of November.

The construction crew were building a new supermarket on the edge of the town, with a parking lot out front and another behind. They poured the tarmac for the first lot, and rolled it flat with the steamroller, and then it was clocking-off time and the men filed out. Marty Callaghan, who drove the steamroller, ruffled Cade's hair. "Poor fella's touched," he said, whereupon Cade hugged him tight – a gesture he'd not made before, and one that caused no end of laughter among the men. "I ain't your daddy, son," said Marty, chuckling. "Your daddy's over there." And he pointed to Tobias, who was standing in front of the steamroller, a blueprint in his hand, making a careful check of the equipment and what there was still to be done before he clocked off.

Cade knew where his daddy was, all right.

Marty Callaghan wasn't just the man who drove the steamroller. He was also, in his youth, what the papers had called a juvenile delinquent, and one of his souvenirs of that wild time in his life was a switchblade knife with a skull carved on the handle in ivory, still as sharp as ever. Marty occasionally liked to show it off, flicking out the deadly blade for the appreciation of his co-workers.

Cade liked to watch him do that.

Soon, all the crew were gone, and Cade looked around himself for a moment, then picked up a loose chuck of brick and wandered down onto the fresh-laid tarmac to say hello to his father.

"Dad?" he said. It was the first time he'd said a single word in about seven months.

Tobias hadn't kept count.

"Not now, boy." he said, not looking up from his blueprint. "Not now, you little –"

That was when Marty's switchblade, which Cade had carefully lifted from his pocket, severed Tobias' left Achilles tendon, and he went down like a ton of bricks, screaming at the top of his lungs. Cade swung the chunk of brick in his other hand and hit his father in the side of the temple with a hard clunk. Enough to put him out.

Then he turned his attention to the steamroller.

He'd lifted Marty's keys from his pocket along with the knife, and he'd watched closely enough over the past months to have a good understanding of how the steamroller was operated. He managed to get it going without too much fuss.

Then he set it rolling.

The big roller moved slowly, rumbling the ground, and Tobias actually had time to wake up out of his daze, although by that time the great steel roller was less than three feet away from him. There was no way he could crawl or roll out of the way in time.

"Jesus!" he screamed. *"Jesus Christ, what the holy fuck are you doing? I'm your father, god dammit! Your father! Your –"*

He didn't say anything else after that. Just screamed.

The roller crunched over his feet first, rupturing the flesh and splintering the bone to fragments, and then slowly crushed the rest of him. Tobias was still alive when the pressure burst his belly open and sent his guts flying, and he may even have been conscious when the hideous weight crunched his ribcage to powder and his heart with it, though that seems unlikely.

Cade waited until the roller had rumbled right over him, and then switched it off, and left the keys in it, and wandered home to the trailer that was now his alone.

He kept the knife.

You killed your Mom and then you ran your Pops over with a steamroller, after you'd driven your Auntie to an early grave. Heartwarming fuckin' story, dog.

Cade nodded. Things had gotten a lot better after that. The orphanage was a pretty decent place if you were willing to get your knuckles a little dirty, and Cade had been more than willing. After they kicked him out, it was a pretty average story – gangs, robbery with violence, a murder here and there. Eventually, the marines had offered him something close to a reason for living, or he'd felt that way at the time.

Bullshit. They just offered you a way to kill a shitload of people without any comeback, that's all. Don't kid yourself you were there for the reasons any other motherfucker was, bitch.

Cade blinked, and looked at the clock. Getting on for half six. The Pastor'd be stewing, and the sun would be getting ready to go down. Probably they were all screwing in the Park by now.

Best to get a move on.

But there was something he had to get done first.

"Won't be needing you for this next bit, Fuel-Air."

Fuel-Air sneered, the metal skin glinting as he leaned forward. *Sure you don't. Want to commit your fuckin' atrocity in peace, right? Fuck you, dog. You're stuck with me, motherfucker, and I'm going to be on your fuckin' back until the day you die about every god-damn fuck-up you--*

Cade took the gun out of his belt.

It was a Magnum .44, big and mean. Cade wasn't a fan of guns, but he'd figured he'd need one that's do the job.

Fuel-Air stared at it, stunned. *Where the fuck did you get that?*

Cade shrugged. "Does it matter?"

Fuel-Air snarled, and suddenly his face was a writhing, suppurating mass of maggots, crawling and slithering over one another, a boiling, oozing sea of putrefaction that seemed to burn into Cade's vision.

You called me up, motherfucker, don't you get it? You brought me out. I'm part of you, you stupid-ass son of a bitch, and I'm never fucking letting you be, not ever again – shit, dog, you honestly think you can put a bullet in me? A fuckin' bullet? You can't do shit. Let me draw you a picture, bitch – you snapped on that fuckin' road you were nailed to, you broke like fuckin' glass. Shit, it ain't no surprise, you know what I'm saying? You had to go a little crazy or a lot crazy, and I'm the crazy you went. I'm your fucking delusion, dog, your bloody conscience, the part of you that doesn't let you get away with this kind of fucking bullshit...

Cade nodded, and shrugged. Wasn't something he hadn't figured out, after all.

So what are you going to do with that fuckin' piece of yours, bitch? Shoot me? I'm a figment of your motherfucking imagination!

"Yeah." Cade shrugged again. Then his eyes narrowed. "So's the gun."

The roar of the Magnum filled the room, and Fuel-Air flew backwards as the bullet hit him right between the eyes. For a moment he didn't look like Fuel-Air. He looked like Sergeant A, or maybe the Captain, or maybe Duke, or maybe his father, or maybe all of them at once. Then his head burst like an over-ripe melon and his body slumped down the wall in a trail of old corpse-blood.

Cade put the gun down on the table, then leant back for a moment and closed his eyes.

When he opened them, there was no body. There was no gun. There was just Cade, sitting in a coffee shop, watching a clock on the wall.

Okay, then.

On the way out, he caught a glimpse of something just across the street. HALLOWEEN STORE. This time he paid a little closer attention.

The glass was smashed, but there was plenty still in the front window of the store, waiting to be taken. Cade guessed there wasn't much call for anything a Halloween store might sell. The whole damn world was Halloween now.

He wondered what it was that kept drawing his eye, and then he saw it, sitting on a polystyrene head, dead centre. The whole plan fell into his head right there. It was crazy – maybe the craziest thing Cade had considered in his whole time in San Francisco, and that was saying a hell of a lot.

Still, he figured it couldn't be that crazy.

After all, Cade wasn't crazy anymore.

When Cade got back to the pickup, the bomb was just a bomb.

The Pastor didn't like being kept waiting. His face was dark as a thunderstorm and his fingers drummed the dashboard in a slow, deliberate pattern while he read through a pocket Bible. His men were slouched around the pickup, cocking and uncocking whatever guns they had like a bunch of kids playing cops and robbers. Cade wondered if they'd done anything sensible with the guns, like cleaning them or sharing out ammo, or if they'd just played and posed with them a while, trying to psyche themselves up for what was ahead, feel a little badass.

He wondered what the rate of misfires was going to be. If he knew anything at all about guns, those ones were going to jam after the first shot.

Hell with it. He'd find out soon enough.

"Brother *Cade*," hissed the Pastor, curling his lip back from his teeth in a cold, mocking sneer, "You've returned to us. I will *confess*, Brother, for a moment I took it in my mind to *doubt* you, even to wonder if you had de-*sert*-ed the true path of –"

Cade got behind the wheel and gunned the engine. "No time. Tell your men to run. Not got long. Sunset came quicker than I figured." That was a lie, of course. Cade had timed it damn near perfect.

The Pastor looked at him a moment, as if he didn't quite comprehend, and Cade wondered how much he'd found out about Clearly's people and their nightly cycle of free love and free hate. Cade didn't figure there was much point in explaining it. The point wasn't for them to live through this, after all.

"They're vulnerable. Let's go." Cade put her in gear and drove the truck forward at a clip, heading down Laguna, keeping just fast enough that the men behind had to run to keep up, but not fast enough to lose them. Not yet.

Cade looked to the passenger seat, and saw that the Pastor had the detonator clutched in his hand, his thumb caressing the button that would blow the both of them sky-high with one press. Not the best situation to work with.

Hell with it. It was what he had.

This was the endgame. This was where everything came to a head, for better or for worse.

If he was lucky, he was about to murder the city of San Francisco once and for all. The thought didn't bother him overmuch. In fact, he was starting to feel a hell of a lot more like his old self.

His palms didn't even itch any more. The corners of his mouth twitched slightly, almost, but not quite, a smile.

Then he gunned the engine, and turned right, heading down Haight Street towards the Golden Gate Park, and the not-quite-human things that were waiting there for him.

CHAPTER TWENTY-FIVE

THE ENDGAME

Haight Street in twilight.

In the end, it was all about the timing. If Cade hadn't killed a few hours in that coffee shop, they'd have hit Haight in the middle of the afternoon, breezing right into Clearly's territory just when it was busiest. That would've started a firefight – the Pastor's men would've held their own right up until they ran out of bullets, and then the mob would've torn them apart, or maybe the Pastor would've pressed his button and gone out in a blaze of glory first. Either way, most of Clearly's people would've made it out – only they'd have been even more ready to burn anything they saw.

If he'd left it any longer than now, the drugged-out mob of love children would've been long gone, most likely slipping right past them on the way to burn the Pastor's territory to the ground along with anybody left in it. Then they'd march on Muir

Woods, most likely. Even if they didn't decide to head straight for Muir Beach, they'd most likely start the worst damned forest fire California had ever seen. It's a wonder they hadn't done that before, and Cade didn't want to take the risk twice.

No, the time to get onto Haight Street was now, with the sun just starting to dip down, and the shadows starting to lengthen. The streets were deserted, but Cade knew the love children were there, all around them, naked, without a thought in their heads but making love... but waiting, deep down, for the shadows to lengthen, for that switch inside their heads to flip.

Any time now.

He kept the pickup truck moving, watching the men running behind in the rear view mirror, noticing they were starting to sweat, panting a little, falling behind. These weren't the Pastor's best physical specimens – just what was left after the war with the cannibals. They weren't soldiers, and they damn sure weren't used to marching double-time.

To the west, the sun was beginning to lower itself below the buildings. The shadows were starting to fall.

The Pastor snapped to attention, his finger hovering over the button on the detonator. "What was that noise?"

His eyes swivelled, staring, while his head turned this way and that. Cade might have smiled, if Cade was a smiling man.

As it was, the corners of his mouth twitched again.

Just once.

"I thought I heard someone... *say* something." He muttered it, almost under his breath, looking to and fro, sweat beading. "Lord, Lord, be my shield in this time of danger..." His finger shook above the button. Cade reached out and gently gripped his wrist, shaking his head slowly.

"Not yet."

The Pastor looked at him for a long moment, then nodded and swallowed. He was scared, Cade could tell – terrified, in fact. Cade figured he was starting to flash back to the last time he was in enemy territory. That had ended with him being tortured for years in a bamboo cage. This might end worse – after all, as far as the Pastor was concerned, each and every man and woman in this part of town was a devil in human form, one of Satan's own, capable of any act of evil.

Cade frowned. He might be right at that. Cade hadn't exactly given the flower children any reason to be peaceful.

"Someone *did* say something! I heard it!" the Pastor hissed, eyes bright. Behind the truck, his men slowed, looking all around them, slick fingers holding wobbling guns that waved in all directions, trying to cover everywhere at once. The Pastor's face was glistening with cold, slippery sweat. "What are they *saying?*"

It was getting darker. Cade could hear it himself, now.

The chant.

"Helter skelter." he whispered, and felt the Pastor's wrist jerk in his grip. "Don't touch it. Not yet."

The Pastor pulled his hand away, lips curling into a snarl –

– and then they attacked.

It was like a swarm. A good two dozen of them, naked as the day they were born, crashing through doorways, snaking from around corners, a couple even hurling furniture through shop windows and launching themselves through the broken panes, cutting their feet on the glass as they landed. Two dozen men and women with foaming, twisted mouths, veins throbbing, faces red and contorted. Some held knives, improvised cudgels – most just had their fists.

The Pastor was white. *"Satan's children –"* he hissed, his finger jabbing down towards the detonator. Cade reached out and grabbed his wrist just in time, twisting it around hard. He heard the bones in the wrist snap first, then a tearing sound as the elbow joint popped. The Pastor screamed, and Cade took the opportunity to wrest the detonator out of his other hand and slam it in the glove box. Hopefully it wouldn't rattle too much. He shot the Pastor a look.

"Told you not to."

Some fools never took a telling.

He slammed on the gas.

The pickup truck roared forward, the front bumper crashing into a red-headed girl and sending her tumbling off to the side, bones broken. Any other of the love children in the way had the sense to get out, although some poor bastard tried to grab hold of the passenger side mirror and got a face full of road rash for his trouble.

In the mirror, Cade could see the small band of the Pastor's men, out of breath and left behind, firing wildly into the crowd, dropping two, three, four – then disappearing under the rest. They weren't soldiers and they didn't know how to carry a gun or keep it from getting taken away, and they sure as hell didn't know how to deal with an army of psychopaths who didn't give a damn whether they got shot or not. They'd dealt with the cannibals, but the love children were a hell of a lot worse than them – at least the cannibals had some self-preservation to them. Not to mention brain damage. The love children had that perfect mix of madness and intelligence, and that was what made them so damned dangerous.

Cade watched as the melee dwindled in the rear view mirror, a severed head arcing lazily up from the centre of the pack. Tough break for somebody. He turned his attention to the road ahead.

So much for the Pastor's army. Still left the two goons with the machine pistols up top – Cade could hear the low, growling *bra-a-aap* of the weapons being fired. The two bodyguards were shooting back at the crowd behind them, for all the good that'd do now. Hell, Zeke and Josiah were probably blowing their own people apart as much as they were Clearly's. They'd be better off firing ahead – Cade was veering through a slalom of love children, all bursting out of the surrounding buildings screaming their battle cry.

"Helter skelter!"

"Helter skelter!"

"Helter skelter!"

Cade kept ploughing into the sons of bitches, and every time one of them went under the truck the whole damn thing shook and he could hear that detonator rattling around in the glove box. Those assholes needed to be shooting in front, clearing a path. As it stood, all they were was extra weight throwing off his driving.

Cade took a second to chew over whether he actually needed those guns or not. Most likely they hadn't been cleaned or treated right in months, so they were going to jam any second, and besides there was the problem of getting them off the idiot twins up top. Hell with it. Cade figured he was better off without them.

This plan, such as it was, had come nearly full-formed into Cade's head when he'd seen what he'd seen in the window of the Halloween Store, but it was still about half actual planning and half improvisation, and this was one of the improvisation parts. Every time he heard that glove box rattle, he was about a split-second away from getting blown sky high.

In the seat next to him, the Pastor was clutching at the side of the seat with his good hand, while the other dangled uselessly at his side, twitching occasionally. His eyes were squeezed tight shut, and his lips were moving in what looked like a prayer. Cade figured he needed it.

This was likely to be tight.

He spun the wheel, sending the truck into a skid, the tyres already slippery with blood – jackknifing the whole rig and spinning it like a top. Zeke and Josiah hadn't had any warning, and, unlike the bomb, they weren't secured. They went down like a couple of ninepins, tumbling off the flatbed of the truck, skidding across the road, the Uzis slipping out of their hands as the roadway tore swathes of skin off of them. Cade fought the wheel, prolonging the skid, inhaling burning rubber and blood, feeling the shock run through the steering column as something burst under his back wheel and the whole truck lurched sideways – he had a glimpse of Zeke in one of the mirrors, head pulped flat by one of the rear wheels – and then he was pulling out of it, getting back control, gunning the truck up Broderick. Behind him, in the rear view mirror, he could see one of the love children screaming their mantra, the Uzi in her hand blazing like a string of firecrackers as it pumped bullets into Josiah's chest. The gun misfired just before he swung the truck left, the tyres screeching again as he drifted onto Oak Street, heading for Golden Gate Park.

When he had a mind to, Cade could drive one hell of a mean truck.

The streets were swarming with the love children now, and Cade figured they were primed to go after outsiders. He hoped so, anyhow. Still, it seemed like a fair guess. The second they saw the pickup, they stopped clawing and punching at each other and ran in his direction, lips curled into bloody clown grins, howling at the top of their lungs. "Helter skelter! *Helter skelter!*" Cade had to fight the wheel to keep from crashing into them and wrecking the truck right there. He didn't know how many more full-on impacts it could stand, and the bastards seemed to have a habit of bouncing off the bonnet. It was already dented all to hell. Cade hoped he could explain it to Woody.

The Pastor was crying now, scrabbling at the gun in the holster at his side. Cade didn't know whether the Pastor wanted to shoot him or shoot himself, but either way he wasn't going to let that happen. He reached over, quick as a snake, and grabbed the gun from the Pastor's trembling hand, tossing it out of the window.

"Fetch!" he yelled, and a couple of the love children did just that, hurling themselves after the gun like dogs. They weren't too far gone to know what could kill.

"Satan." sobbed the Pastor, fat tears rolling down his face. Cade almost felt a pang of sympathy for the man. This was the battle he'd spent two years waiting for, the final confrontation against the devil he'd built up in his mind, and in one hot second Cade had taken it for himself, like a director stealing the leading man's part on the first night of the play. "Oh, Satan, why do you *torment* me?" The words were whined between hitching breaths.

"Be over soon." muttered Cade, keeping one hand on the wheel as he skidded the speeding truck between the Clearlyites, keeping one eye on the crowd building in the rear view mirror. Word spread fast, and they were running like a stampede of rats, like the casts of three horror movies at once, just waiting for the truck to spin out or flip over so they could tear it open like a turtle's shell and rip out the meat. His other hand reached into his pocket for what he'd got from the Halloween store. For half a second, he was almost sorry he'd had to kill Fuel-Air the second time. He might've gotten the reference.

They're selling hippie wigs in Woolworth's, man.

Keeping the truck steady, Cade pulled on the shaggy blond wig – a cross between a seventies rock star and some kind of show dog – and then covered his own beard with a larger, shaggier one the same blond. It wasn't about to fool anyone, even in the twilight, but he was counting on the Pastor to help him out with that.

Cade was a brutal man. He was a man who'd kill at the drop of a hat, without even breathing hard. He was a man who'd shot his own conscience in the face so he could murder easier when it came time to. But that didn't mean he couldn't be smart.

And it sure as hell didn't mean he couldn't be sneaky.

He unlocked the glove box and grabbed the detonator.

Ahead of him, he could make out the gates of Golden Gate Park, and just inside them, another massive crowd, easily as big as the one running to catch him up. He could make out Clearly, standing at the front, facing the crowd with his back turned to the truck, yelling about something. Some reason to set them moving. Cade figured he'd taken a dose of his own drug – from this distance, he looked like a fire and brimstone preacher, not so different from the Pastor at that. Cade had figured they'd turn out to be the same in the end.

Cade knew what Clearly was saying, even without hearing the words. He was giving them a direction to follow, a target to burn, the way he had when the bad times had come the first time around. He was being the ruler, the man in charge, the Daddy, letting his children play outside to keep them from wrecking the furniture. Oh, it was all for the good of the people. It was all excellent therapy. They needed it. It was the only way the community could survive. There were a hundred excuses you could make, but at the end they were all just more bullshit from Doctor Len Clearly, PhD.

Hell with that.

"There he is, Pastor," growled Cade. "This is it."

The Pastor blinked, sniffling, then straightened in his seat. Some of the old fire seemed to creep back into him, the serpentine bastard who'd nailed Cade to the street and killed anyone he didn't agree with.

Cade figured a man should die as he lived. "Go on." he muttered. "Let him know."

The Pastor breathed in hard, a snuffling, snot-filled breath, then screamed as Cade gunned the engine, his eyes almost popping from their sockets, face red, mucus flying from his throat with the force of the shout.

"SAAATAAAAAAAN!"

Cade hit the accelerator hard, slamming his foot to the floor, hurling the truck forward at the maximum speed, heading right for the Doctor.

The truck hit Clearly first, snapping his legs like twigs and cracking his pelvis with a sound like a gunshot, sending him flying over the bonnet until his head smashed through the windscreen, almost landing in the Pastor's lap as the truck ploughed into the crowd, crashing into three dozen bodies with the force of a sledgehammer smashing into a box of breadsticks.

Carnage wasn't the word.

"Satan!" screamed the Pastor, howling at the top of his lungs as Clearly blinked up at him, blood beginning to seep from his open mouth, somehow still conscious. *"Satan! I know you! Devil! Spawn of the goat! I know you! I know your works! Your time is come and into hellfire will you be delivered! Satan, the time is come! The time is NOW!"*

The love children had a habit of turning on outsiders, and Cade figured you couldn't get much further outside than that. He popped his seatbelt and checked his wig was straight, then started yelling at the top of his lungs.

"HELTER SKELTER! HELTER SKELTER! HELTER SKELTER!"

In the movies, there's often a part of a plan that involves something being done 'in the confusion'. Cade had never actually been in a confusion before, but he'd been in a clusterfuck, and he understood them pretty well.

He rolled out of the truck, and then started kicking and punching at it, driving his fist through the side window, shrieking like a madman. "HELTER SKELTER! HELTER SKELTER! HELTER

SKELTER!"

Cade figured pretty much everybody in this crowd hated his guts about as much as they hated the Pastor's. If the Pastor was sitting in the truck that'd just mown half their people down, screaming his Jesus talk at the top of his lungs, Cade figured they'd pay less attention to the blond dude who looked a bit like some other dude they hated. Especially if they were fucked up on Clearly's compound. Cade had been on it and he hadn't even recognised himself, never mind anyone else.

Oh, if Cade had tried a stunt like that on his own, they'd have torn him into pieces, no doubt about it. They'd have hung his guts from the railings and played softball with his skull.

But the Pastor made a pretty damn good distraction. He had his good hand locked around Clearly's throat now, trying to strangle him before he died of his internal injuries. He looked like he might do it, too.

"Satan! Oh horned goat! Oh corruptor! Oh scavenger of men's souls! I know you! I know your stench and your rot and I will END you –"

Clearly was staring out, eyes bulging, looking right into the Pastor's, and the Pastor was the only one to see what look Clearly wore as he went to his grave. Confused, maybe. Sad. Apologetic. Raging with the fury of his own drug. Any of those might have done.

Clearly's shattered legs weaved and twitched on the bonnet like a spastic doll.

Hell of an undignified way to go, Cade figured.

The crowd seemed to agree. They rushed at the truck, pushing each other back to get at it, tearing at the doors and windows, reaching in like zombies in a motion picture, trying to claw Clearly free and tear the Pastor apart. Cade let himself be muscled back, shoved out of the way by the love children. He kept on yelling, trying to get the timbre right, to keep that cracked edge of madness in his voice. "Helter skelter! Helter skelter!"

Then he just dropped back, heading towards the west side of the park, making as good a pace as he could without drawing attention. He figured pretty much all of the love children would be swarming around the truck soon enough, trampling each other for the chance to take vengeance on the Pastor, never mind that he'd not even been driving.

He could still hear the Pastor screaming in his maddened voice, yelling about danger and terror and lust, howling like a banshee. There was pain in those cries, now – Cade figured they'd got their hands on him and they were tearing him out of that truck piece by piece.

He figured he'd got about eighty metres away from the truck now, but with a Fuel-Air Bomb that was definitely danger close. And then some.

"Oh lord! Oh spare me the torments of hell! Didn't your servant do right, oh lord, oh god... Dei! Dei! Deiiiii!"

The voice drifting over the screaming roar of the crowd was an agonised shriek, bubbling up out of a throat full of blood. The Pastor had about run out of time.

So had Cade.

As soon as the Pastor's body was cold, they'd look around them and go for the next outsider, and hippie wig or not, that was him. Hell, even if they didn't, they'd scatter in all directions, and then next night they'd probably do it all over again.

He thought about what they'd likely do with Woody and the Duchess.

A hundred metres.

Still danger close.

Cade saw the Pastor's head shoot up into the air, ripped off of his body, a length of spine flapping out of the neck. They were playing football with it.

Hell with it, thought Cade, I guess danger close really is coward talk after all.

He pressed the button.

CHAPTER TWENTY-SIX

AND THEN

THE SKY BURST OPEN
AND A HAND OF SOLID FIRE
SMASHED HIM TO THE GROUND.

CHAPTER TWENTY-SEVEN

THE AFTERMATH

He came to three days later.

Or it may have been four.

He'd got third degree burns over a fair amount of his body, probably more than a man should have and still be walking or even breathing. In other places, the skin was cracked and leaking something that looked like pus. He was blind in his right eye, which was a smashed, shapeless blob of jelly oozing from the socket. There was a constant ringing in his ears that, in the end, took a full three weeks to go away. He'd lost two of the fingers on his left hand. His eyebrows and most of his beard and the hair on his head had been singed clean off.

He was halfway down Nineteenth Avenue, and everything on all sides was a blackened ruin. He had no idea how he'd gotten there or what he was doing there.

He stood, swaying, blinking with his one good eye, and ran a dry, sandpaper tongue over cracked lips.

After a couple of minutes, he remembered what his name was.

Cade.

Then the blackness rushed up to claim him all over again.

He wasn't sure how much time passed, but when he opened his eyes he could have sworn the Duchess was standing over him, soaking a cool sponge loaded with ice water over his skin, and he was seeing her with two eyes.

Then he blinked, and realised that everything was flat and a little blurred and his skin was in agony. The pain came in waves, washing over him like chips of broken glass rubbing into his flesh. Hadn't there been a fella with a laugh like broken glass at one time? A laugh like broken glass and a walk like a snake. Cade maybe killed him, or somebody else did. Probably Cade.

Cade winced. His head was like crazy paving, one thought running into another. It came to him that he was in a coffee shop somewhere, which made sense. He seemed to pass a lot of time in coffee shops. He realised he was laying on his side, on a leather bench that was sticking to his suppurating, pus-coated skin. That didn't make as much sense, on account of every time he moved, the leather tugged at him. Moving hurt so much that he figured he should just pass out again. Pass out and maybe not wake up this time.

He tried for a while, but he couldn't.

Hell with it.

Somehow, Cade got himself onto his feet and wandered into a back room. He didn't see any corpses around, and that meant something, but he wasn't sure exactly what right at the moment.

On a table in the back room, there were bandages and antiseptic, and some kind of shiny hinged blades that Cade couldn't remember the name of. Handle-blades. Finger-blades. Dammit. Skin-blades. Skin-saws. Scythe-saws. Something close.

Scissors. That was it.

He looked at them for almost a minute.

Then he blacked out again.

The first couple of weeks were like that.

It was kind of a wonder that Cade didn't lie down and die at any point during this, but Cade wasn't the lying down and dying type, even in as much pain as he was in. Gradually, agonisingly, his body started to put itself back together, and his mind followed suit.

Somehow, he managed to keep his burns from killing him and do what he needed to do to bandage and treat them. To begin with, he did this using the contents of medicine cabinets and whatever drugs he could scrounge from other places, but after a while he was spending whatever time he could stand on his feet scavenging around Haight Street and the surrounding blocks, looking for any storehouses of medical supplies Clearly might have had. The Park was a ruin, of course, and big sections of Stanyan Street, Oak Street, Fell Street... it was a big blast, and it'd damaged a hell of a lot of the area. Cade still wasn't sure how he'd survived it.

Hand of a generous God, he figured.

He knew there were a couple of the love children left – he hadn't got all of them with the Pastor's bomb – but whenever he saw them they were wandering the streets like broken dolls whose clockwork had yet to come to a halt. It took him a day or two to realise that anyone who knew where Clearly's compound was stockpiled had taken their knowledge into the grave with them.

After a while, he didn't see the love children anymore. They just wandered away, whether to start again somewhere new or just to die away from the memories of their strange, good, evil community, Cade didn't know.

He didn't much care, either.

The last love child he saw on the streets was Thelma. He came across her suddenly – just a matter of turning the corner and seeing her at the other end of the street. She was looking broken – she'd lost an eye too, and it looked like she had a broken arm – but instead of running, or cursing him, like the other flower children did, she'd smiled, and raised something up in her hand.

The burnt remains of a blond wig.

"I told you!" she yelled at him, laughing. *"Disguises! I told you!"*

Then she ran around the corner, laughing giddily, as if the world had just begun to make sense.

He never saw any of the love children again.

It was another week before he found Clearly's medical stores, in a warehouse just outside the blast radius on Frederick street, complete with an eighteen-wheeler sitting outside. The Doc had been right – there was enough insulin there for hundreds of people, maybe thousands.

Enough to keep the Duchess going until she died of old age, Cade figured, and he'd still have enough space left in the trailer for some other bits and pieces that'd come in handy.

Of course, he couldn't load it as quickly as he'd have liked to, not in his condition. Time was, it'd have taken him less than a day to fill the damn thing top to bottom, but now it was a full week of agonising labour as every inch of his body screamed at him, every damn box of insulin like hefting blazing lava against his burned flesh. Loading that damned eighteen-wheeler up was like a punishment from the depths of Hell, and Cade was still messed up enough in his mind to wonder if he hadn't ended up there, if the Pastor hadn't been right. If he hadn't damned himself by standing against the snake-legged little bastard. Cade had never in his whole damned life been in so much pain.

Cade being Cade, he loaded the damned thing anyway.

And then he spent a couple of days sleeping, drinking any whisky he could find and getting ready to find the gasoline.

Another week, or near as. Five and a half days of trudging

from gas station to gas station, all over San Francisco, trying to find ones that hadn't burned to the ground, ones that still had gas in pumps or in cans, and the right kind of gas for an eighteen-wheeler at that. And on those rare occasions he found it, Cade had to drag it back to Frederick Street in the hot sun, with every muscle screaming at him.

Hell with it. Cade figured he could rest when he got back to Muir Beach.

In the end, he got most of the gas he needed from the Pastor's people, or what was left of them. It was just women and children now, as well as a couple of shaky-looking fellas, the people who'd cracked during the battle with the cannibals. When Cade limped back into the supermarket parking lot, he was greeted like some kind of returning royalty, and they pretty much let him take what he wanted. Things were changing a little – they had clean mattresses now, and he saw one kid with a colouring book, and another with a GI Joe figure. A woman named Emily was the head of the community, and she was talking a lot about planting seeds and raising some kind of crop. And about Jesus, too. Cade figured it was better than nothing at all.

After he'd fueled up the rig, and checked the engine over, and loaded the trailer, and gotten a couple days rest to make sure he wasn't going to pass out on the way back to Muir Beach, Cade figured it was about time to go. He'd seen enough of San Francisco, and he had a strong feeling San Francisco had seen enough of him, given that he'd killed about ninety-eight per cent of it with his own two hands.

He threw the eighteen-wheeler into gear, coaxing the engine into life and feeling the vibration of it rush through the leather seats of the cab and into his body. It was painful, sure – pretty much anything was going to be painful for at least the next year – but it felt pretty damned good, all the same. Gave Cade the feeling of a job well done. The roar of that engine was as good a note as any to end on, at least the way Cade figured it.

Still, there was an itch in him – something that went deeper than the crawling feeling of his burned skin as the hot leather hummed underneath him.

It wasn't like he'd had fun, exactly. He'd been carved up, staked out, damn near fed to a bear, blown up, drugged and had his shoulder cried on a couple times, which he wasn't used to.

But.

Cade thought about the routine of life in Muir Beach. Whittling down wood. Screwing the Duchess every day. Playing solitaire. A beer with Woody once a week.

It could be a lot worse, Cade figured. That wasn't a bad routine at all for a man to have.

Cade sighed.

No killing, though.

He'd have to get used to that.

Halfway across the Golden Gate Bridge, Cade realised he owed Woody a new pickup truck and he was going to have to go get one from somewhere.

He figured San Diego.

THE END

AL EWING'S written a mess of stuff over the years. He wrote a couple of novels before – *El Sombra* and *I, Zombie,* they were called. Mainly, though, he writes for comic books. He's one of the fellas who write that *Judge Dredd* – never much cared for it myself, though I did see the film once. He's not much of a man, or much of a God, come to think of it. But he tries, and I guess when all's said and done that's the important thing.

THE AFTERBLIGHT CHRONICLES

BROKEN ARROW

PAUL KANE

ISBN: 978-1-906735-27-2

UK RELEASE: November 2009
US RELEASE: February 2010

£6.99/$7.99

WWW.ABADDONBOOKS.COM

CHAPTER ONE

It was a blood moon. A hunter's moon.

And she was most definitely being hunted. As she ran down the road, almost slipping on the icy surface, she looked over her shoulder. She couldn't see her pursuer, but she knew he was there – and he was close.

The light from above gave the snow-covered streets a crimson tinge. She pushed on, dodging the rusted carcasses of vehicles that hadn't been used in an age. Not since before the world went to Hell – and you could actually believe you *were* there tonight. Once this road would have been jam-packed with motorists making their way through the city. Now it was simply full of memories and ghosts.

It was a different place, and it wasn't safe anymore to be out at this time of night. She knew that, yet she'd ventured out anyway. Clutching the bag containing a half dozen cans she'd managed to scavenge from various shop, she was beginning to wonder if it had been worthwhile. After this amount of time most of it had already been picked over by the starving survivors of the virus.

There weren't that many, granted, but they'd been living on their wits and whatever they could find for a long while.

Folk had raided houses first, homes on the outskirts – rather than head into the towns and cities; because gangs of thugs had banded together there, hoarding the lion's share of food and other items. Only those stealthy enough to creep in and out could get away with it.

Or at least that had been the case before...

Word had reached people far and wide that the gangs were no longer in control. That they were being driven out. Whether it was true or not, nobody could confirm, but when people are hungry enough they'll believe anything. She'd believed it. And she'd risked her life because of it.

Now she was paying the price. She ran as fast as she could, skidding as she turned a corner, legs everywhere. Looking up, she saw it: a dark shape on top of a hill, the edges defined by that glowing red sphere above. A castle, that was the very heart of this city. For a moment she considered making for it, but she knew she'd find no refuge there. Whoever was following just out of sight would surely follow her there, too. Then she'd be trapped.

Might be help up there? Might be someone who could –

She shook her head. There was no-one living there, no lights, not a sign of life at all. No, her best bet was to try and lose them in the narrow streets.

Cocking her head, she heard the footfalls behind – boots crunching the snow. She had to keep moving, didn't have long before they caught up with her. Pulling the bag in closer to her chest, like a mother cradling her baby, she ran down the nearest street, into the labyrinth: a warren made up of houses that seemed to be leaning in and watching her progress. It shouldn't be too hard to get lost in here, to hide until the hunter had passed by.

Another quick glance over her shoulder told her it would be harder than she thought. Now she saw him, and the fact that he was revealing himself meant the hunt was almost at an end.

The man was wearing a hood, which prevented her from getting a good look at his face. But the hood was only part of his attire, attached to a robe of some kind, which also appeared red in the light from the moon. She caught something glinting, something the man was raising up.

A knife...except this was a really big knife, a good twenty inches or more long. She'd seen their like before in old horror movies back when she was in her teens, usually wielded by indestructible masked killers. One slice could virtually cleave someone in half. If he had been alone, she might have reasoned that this was just some nut, using the apocalypse as an excuse to live out his horror film fantasies. But there were more where he came from: many more.

They came out of the shadows now, all hooded, all wielding those deadly weapons. She froze, realising that her situation was so much worse than she'd thought. The lead figure came closer, reaching a hand up to pull down his hood.

She let out a gasp when she saw his face – or what there was of it.

It's a skull, her mind was telling her. Perhaps this place wasn't only populated by ghosts, but by the living dead as well? The skull was quite obviously white – or at least would have been were it not for the moon's influence – but that wasn't the only giveaway. The eyes were sunken and black, merely sockets from which this thing stared out. And in the middle of the forehead was a symbol she couldn't quite make out, etched into the bone.

I'm going mad, she thought. *I must be.* But there was time to worry about that later. Now she had to get out of there, just run. When she finally found she could move again, what she'd witnessed gave her feet wings. Head down, she sprinted faster than ever: up one street, down another. The ground beneath her was still unstable, but somehow that didn't matter anymore. She lost her footing a couple of times, but ignored it, desperately trying to get away from the nightmare she knew was behind her.

Rounding one final corner she let out another gasp. It was a dead end. The houses seemed to lean in even more, as if to ask: "Well, what are you going to do now, then?"

She had no answer. Looking quickly to the left and the right she thought about trying a few doors, bobbing inside the buildings that were mocking her. But she'd be just as trapped inside as she would have been back at the castle. More so perhaps, because they were smaller, easier to search.

Instead, she headed back up that same street in the hopes she might reach the only way out again before the dead men arrived.

She'd taken only a few steps before her exit was cut off.

As before, one appeared at the mouth of the street: materialising out of nowhere. Then, seconds later, the others joined him. She counted ten at least. The leader, slightly taller than the others – the one who'd initiated the hunt – began to walk towards her. She backed off, knowing that she didn't have much street left before she hit the wall, but in no rush to meet her fate.

"P-Please...Please just leave me alone..." she cried.

He took no notice – *they* took no notice – approaching now as one, swinging their machetes.

She screamed at the top of her lungs: "*What do you want from me?*"

The dead man at the front paused, contemplating this question. Then he answered in a hollow voice: "Sacrifice."

It told her nothing, yet everything. They didn't want her physically, as so many had before. Didn't want to paw and molest her – why would dead men want that? They wanted her to join them; to become one of them. To give up her life so that she could exist forever walking these streets, preying on the warm blooded. Maybe living forever wouldn't be so bad?

But what if when they killed her she stayed dead? Or, even worse, went to a place that made this look like Heaven – as impossible as that might seem? She looked again to the sides, searching for a way out, a way *up* perhaps?

Then she saw it, another hooded figure on the rooftops. The bastards were up there as well! She was well and truly finished. The hunt was over. Bowing her head, she sobbed, accepting the inevitable.

One of the walking dead fell. At first she thought he might have slipped on the wintry ground. Blinking the tears from her eyes, though, she saw something sticking out of the dead man's shoulder. Something long and thin with feathers on the end...

She traced the shot back to the figure above her, the person she'd assumed was another one of their number. But even as she looked up, he was falling, legs bent to take the strain of the landing. The shape rose, standing between her and the dead men... except she knew now they weren't dead at all, not if an arrow from this man's bow could fell them. This man who wore a hood just like her enemies.

With his free hand he waved her back. Then, with that same

hand, he plucked another arrow from the quiver on his back. He'd loaded it and fired quicker than she had time to register, already reaching for another.

Two more of the 'dead' men dropped before they could get any nearer. But that didn't stop more taking their place, charging at her rescuer. He had time for just one more shot, but it went wide – his aim spoilt because he had to avoid a blow from one of the swinging machetes. Too close to rely on his bow, the hooded figure let go of it and pulled something out of his belt. To her it looked like another of those long knives, but on second glance she realised it was a sword. He used this to block first one machete swipe on his left, then another to his right. Metal clashed against metal, but the man seemed as quick with this weapon as he had been with his arrows.

As she watched, he pushed one of the robed men back, headbutting a second – which dropped the man like a stone. A roundhouse kick sent a third into the wall, and she heard a definite crunch of bone. But he couldn't be everywhere at once, in spite of how it seemed. A couple broke through, machetes high, ready to be planted in her.

The hooded man punched one attacker and elbowed another in the face, before swinging around and chasing after the ones making for her. He leapt and landed on them, taking them both down just inches from her. She fell backwards, landing on the snow, her bag falling from her grasp.

The three men struggled to their feet, each one determined to get up first and have the advantage. The hooded figure narrowly avoided a machete swipe to the stomach, arcing his body then bringing his sword down to meet the challenge. No sooner had he thrown off that man than he had to meet the other's blow. This he did but the force knocked him back hard into the wall. A flash of gritted teeth, and he slid the hilt up to the man's hand as they struggled to force the weapons out of each other's grip. The stalemate was ended when the first man, now recovered, swung again; but the hooded man dragged the figure he was locked onto around, creating a human shield, and the sword buried itself in him instead. The injured man fell to the ground, but her hero wasn't quick enough to avoid a punch that caught him a glancing blow on the chin. Shaking his head, he brought his sword up and into that first attacker, the point emerging from his back.

Breathing heavy, each puff turning to steam in the night air, he looked across at the woman and she caught just a glimpse of those intense eyes under the cowl; searching her face to see if she was all right. Then she saw one last glint of metal just behind him, a machete whipping through the air to connect with her rescuer's neck. She didn't have time to scream or point, but he heard the sound anyway... just not in time to do anything about it.

Then the machete halted in mid-strike. The blade quivered. As she lifted her head she saw what had stopped it. A large wooden staff was in the way, being held by an equally large man. He was wearing a cap and sported a goatee beard.

"Whoa there, fella," said the big man, with a trace of an American accent. "That's enough of that." Taking one hand off the staff, he punched the robed figure in the face, knocking him clean out. The machete clanged to the floor.

Beyond the giant she saw others: *his* men. The Hooded Man's. She could tell because they were armed as he was, with bows and arrows, with swords. They were grabbing hold of her attackers, pinning them against the wall. Two or three of the skull-faced figured who'd been taken down by Hood seized their chance to get up and barged past these newcomers, shouldering them out of the way.

"Don't just stand there," the large man barked, "get after 'em!" Then he held out his hand, helping her saviour properly to his feet. "Don't worry, they won't get far."

"They'd better not," said the hooded man – a hood she realised was not attached to some robed outfit, but part of a winter huntsman's jacket (sliced across the front where the machete blade had almost cut him). She smiled at the irony; the hunters were now the hunted.

"If you'd waited for the rest of us, we'd probably have got them all," replied the man in the cap.

"This woman was in trouble."

"Yeah, and so were you Robbie."

"What's that supposed to mean, Jack?" asked Hood.

"You've... Well, you've been out of the game for a little while, boss. You're rusty. That psycho almost had you."

Robbie grunted at this, ignoring his friend. Then he turned to her, pulling down his hood. She saw him for the first time, in the glow of the moon – a glow that gave his features a strange kind of warmth. He was clean-shaven and handsome, just like folk said. Oh, she'd heard the stories. Who hadn't? It was why she figured it might be safe to come into York that evening. The Hooded Man and his forces were cleaning up the area, or so went the rumour.

Finally, she found her voice again. "Y-You...You're him, aren't you? The Hooded Man?"

"What gave it away?" Jack answered before the man could say a thing.

Though it was hard to tell in this light, she could swear Hood's cheeks were flushing. He nodded shyly, like he was embarrassed to admit the fact.

"Are you going to help the lady up then, Robbie, or should I offer my services? Which, I might add, I'd be happy to do..."

The leader of these men held out his hand and she took it, feeling its strength. Her heart was pounding, not because of the skirmish, not because she'd been seconds away from dying, but because she was this close to *him*. Could he feel it too? Their connection?

As she rose, she stumbled slightly, unsteady on her feet. She fell into him and he held her there for a second... before the embarrassment crept back and he righted her, letting go. She felt somehow bereft, but still managed a, "Thank you... Robbie."

"It's Robert," he corrected, stooping to pick up her bag and handing it to her, "or Rob."

"Or sometimes even Robin," added Jack, grinning.

Robert sighed. "Only this big lug calls me Robbie, I suspect because he knows how much I hate it."

The bigger man feigned a look of mock offence, then grinned again, resting his staff on his shoulder. "And I'm Jack. Always a pleasure to help out a damsel in distress...'specially one as pretty as you are, ma'am." Once he'd got a smile from her, Jack turned to address his superior again. "Looks like all those hours of stake-out actually paid off, anyway. We got most of 'em."

"I wanted *all* of them," said Robert.

"Who are they?" she asked as they walked towards the men having their hands bound behind their backs.

"We're not entirely sure, some kind of cult," Robert said. "We've had reports of them cropping up in various locations. It never ends well for their victims."

She remembered what one of the 'dead' men had said to her during the chase.

Sacrifice.

She could see now, though, that the grinning skulls were merely wearing make-up. Their faces and shaved heads had been painted white, with the area around their eyes black. They'd done this on purpose, of course; imitating the deceased to intimidate the living. She peered closer at one of them, trying to make out the tattoo on his forehead. The robed figure bared his teeth, snapping like an animal before the young man holding him could pull the guy away.

"You might want to get back a bit, miss," he told her. "They're kind of unpredictable."

Jack clapped him on the shoulder. "You did good work tonight, Dale. I'm proud of you."

The youth beamed, clearly delighted by the praise. "Are we taking these back to Nottingham?" he asked Jack.

"I believe that's the plan. Robbie wants to find out more about them."

"You're going back to the Castle? To Nottingham Castle?" the woman asked Robert.

He nodded.

"Then please... take me with you." Robert was silent and she looked at him pleadingly. "I'm begging you. I have nowhere else to go. I've got no-one... not since my mum... my family..." She didn't need to finish that sentence; they'd all been there, it was reflected in the eyes. *Him* especially. The hurt, the pain he'd tried to bury but which still lurked there.

"Come on, Robbie," said Jack. "The lady's been through a lot tonight; what harm can it do?"

"All right, all right," said Robert. "You can come along."

She flung herself at him, giving him a big hug. "Oh thank you, thank you." Jack coughed and she felt Robert tensing up; this was obviously too public a display of affection. Pulling back, she then gave Jack a hug as well, so he wouldn't feel left out. "Thank you. Thank you both."

"Er... Jack," Robert said, "when the others get back ready the horses."

"Sure thing," said a happy Jack, walking out of the alley and taking the men and prisoners with him.

"So," Robert continued, turning to her; he'd looked more comfortable facing death than he did right now. "What's your name?"

"Me?" She hesitated for a second or two. "Do you know it's been so long since anyone asked me that? It's Adele."

Robert stuck out his hand for her to shake, noticeably more formal. "Well then, Adele. Pleased to meet you."

She smiled a big smile. "And I'm so very pleased to meet you, Robert... The Hooded Man."

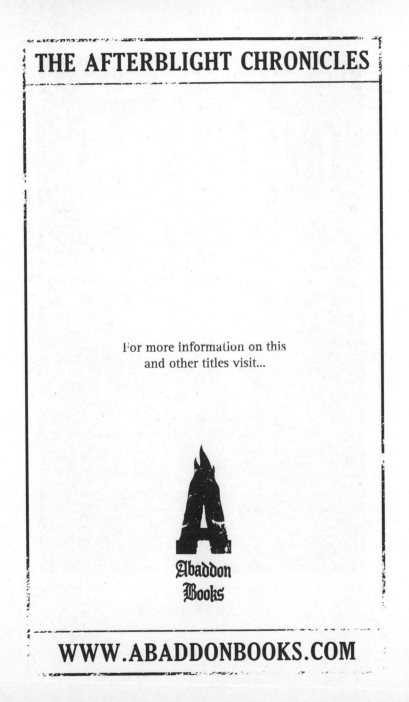

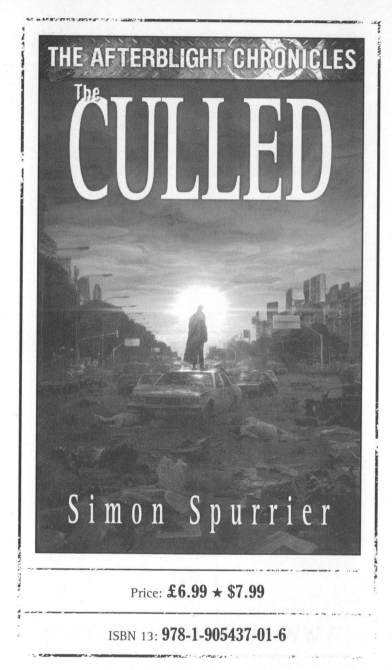

THE AFTERBLIGHT CHRONICLES

The CULLED

Simon Spurrier

Price: **£6.99** ★ **$7.99**

ISBN 13: **978-1-905437-01-6**

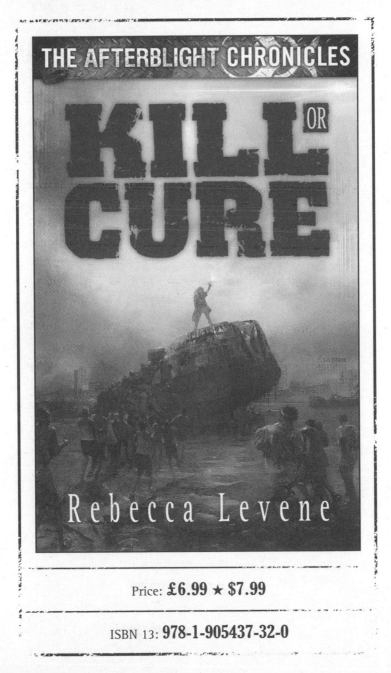

THE AFTERBLIGHT CHRONICLES

KILL OR CURE

Rebecca Levene

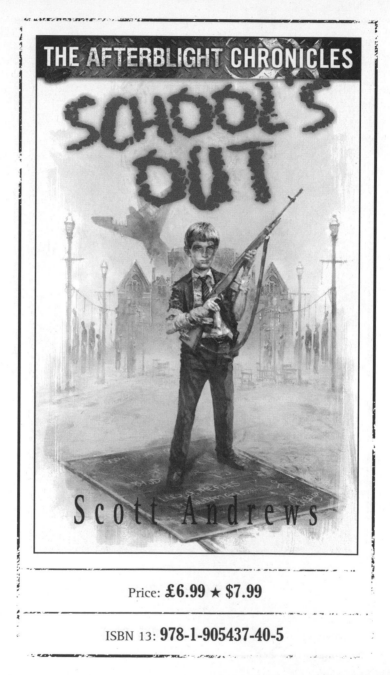

THE AFTERBLIGHT CHRONICLES

SCHOOL'S OUT

Scott Andrews

Price: **£6.99 ★ $7.99**

ISBN 13: **978-1-905437-40-5**

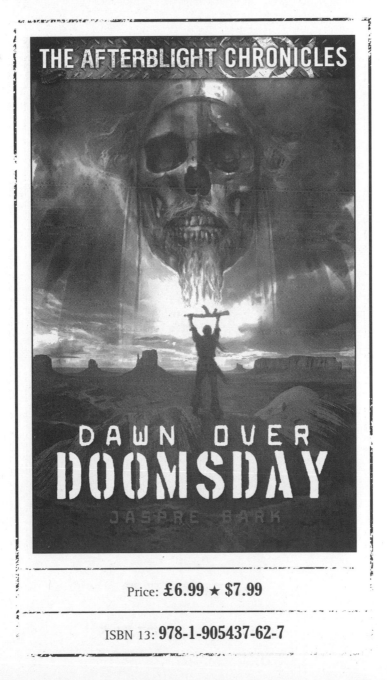

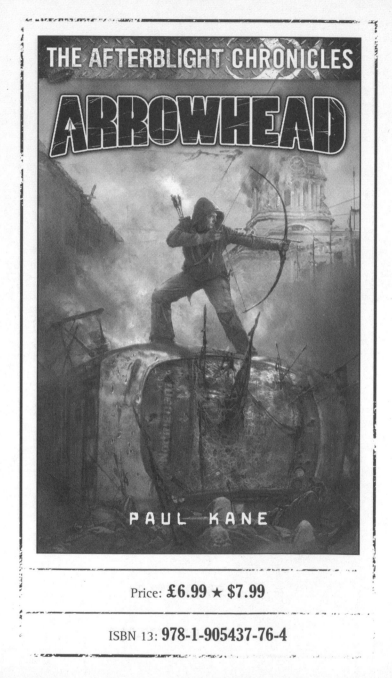

THE AFTERBLIGHT CHRONICLES

ARROWHEAD

PAUL KANE

Price: **£6.99 ★ $7.99**

ISBN 13: **978-1-905437-76-4**

THE AFTERBLIGHT CHRONICLES

OPERATION MOTHERLAND

SCOTT ANDREWS

Price: **£6.99** ★ **$7.99**

ISBN 13: **978-1-906735-04-3**

Price: **£6.99 ★ $7.99**

ISBN 13: **978-1-906735-27-2**